# BOATS ON LAND

## A COLLECTION OF SHORT STORIES

### JANICE PARIAT

RANDOM HOUSE INDIA

Published by Random House India in 2012
1

Random House Publishers India Private Limited
Windsor IT Park, 7th Floor, Tower-B
A-1, Sector-125, Noida-201301 (UP)

Random House Group Limited
20 Vauxhall Bridge Road
London SW1V 2SA
United Kingdom

978 81 8400 074 0

Typeset in Sabon by Eleven Arts

Printed and bound in India by Replika Press Private Limited

*For my parents*

*I found the marvelous real with every step.*
—Alejo Carpentier

# Contents

*Contents*

# A Waterfall of Horses

*H*ow do I explain the word?
*Ka ktien.*

*Say it. Out loud. Ka ktien. The first, a short, sharp thrust of air from the back of your throat. The second, a lift of the tongue and a delicate tangle of tip and teeth.*

*For I mean not what's bound by paper. Once printed, the word is feeble and carries little power. It wrestles with ink and typography and margins, struggling to be what it was originally. Spoken. Unwritten, unrecorded. Old, they say, as the first fire. Free to roam the mountains, circle the heath, and fall as rain.*

*We, who had no letters with which to etch our history, have married our words to music, to mantras, that we repeat until lines grow old and wither and fade away. Until they are forgotten and there is silence.*

*How do I explain something untraceable? The perfect weapon for a crime. Light as pine dust. Echoing with alibis. Conjuring out of thin air, the ugly, the beautiful, the terrifying.*

*Eventually, like all things, it is unfathomable. So, how do I explain?*

*Perhaps it's best, as they did in the old days, to tell a story.*

I learnt about the word long ago, when I was young and had seen no more than thirteen winters. In those days, the nights were so cold that frost gathered on our roofs and gardens like snow. Well, that's what the bilati men said it looked like, for we had never seen snow in all our lives. They would huddle by the fire at the gate to Sahib Jones's bungalow and talk about their homes far away across the sea. I would bring wood and coal to bolster the flames, and eavesdrop; they paid no attention to this dark, snotty-nosed boy in his threadbare clothes and frayed woollen shawl. They'd speak of places I'd never heard of, names that slipped through my memory like little silver doh thli I tried to catch in the streams. I dreamt about it sometimes, the land of gently rolling hills, thatch cottages, and women white as the 'tiew khlaw that grew wild by the roadside. The bilati men had come to guard the land and tea plantation of an owner we hardly saw; their presence there forever changed the lives of the people of Pomreng village.

It was the 1850s, and Pomreng was a smudge that probably couldn't be found on any map of the area at the time. It lay nestled on a bit of grassy flatland, a cluster of fifty huts, ribboned by a river that flowed languid and deep before plunging down a steep rocky cliff. Shillong, then called Laban, lay at the end of a rough, day-long, horse-cart journey on a dirt track twisting through forested hills or miles of desolate countryside. Our people rarely ventured out except for the occasional family visit or trip to the big market. Nothing ever happened at Pomreng; it was a quiet life, marked by sowing and harvests, steady as the seasons. Which was why there was great excitement at the news that a judge from Sylhet had bought vast swathes of land outside our village, to grow tea and build himself a pleasure palace full of wondrous things. 'The ceiling will be high as the trees,' it was reported. 'They're bringing maw-Sohra all the way here for the floors.' It would have a hundred rooms and a hundred servants. Eventually, the palace turned out to be a humble lime-washed, stone bungalow atop a hillock, with a smaller cottage and sheds and stables further down the slope. But we weren't disappointed; it was still the largest construction we'd ever seen. The judge arrived with his family on a short vacation at the end of the monsoon, and departed soon after, but they left behind a unit of soldiers and their horses. The estate was managed by a missionary named Thomas Jones, and rumour had it that he was on the run from a rascal bilati businessman in Sohra who wanted him hanged for encouraging the locals to question the price of his goods. We didn't know if that was true, but Sahib Jones did look perpetually worried, his sombre face pale as a stub of bitter white radish. He strode around dutifully inspecting the tea bushes and large garden, checking every once in a while on the men and their animals, yet there hung about him an air of nervous disquiet.

My young mother worked as a maid for his wife Memsahib Greta, which was how I ended up employed as help around the house and estate, doing various odd jobs and running errands. I didn't mind; we needed every bit of spare cash since my father walked out on his wife and five children one night in a drunken fury and never returned. I also worked extra hard because my secret ambition was to some day get out of Pomreng and make my way to Shillong. If I could, I would take my mother and siblings with me. The little money I saved I hid in an old sock under my mattress. Every morning, I'd crawl out of bed as dawn broke outside our shuttered windows, bathing the hills in milky white light, and head to Sahib Jones's kitchen, a stone building separate from the main house, where my mother would be preparing sweet red tea in a large blackened kettle. From there I'd carry the cups on a tray out to the men—first the ones who'd been up all night at the gate, and then to the others. After a while, I came to know them well—Pat, a big man the size of a bear; Roger, the one with blazing orange hair; Trotter, a stout red-faced soldier with the loudest voice in camp; and Sahib Sam, the only one who thanked me when I handed him his cup of tea. I marvelled at the strangeness of their skin, their eyes like bits of coloured glass, the unfamiliar intonations of their language. Even their smell, I thought, was different. I wondered why they'd given up their homes and families to protect a cold, muddy slice of land in a place they couldn't possible care about. But as Mama Saiñ, the village headman, said, it was the bilati men with their guns and cannons who ruled us, and hence this was their territory too. Besides, he added, they were also probably people on the run, like Sahib Jones, who found shelter and safety in Pomreng's isolation. I wouldn't have been surprised to discover that Trotter, Pat and some of the others were criminals—they were rough, filthy-mouthed men who grew more garrulous and aggressive by the day. Sometimes I saw them whip the plantation workers or knock them down with their horses.

'Move, you bastards,' they'd shout. 'Get to work before we peel the flesh off your bones.'

I was petrified of them and kept out of their way as much as possible. Since I was small and insignificant, it wasn't too difficult to slip past them unnoticed. I did quite well until one morning when I tripped while carrying a tray, and spilled hot tea on Trotter's lap.

'Bastard,' he yelled, jumping up from the moora, and cuffing my ear so hard I fell to the ground bleeding. He was about to strike again when suddenly a pair of legs in muddy black boots appeared in front of me.

'Leave the boy alone, Trotter, it was an accident.' It was Sahib Sam.

'Burnt my balls, the little son of a bitch.' .

'That's good to know, Trotter. Some of us were worried you didn't have any.'

The laughter that followed drowned out Trotter's belligerent shouts.

'Are you alright there, boy?' A pair of bright blue eyes looked into mine. Sahib Sam had bent over me, his hand on my shoulder. I nodded, too scared to speak, and as soon as I was on my feet, I ran like I was being chased by a wild animal.

From that time on, I saved the largest cup of tea for Sahib Sam, and the choicest piece of meat for his dinner, the sweetest 'pu khlein cakes bought from our local market, and the largest, driest logs of wood for whenever he was on night duty. As captain of the unit he had probably warned Trotter as well, for apart from a string of verbal abuses if I happened to pass by, the red-faced pig left me alone.

For almost a year, we existed companionably enough, mostly because the bilati men were indifferent towards us, and all we felt on our part was awe and more than a little fear. They stayed within the confines of the plantation, training, taking care of their animals, settling in, and we kept to our village and the countryside beyond, preparing for weekly market days, attending archery competitions and quietly ploughing our fields, eking out a living from

7

Pomreng's hard, red soil. I think trouble started when the soldiers ventured into the village. Around the camp I heard them talk of the tedium of their work, the place, their lives. Of having nothing much to do, and nowhere to go. Sahib Jones, though a fair and just master, frowned upon epicurean revelry, so the men weren't given many days leave to travel to Shillong. Although they didn't lead what could be called a tough life. Far from it. Apart from a few instances where cattle were carried off by tigers, there was no great danger from other perpetrators. The men were filled with boredom and restlessness. They started attending market days, and bullied the sellers over their prices, sometimes walking off without bothering to pay. Sahib Sam and his friends didn't do this, I noticed, but among the villagers who didn't know one soldier from another, grumbled murmurs started about them in general. 'When are they going to leave?', 'Who do they think they are, stealing from us.'

The place where the men liked to meet and play cards was Bah Lumen's jadoh stall located at the end of the only main road that ran through the village. Apart from tea, the stall also served local kiad, a clear, strong alcohol made from rice, that the bilati men enjoyed immensely. At first the owner was pleased—'They all drink like fish…it's good business'—until fights started breaking out, food and drinks were ordered on credit, and women of (what my mother called) unsavoury character started appearing on the premises. They seemed alright to me, cheerful and friendly, and generous with their laughter. Sometimes when I helped out at the jadoh stall for a little extra money, I'd see the men call a girl over, negotiate a price, and then disappear to the barracks.

'The brothels are in Laban, not in my food shop,' complained Bah Lumen, and Mama Saiñ would tell him that the town was too far for hot young blood to travel and he might as well start charging a commission from the whores. There were rumours that some soldiers, Trotter and his gang I suspect, would pick up village women returning from the fields or from fetching water from the river, and carry them off on their horses. Sahib Sam, I was relieved to see, paid attention only to one young lady—Bah Lumen's eldest daughter, Haphida, a pretty girl with clear skin, bright eyes and hair so long it touched the back of her knees. She would shyly bring over his food and tea, and he'd try and converse in the few Khasi words he'd learnt, but, as I came to understand later, you didn't need language to decipher a lingering glance or touch of the hand. If Bah Lumen disapproved, there was nothing he could do, and he only voiced his objections to Mama Saiñ or to no one in particular as he chopped onions or stirred a pot of lumpy yellow rice.

'These outsiders, what do they think? He'll get my daughter pregnant, and we'll have a half and half on our hands. I've heard it happens. All over the place, little bastards running around with blue eyes and white skin.'

While he and the village seethed in slow resentment, Sahib Sam and Haphida, oblivious to the world outside their own, met every day, in the lull between afternoon tea and the evening revelry. Often, I saw them go for walks, and though I followed close behind, I hardly heard them converse. They'd stroll leisurely by the river, while twilight hovered over the valley, darkening the hills around us, and make their way to the waterfall. There, they'd sit on one of the large boulders,

Haphida's hair flowing onto the ground. He'd gather it up carefully and place it on her lap, or pluck wild 'tiew khlaw for her to braid into her locks. Once, they kissed, tentatively at first, and then suddenly with great urgency, as though time and the world were passing them by. Other kids from the village, who'd been bathing nearby, whistled from the undergrowth, sending a shower of stones from their catapults.

'Ei, Sahib bilat, kbih noh,' they shouted, while Haphida flushed a deep crimson. She refused to tell Sahib Sam what they'd said but I presume he guessed for he shouted back, saying he'd have them whipped.

The breaking point, though, between the village people and the soldiers, had nothing to do with the two lovers. One market day, when Trotter walked off with a bunch of corn cobs he didn't pay for, the local farmer spat at the soldier's boots.

'What did you just do?' shouted the red-faced pig.

'You're a thief,' said the farmer in Khasi, 'a thief with no balls.'

Or something like that. The versions vary. Yet I suppose it didn't matter what he said, Trotter would have had his revenge simply for being talked back to. The man was tied to Trotter's horse, and dragged behind him for a day. When he was finally released, his body was caked in blood and dust, his skin shredded to mulch. He didn't last the night.

The village council met in Mama Saiñ's hut, and gathered around the heath. Close to the glowing embers stood a wooden thlong, perpetually filled with water. Our people believed it could predict the future—the higher the water level, the better the harvest. Right now, though, no one cast a glance at the vessel. There were other, more tragic things to discuss. I was there to stoke the fire and serve tea spiked with kiad to bolster their ravaged spirits. A muted rebellion ran through the crowd in the room. One young man couldn't contain his anger any longer. 'Something must be done,' he spluttered.

Mama Saiñ, flames dancing in his eyes, sipped his drink in silence. A murmur rose around him, voices filled with anger and grief. It was cruel what the bilati men had done (what *some* of the bilati men had done I wanted to add, but didn't dare), they needed to be punished, to be driven out of the land, the village would fight them and take its revenge for all the wrongs the outsiders had committed.

Finally Mama Saiñ spoke. 'What will we fight them with?'

A silence fell broken only by the hiss and crackle of the fire. The bilati soldiers had guns, while we wielded only primitive swords and shot inadequate wooden arrows.

'There are enough of us against them,' someone shouted. 'Damn their guns, we can overpower them by sheer strength and numbers.'

A chorus of agreement swelled in the room.

Mama Saiñ shook his head. 'We would lose too many men. Would you have your own brothers slaughtered in vain like chickens?'

The debate continued for almost an hour, until an old man, whom everyone called Nong Kñia, spoke up. He'd been sitting in the corner, quietly observing the proceedings. 'Rangbah,' he said softly, 'we can fight them with words.'

Gasps of disbelief and laughter escaped the crowd. The old man remained stoic and silent, his silver beard catching the firelight. His face, though lined and aged, held the resolute stamp of pride. Mama Saiñ nodded, and looked around at his people. 'We have one weapon, poor as it may seem, the power of ktien—the word. It is our last resort because it is dishonourable to fight an enemy without giving him a chance to defend himself.'

'That could be corrected,' said the old man. 'We won't strike the men.'

'Then what?' said a man sitting closest to the fire. I recognized him as the younger brother of the farmer who'd died. 'They killed Jymmang. We need to kill them.'

The old man shook his head. 'There are other ways to render them powerless.'

Late that night, after my younger siblings were put to sleep, my mother and I warmed our hands by a small coal chula. I asked her who the Nong Kñia was and what he meant by ktien. My mother, her face sunken in tiredness, looked at me and smiled. 'He is the bearer of the word. The one who performs our rituals and communicates with the gods. The memsahib says she would like to teach me to read and write, with something called "alphabet" that her husband has invented for our language. I explained to her that we have no need for these things—books, and letters, and writing—and that everything we know about the world is in the sound of our words, ki ktien. It has the power to do good...'

'Like what?' I asked quickly; I rarely heard my mother talk of these things. She was always too busy or, at the end of the day, often exhausted. 'Like your grandfather,' she replied. 'He could heal a person by uttering a mantra. Once, I remember I cut my hand while splitting bamboo...and he held it, and spoke into it, and the bleeding stopped. People would come to him if they had fish bones stuck in their throat—he'd chant the words and rub their neck with oil and ash, and the bone would be gone. He told me there are mantras that hungry travellers can chant for an animal to appear before them so they can feed, and to bring clean water from a river, or fruit from a tree.'

The embers in the chula were dying; I knew we wouldn't be sitting around it for long.

'But can it also be used to bring harm?'

My mother nodded.

'Is that what Nong Kñia and Mama Saiñ will use on the bilati men? All of them?'

She pushed herself away from the chula. 'Who can say what mantras the Nong Kñia knows...'

For days after, I moved around distracted and restless. The hours passed by glistening with sunshine and sudden autumn showers, yet they'd shifted, a little askew and out of line. I was nervous, constantly waiting for something to happen. The other villagers seemed to feel the same as they left to work in the fields or opened their makeshift shops for business. They talked about it endlessly in hushed whispers over smoking pipes and cups of tea, but no one knew exactly what the elders had planned. I tried to keep the soldiers, especially Sahib Sam, within my sight as much as possible—following them around, an unobtrusive shadow. One afternoon, the bilati men were exercising and training their horses in the field at the bottom of the hill; soon they would take them back to the stables and it would be time for lunch. I was helping my mother with the washing, hanging it out to dry. I glanced at them repeatedly; when would they all drop dead? Or would they fall ill and languish slowly? Whatever it was going to be, I had to do something, I decided. I had to warn Sahib Sam. When I finished wringing the bedsheets, I hovered as inconspicuously as I could by the gate leading to the field, trying to spot him. After a while, I realized he wasn't there. Had something already happened? I could feel my heart thump heavily against my chest. Perhaps I was too late. Then I remembered that at this time, he usually met with Sahib Jones and retired to the barracks until lunch. I raced up the hill, scattering a hen and her family of chicks, and headed to the long rectangular stone building that housed the soldiers. To my relief, I could see Sahib Sam sitting on the veranda, smoking, reading a book. I crept up to him and waited to be acknowledged.

'Hello, boy.' His eyes were the colour of our April skies.

Suddenly everything I wanted to say sounded silly to my ears. What would I tell him? That a couple of old men were plotting to murder the entire regiment? And how? Through a mantra? But he was looking at me expectantly, and I had to say something to explain my reason for being there.

'Is everything alright?'

'The people in the village...they are angry about Bah Jymmang,' I said, hoping his Khasi was good enough for him to understand me. He frowned, but I could see comprehension dawn on his face.

'Yes, I heard about what happened. It was terrible...'

'They plan to harm you,' I interrupted. 'Be careful.'

And then I fled, leaving him staring after me, the book open on his lap.

Yet I suppose no amount of warning could have prepared Sahib Sam and the other soldiers for what happened. Or saved them. It took everyone by surprise, including the people from the village. As the Nong Kñia had promised, his mantra didn't harm the bilati men; it was much worse. It happened a fortnight after our village meeting, when everyone had almost given up on the elders taking their revenge, when dark murmurs spread of the younger men wanting to sneak into the barracks to slit the soldiers' throats while they were sleeping. That afternoon, they say it started with Trotter's horse who refused to be led into the stable; he whipped and yelled at the creature until it obeyed. Inside, while the animals were being rubbed down, they appeared unusually restless, swishing their tails, flaring their nostrils, and pricking their ears, as though listening to a sound no one else could hear. Then they began shifting fretfully in their stalls, stamping on the hay, kicking against the walls. I could hear the bilati men shout out orders to the animals—'Stay, boy, stay'—and to each other. Soon, the horses grew impossible to control or contain—they reared and neighed, baring their teeth, knocking over their masters, trampling on bodies fallen to the floor. A fierce madness overtook them, their eyes turned white and wild, and, full of a great and invisible terror, they dashed blindly out of the door with men trailing behind them. I saw them charge down the hill, a herd of savage horses, their bodies steaming, their manes flying out behind them. People tried to move aside but some were slow and got crushed beneath their hooves. They barely had time to scream. Once the horses were outside the village, they galloped down the road by the river, the one which Sahib Sam and Haphida had walked down so many evenings. They made straight for the waterfall, and leaped, soaring over the emptiness and falling into the mist. The pool at the bottom was the colour of blood for almost a week.

'It was like they were possessed by the devil himself,' the soldiers told Sahib Jones later, while he was tending to their wounds. I followed behind him, carrying a tray of clean rags and medication. 'They were out of control.' Most of them said they'd never seen anything like this before, even though they'd worked with horses for most of their lives. 'It doesn't bode well,' I thought I heard Sahib Jones mutter.

That night the fires in the camp burned brighter and longer as though to keep away the forces of darkness. The air was pungent with fear. No one slept. The soldiers huddled together, if not for warmth, then comfort, drinking, speaking of England, of their homes across the sea. The Nong Kñia had been right; there were other ways to render them powerless.

After that began the gradual disintegration of the camp. Some men fled the barracks, convinced the place was cursed, and that they'd be next to go insane and fling themselves over the waterfall. A few others drank themselves to death on local kiad. Sahib Jones buried them in the corner of the field where once they'd exercised their horses, their graves marked by wooden crosses painted with their names. A few months later, news spread that the goons hired by the rascal businessman in Sohra had traced Sahib Jones's whereabouts and were on their way to Pomreng to find him. He left in haste one morning before dawn for Guwahati and some say he made it to freedom, while others believed he died of malaria on a steamer on his way to Calcutta. When his wife followed a fortnight later, my mother was dismissed from service and so were the remaining men. There was no one left for them to guard and protect. Sahib Sam was the last to leave even though he had no reason to linger. On the day of the horses' madness, amid the carnage along the road, we'd found Haphida. She must have been bringing back water from the river. Her face was trampled beyond recognition, but we knew her from her hair, tangled in the dust. Before his departure, Sahib Sam took a walk to the waterfall, and I followed him, fearing the worst. He stood there a long while, and I waited anxiously, hidden in the shrubbery. Did I have a right to encroach upon his grief? When he took a step closer to the edge, I stepped out of my hiding place onto the road. I tried to make it seem casual, as though I too had decided to take a stroll and happened to be in the same place. I was sure he'd heard me, for I shuffled my feet on the gravel, but he didn't turn. I stood by him, at a safe, respectful distance. The view before me is etched in my mind so clearly I can close my eyes and remember it all—the waterfall sweeping over a rocky cliff patched with damp moss and long, feathery ferns, falling like liquid mist into a pool and winding unseen into a forest. Beyond this, trees covering the expanse of valley and hills, until they appeared in the distance not as single entities but a smooth carpet of green.

'What happened that day?' asked Sahib Sam.

I didn't know whether he was referring to the horses or Haphida, so I remained silent.

His eyes were shiny; his hair and moustache, I noticed, looked untidy and unkept.

'They went over. Just like that...why?' He laughed. 'Perhaps it was a relief.'

I tried to disprove politely, to speak of the sheer drop, the seemingly endless fall...

'There must have been something...' he interrupted, shaking his head. 'Do you have a name for it, boy? In your language.'

'For what, sir?' Did he know about ktien and the mantras?

'This.' He gestured in front of him. 'It's difficult to explain... they say it's the call of the void, you know...the pull you feel when you stand looking down from a great height. The urge to jump...'

'No—I don't think so. Do you?'

He shook his head. 'It's strange, all the things that language cannot say.' He stood there a while longer and then turned and walked away.

Nobody lives in Pomreng any more. One by one, people packed up and left the village. They say dark magic always leaves a trace, and our harvests failed year after year, despite the usual turn of seasons. The water hardly rose halfway up in the thlong. Bah Lumen, grieving for Haphida, was one of the first to leave, along with others who'd lost family that day. He said he could never forgive the village elders for what they'd done, that nothing was worth losing his daughter. My mother and I eventually pooled our money and resources together and left for Shillong, where she found a job in a memsahib's household and I worked in a jadoh stall in the Laban market. Mama Saiñ, I heard, passed away in a relative's house in Sohra. I don't know what became of the Nong Kñia; as the world changes and its mysteries diminish, there are fewer people like him to be found. Pomreng is an abandoned village now with barely any recognizable markers of its past. Only a few stones stand atop a barren hill, a cluster of tea bushes grow wild; while the wooden barracks and stables have crumbled into dust. The wind and the wilderness have had their way with the roads and fields, making them indistinguishable from each other. The one thing that remains is the waterfall, throwing up a sound, a word that is ungraspable and constant.

# At Kut Madan

Today, nobody had come to the doctor possessed by a ghost. Kem ksuid it was called. Caught by a spirit, forced to languish and waste away. No one had blamed their illness on thlen either, the evil eye, cast ruthlessly on unsuspecting souls.

Often, he was more shaman than doctor, but today, it had been simple—a child's hollow, persistent cough, a pregnant lady's erratic bleeding, a spade wound on a farmer's ankle, arthritis in an old woman's fingers.

Doctor Wallang stepped out onto the veranda and lit a cigarette. The wooden bench outside his room was finally empty. In ten years of clinical service, no matter how late, he'd never turned away anyone who'd sat there. Sometimes his patients travelled for days from their villages deep in the folded valleys of Sohra; he knew for he'd visit occasionally to distribute medicine and clothing donated by the Welsh missionaries. He hadn't been there recently though—with the outbreak of the second great war four years ago, these rations were hard to come by. Yet Father Bevan, the church elder, did his best, as he said, 'for God and his people'.

Usually Doctor Wallang would head indoors to his study, but this evening, with the last of the fine autumn weather, he decided to stroll down the garden path towards the main road. He passed the vegetable patch tended by his wife, and, to his left, a stone wall overhung with 'knupmawiang. He liked these large creeper orchids with their flat, ribbed leaves and pale yellow flowers that opened during the rains and blossomed all through winter. It was October now, and they would be the sole floral survivors of the next few cold, crippling months. He leaned on the gate and watched the evening settle around him—in the fading light, the lime-washed missionary building opposite glowed an iridescent silver, smoke drifted from a cluster of small stone houses on a nearby hill, and the smell of wood fire rose in the air. Across the valley, the faint drone of an airplane broke the primitive silence. It was carrying passengers and rations from the American base camp in Dhaka to Shillong. The war had placed even this part of the world on the map.

Further down the road, Flynn, the manager of a tea plantation over the next hill, was walking his dog, a large, scruffy-haired Bhutia from Sikkim.

'Good evening, Sahib Flynn.'

'Nothing good about it, doctor.'

The Irishman's gruffness stemmed not from impudence but worry. Almost a decade ago, during his first Sohra monsoon, it had crept into his voice, a raspy insidious shadow, and outlined his rough, thickset features. It had deepened over the years, when every summer, his life savings were washed away by rain, eroding like mud into a river. It wasn't as though the locals hadn't warned him—'It doesn't stop for weeks, Sahib Flynn,' they'd said, 'and nothing grows. See, the topsoil is all gone, nothing grows.' Tea bushes, they tried to tell him, no matter how resilient, probably wouldn't survive either.

The doctor knew better than to ask how things were at the plantation, so he made small talk instead—the bishop's impending visit to the village church, the fast approaching winter, the price of coal. Whilst they discussed rumbling rumours of plans to construct an industrial factory near Mawmluh village, the hound at Flynn's feet looked up and growled.

'What's up, Sonny?' Sahib Flynn placed a hand on the dog's collar. Apart from them, the road was empty, disappearing on either end into rising mist. The garden in front of the missionary building was also vacant; Father Bevan and the other priests were probably at evening prayer. Sonny growled again, and barked.

The sound of hooves echoed in the distance.

'Don't know why,' Flynn muttered, 'but this dog hates horses.'

Soon, the rider was close enough to be recognized—it was Jonah, son of Mr and Mrs Smithson who lived in a bungalow at Kut Madan. Doctor Wallang expected him to stop at his gate—somebody had probably taken ill—but instead Jonah dismounted at the missionary building. He tied his horse to the gate, his walk marked by a limp, the remaining trace of a childhood illness.

Flynn still had his hand on Sonny's collar. 'Last rites?'

'Maybe,' said the doctor, and stubbed out his cigarette on the gate.

That evening Doctor Wallang's family sat down to dinner in the kitchen as usual. In one corner, a fire spluttered, drying out ragged strips of fish and meat hung above the flames. At the table, the children wrestled for attention, while their mother dished out pork stew and steaming rice. Everyone fell quiet for grace. Their father could be strict about these things.

For a few moments, only his voice echoed in the room—'Bless us, O Lord, for these, Thy gifts, which we are about to receive from Thy bounty. Help us to be mindful of all our blessings, and the needs of those who have less.'

In chorus, the family murmured 'Amen'.

Halfway through the meal, when chatter and gentle teasing had resumed, an urgent knocking sounded on the door. It was a helper from the Smithson household.

'Please,' he uttered, out of breath, 'could the doctor come at once to Kut Madan?'

As Doctor Wallang washed his hands, his children fetched his bag and his wife brought him a shawl. 'Who knows how late you'll be there,' she said. He rushed out of the house with a familiar tug in his stomach. No matter how long he'd been doing this, it always made him nervous—the sudden summon of illness or death. As they hurried down the road, he asked the helper what had happened. The torch in the doctor's hand threw a feeble jaundiced light on rough mud and stone. Around them the wind blew over the barren hills like a restless spirit.

'The memsahib, she has taken ill. The young one.'

It would have been difficult to imagine Mrs Smithson—a tall, thin woman with a steely tongue and constitution—being anything apart from ruthlessly fit. The 'young one', he presumed, was Miss Lucy, Mrs Smithson's orphaned niece from England. She'd arrived earlier that year with the monsoon. The doctor had seen her a few times out riding alone, and occasionally with Jonah.

The bungalow at Kut Madan lay ensconced in a thick forest of pine, brooding in the darkness like a mournful ruin. To the back, the trees spilled over a sudden sharp cliff that gave the place its name—'the end of land'. There were dim lantern lights flickering at several windows, the household was up and waiting. Jonah opened the door.

'Thank you for coming, doctor.' He was twenty-two, yet carried the formal, sombre manners of a much older man. As he was ushered in, the doctor noticed that Jonah's limp had worsened—he'd advised him to ride less often; clearly the boy hadn't listened.

In the living room, Mr Smithson's expansive frame stood in front of the fire, while the lady of the house sat still and silent by the window.

'We're sorry to have disturbed your evening, doctor. I know you close the clinic at five.' Mr Smithson's usually genial manner was subdued, despite the trace of whisky on his breath.

'It's no trouble, Sahib Smith, how can I help?'

'It's Lucy...' he began, and faltered.

'Yes?'

'Well...'

'What is the matter with her?'

Mr Smithson glanced at his son.

'That's the problem, we're not quite sure...' answered Jonah. 'She is—'

He was interrupted by his mother. 'The girl has been complaining of headaches and dizzy spells.'

The doctor turned. 'For how long now?'

'About a week.'

The doctor didn't ask why he hadn't been summoned earlier; despite his profession, in a white household, it wasn't his place to do so.

The family lapsed into silence. Jonah spoke first, 'Perhaps you ought to see her.'

27

Mrs Smithson said she'd check on the girl and left the room. A burning log crackled and spat in the fireplace. Jonah and his father stood quiet as ghosts.

'Sahib Smith, was there anything that happened today, that made you send for me?'

Mr Smithson moved to a side table and poured himself another drink.

'Lucy's been a little under the weather lately…I put it down to pining for something or other, you know young people these days. You see, there was a small matter concerning the stable lad—'

'Father, it isn't necessary to bring that up.' Jonah's tone was sharp, and his face, the doctor noticed, had reddened.

But the elder gentleman continued, unmindful. He was a little drunk.

'Don't know what they were up to…probably nothing more than long walks, really, but I noticed she seemed rather dispirited after…well, after her aunt had a word with her about him.'

Doctor Wallang knew who they were talking about; Kyntang had escorted his ailing father to the clinic about a month ago. He was a quiet, good-looking boy even if he did bring along with him a faint odour of horses.

Mr Smithson sat back heavily in his chair; he looked tired.

'This afternoon she was…I suppose you could say, delirious…not herself at all. Kept talking about a golden…a golden, what was it? Anyway, it was most worrying and we thought, perhaps, it could be one of those things, what you people call…' He struggled with the words.

'Kem ksuid?'

Mr Smithson nodded. 'My wife thought we should call Father Bevan...'

'And he suggested we summon you,' finished Jonah, 'because he says you...have some experience in these matters.'

The awkwardness hung in the room like a blind, lost creature unable to escape until Mrs Smithson beckoned from the door.

The lantern she held threw long, loping shadows on the walls of a narrow corridor leading to the bedroom.

'How old is Miss Lucy?' asked the doctor.

'Nineteen. A most trying age, when a girl's mind is full of fanciful things. We must not be indulgent, doctor.' It sounded more an order than a plea.

'And her parents?'

'Both dead, bombed in the Blitz. It's a miracle she escaped.'

Mrs Smithson stopped and pushed open a door. 'I'll be right outside, doctor.'

He paused. With cases like these, he was never sure whether he'd need to be shaman or doctor. Sometimes, there didn't seem to be a difference.

The room he entered was large and spacious, with a heavy chest-of-drawers and wooden bed on one side, and, on the other, a small table and chair by a window. A lantern placed on the mantelpiece above a cavernous fireplace shed limpid light on a girl as pale as the snowy quilt wrapped around her. Even when he moved closer, she lay still, propped on a pillow, her wavy chestnut hair spread out in a wild, flaming tangle.

'Miss Lucy, how are you feeling?'

His question was met with silence.

'Your aunt and uncle are worried about you.'

He thought there might have been a quickened breath.

'If you prefer to sleep, I can come back later...'

This time she laughed, a hollow shaking that subsided when she turned to look at him. 'Nobody else cares that I want to be left alone, why should you, doctor?'

'They only want you to get better, as I'm sure you do too, Miss Lucy.'

He gestured to a chair. 'May I sit down?'

She shrugged in indifference.

'Why don't you tell me what's troubling you?'

She stared straight ahead, out of the window into consummate darkness.

'Your aunt says you have headaches?'

She nodded slowly.

'I can give you something for that, but might I examine you first?'

She sat up and responded mechanically to all his clinical instructions—to take a deep breath, stick out her tongue, open her mouth wide. Apart from a slightly increased pulse rate, she seemed physically well. Perhaps Mrs Smithson was right, that she was merely seeking attention.

'I'll give you a tonic for your headaches.'

As he reached for his bag, she turned to him. 'Can I ask you something, doctor?'

'Yes, of course.'

'Do you think I'm mad?'

Her eyes were green—he'd never been close enough to notice before—like the pools of water at Laitkynsew, undisturbed for a thousand years.

As a good medic should, he turned the question around to her. 'Why would I think that?'

She sank back into her pillow and closed her eyes. 'They all do, I know it, except... It's always there—that look on their faces, those hushed conversations. Following me...like flies. Only when I go riding, they can't catch up. Everything disappears.'

An image flashed through the doctor's mind—the girl against Sohra's expansive sky and desolate hills. Perhaps this was a strange place for a girl like her to spend her time.

'Your uncle told me you were...not yourself this afternoon.'

She answered quietly, 'It's my migraines, they explode in my head.'

'Where does it ache?'

'Everywhere. It's like a light—a bright, blinding light. As though I'm having a vision of another life, or the end of time...'

She was much too young to speak of such things, the doctor thought, but didn't say so.

'Have you had them before?'

'Sometimes. In London.'

'Have you been sleeping well?'

She shook her head and reached for a glass of water on the bedside table.

'What keeps you awake?'

'Nightmares.' She laughed. 'Or "juvenile blarney" as my aunt calls them.'

Somehow, the doctor didn't find that hard to believe.

'She says it's silly to pay any attention to dreams.' Lucy turned, her eyes, bright and wary, met his. 'But you, doctor, you don't think so. Kyntang told me that here dreams are as important as waking life. Do you believe that too?'

'Well, there are many things that Khasis believe—most of them born of centuries of stories and superstition.' He spoke lightly, trying to calm her sudden restless excitement.

'But is it true that people can be possessed? You've seen them... Is it true?' A flush of colour rose on her cheeks. Her hair glinted in the lantern light.

The doctor took off his stethoscope and placed it in his bag. 'I have seen people who are deeply unhappy. And within this emptiness, many demons may reside. Like creatures in the hollow of a tree. I don't know if the demons come from outside or within.' He added gently, 'But if you dream of loved ones who are no more, the Khasis say they come to visit you...'

'I used to dream of golden eggs,' she interrupted. 'They fell all over like rain, whistling through the air, bursting when they touched the ground. And now, a fire bird.' She turned to him. 'What does it mean? If you dream of being inside a fire bird.' The girl suddenly pushed the quilt away and climbed down from the bed. Standing barefoot in her white nightdress she looked like an angel who'd stepped out of a painting—like the ones he'd seen hanging in Father Bevan's office. She moved to the window at the other end of the room and flung it open. A gusty wind tugged at the curtain and the edges of her clothing.

'It's what I dream of...floating around there,' she gestured towards the sky. 'A dazzling fire bird comes crashing down to earth, like a star that's burst into a million flames. It drops fast, lower and lower, shrieking loud and clear...' She placed her palms against her ears, shivering in the cold. 'I'm dizzy…I'm dizzy,' she murmured, and crumpled to the floor, knocking over the chair and table.

Doctor Wallang lit a cigarette as he stepped out of the bungalow. It was a clear night, and far away a half-moon hung over the gentle rise of a mountain. He stood at the edge of the garden path, unsure whether he ought to have left. Yet there didn't seem to be anything more he could do. Moments after Lucy had fainted, her aunt rushed in, followed closely by Jonah. From her dress pocket, Mrs Smithson whipped out a packet of smelling salts and, with practised ease, slipped it under her niece's nose. When Lucy came round, the doctor carried her to the bed—she was light in his arms—laid her down, and covered her with the quilt. She was too exhausted to speak, and soon enough she fell asleep.

'She's alright,' he'd reassured the family. 'It was probably the cold from the window… We should let her rest.' As they walked out, he'd glanced back to see Jonah pause by the bed. He'd never seen that expression on the boy's face before—it was an odd and unusual tenderness.

In the living room, Mr Smithson had asked the doctor what he suggested they should do. Doctor Wallang hadn't been able to prescribe anything specific. Lucy needed to eat better, put on some weight, perhaps meet other English girls her age.

'I know Miss Lucy sometimes helps out at Sunday School,' the doctor added, 'but it'd be good if she had more friends to keep her occupied.'

'When she's better I'll take her to Shillong,' said Jonah.

With the striking of the clock Mr Smithson had exclaimed at the lateness of the hour, and insisted the doctor go home.

Doctor Wallang stubbed out the cigarette and looked back at the bungalow. It lay shrouded in darkness; the household had retired and the lanterns put out. He wrapped the shawl closer around him, glad for its warmth against the frosty night air. From the pine forest came the wail of a niangkongwieng, its shrill, tremulous notes carried to him on the wind.

'Next,' the doctor called, wondering how many patients were left before he was done for the day. He'd seen more cases than usual and was tired. From the window, he caught a glimpse of his wife watering the vegetable garden, leaving neat lines of dark, wet soil. On his desk lay a note from Sahib Flynn, requesting for an antiseptic cream to apply on a cut on his hand. As Doctor Wallang mixed the medication in a mortar, his back to the door, someone entered the room.

'How can I help you?' he asked.

'Doctor, will she become well?'

The young man, with windswept hair and lean, wiry limbs, seemed uneasy indoors—perhaps he was more at home in the stables or out on the hills.

'They won't let her come out any more now. I hear she's ill...lah kem ksuid.' The boy struggled to stay calm.

It had been a week since Doctor Wallang's visit to Kut Madan. He would have liked to check on Lucy, but he hadn't been summoned, and he couldn't drop by at the bungalow unannounced.

'Why are you concerned about her?'

34

The young man flushed.

'I'm Kyntang...'

'I know who you are. That's why I'm asking.'

'You won't understand,' he said, with the martyric certainty of youth. 'Everyone told me I'm mad, I must forget her because this—it's not possible.'

'It's not possible,' said the doctor. 'You know that.'

'I'm the only one she can talk to in this place.' His voice contained a quiet relentlessness. Doctor Wallang encountered it everywhere in Sohra—the 'knupmawiang blossoms, the hardy villagers. It was what enabled them to survive their valleyed isolation, the perpetual rain, the long winters.

'One day, she came back crying,' the young man continued, 'after going riding with Bah Jonah. She looked upset so I asked her what was wrong. She couldn't believe I spoke their language...but I've worked with bilati people all my life.'

'It will never make you one of them.'

'I don't want to be one of them.' He sounded mutinous. 'I just want to know if she'll be well.'

'She's young and strong, but beyond that I can't say. Who knows what demons people wrestle with on their own.' The doctor carefully emptied the antiseptic preparation into a bottle. 'Did she ever tell you about her dreams?'

The young man hesitated. 'I don't remember but the next time she...'

'You cannot see her again, Kyntang. Not if you know what's good for her.' He gestured to the door. 'And for you.'

When the doctor was summoned to Kut Madan a fortnight later, he found Mrs Smithson waiting for him by the front door. On her face were hints of how she must have once been beautiful, yet now, her high cheekbones only served to emphasize the long hollowness of her cheeks, and her eyes, though startlingly blue, were cold and distant.

'How is Lucy?' asked the doctor; he wished her husband was around to take the formal, disquieting edge off the air.

'The foolish girl has stopped eating.'

'For how long?'

She paused. 'Four days...nothing but bread and water, some fruit. And only when we force it down her throat.' Her voice carried a trace of exasperation. He had a feeling Mrs Smithson was accustomed to people submitting to her orders; presumably she didn't know what to do with her niece.

'She's stubborn,' the lady blurted. 'Just like Eve. I told my sister to get out of London, the city was being bombed to bits, for god's sake...but no, she stayed on, to nurse the wounded. And now...well, now I have an impossible situation on my hands.'

Doctor Wallang wanted to say he was sure it was traumatic for Lucy too.

'May I see her?' he asked.

She gestured for him to follow. They walked down the narrow, airless corridor that led to Lucy's room; without a lantern it appeared darker during the day than at night. At the door, she stopped. 'See if you can talk some sense into her, doctor.'

He found Lucy sitting by the window, a shawl wrapped around her knees, an unfinished embroidery hoop on her lap. On the table was a plate of winter fruit—small soh um berries and thick, fleshy soh mon—lying untouched and unpeeled.

He wasn't expecting to find his patient looking well, but he didn't think she'd have deteriorated this quickly either.

'How are you feeling?' he asked, trying to avoid her dark-circled eyes.

She glanced up at him, her skin translucent in the light. 'May I go riding, doctor?'

It was too cold, and she much too weak. 'When you get better, of course you may.'

She turned to look outside; a series of frosty nights had left the landscape pockmarked with patches of burnt, shrivelled grass.

'I will not get better.'

'You won't if you carry on this way. Your aunt says you're refusing to eat...' He sat on a stool beside her. 'How are your headaches?'

'They come and go.'

Around her were layers of fog far thicker than the clouds that rippled over the hills.

'Have you been sleeping well?'

'Yes.'

'And your dreams?'

A small smile flitted over her face. 'They visit like old friends.'

They sat in silence, a faint drizzle had begun; it pattered softly on the tin roof.

A maid entered and placed a coal-filled chula in front of them.

Lucy drew her hands out from under the shawl and held them over the stove. They shook slightly.

'Doctor, if I'm not permitted outside...no matter how

much I long to...I'd like to bring it in...the sun, the wind, even the rain.'

He said he wasn't sure he understood.

'What I mean is...I'd like to see Kyntang.'

The doctor began to say it wouldn't be possible.

'They've dismissed him from service at the stables here... I overheard the maids talking...he was good with the horses.'

Lucy sounded as though her mind was far away on the open hillside.

'I know my aunt and uncle won't hear of it, even Jonah... they don't understand. I was sent here to be safe.' Her voice dropped to a whisper. 'But it follows me everywhere.'

'What does?'

'There's no escaping it,' she continued. 'I told you. Yet sometimes when I'm with him...' Her eyes were the colour of the hills after the rain.

'I don't see how such a thing could be arranged.'

Her shoulders drooped. Under her shawl, she seemed a captive, fluttering creature. Outside, it was growing dark, the days were short and graceless in November. He stared at the coal in the chula, burning amber-golden, in between liquid and light, solid and shadow. Lucy had her eyes closed, her breathing flimsy and shallow.

'Will you tell him at least, doctor? What I said...'

Doctor Wallang hesitated.

'Please.'

'If I see him.'

The embroidery hoop slipped to the floor; the doctor picked it up and placed it on the table. She was stitching a wreath of white lilies.

'Are these your favourite flowers?' he asked.

'No,' she replied quietly. 'Somebody else's. I couldn't find any to place on their grave.'


One evening in late December, Doctor Wallang was summoned to a house close to where Kyntang lived, to perform an exorcism. The woman had lost her child, but the dead baby, the villagers said, refused to leave her. Since the stillbirth three days ago she'd been lying in bed muttering incoherently and weeping.

'She might be in shock,' he said, 'and grieving.'

'But, doctor,' they insisted, 'we've heard it crying at night, hungry for her milk.'

So he sprinkled holy water around the room, chanted a mantra, and spoke into the air, commanding the child's spirit to leave its mother in peace. Finally, he asked to be left alone with her, and spoke to her gently, telling her that she was young and had many more years to give birth to healthy children. He then gave her something to make her sleep and instructed the household to allow her to rest. The doctor walked back, exhausted, wishing he hadn't missed the last bus home. Along the way he passed people from the village returning from Sohra market, carrying khohs, conical cane baskets, filled with vegetables, grain and fruit. Trailing behind them was Kyntang, doubled over with a gunnysack on his back.

The young man didn't see the doctor. He looked weary, and his face more lean than usual.

'Kyntang...'

The boy stopped and slung the sack to the ground.

Once, Doctor Wallang had taken his children to see the Mawsmai caves, an hour away from home; they were cold and hollow, running for miles into the earth. Standing in front of Kyntang, he felt a similar sense of emptiness.

'How is your father keeping?' the doctor asked.

'Not too good over the winter.'

'And you? Where are you working now?'

'There's a bilati man who's building a house near Mawmluh…I look after his horses.'

The doctor hesitated. 'I saw Miss Lucy about a month ago. She is…'

'Better, I'm sure.'

Dusk had fallen heavily around them and he found it hard to decipher the look on Kyntang's face.

'She said to tell you…'

For a moment, the young man's eyes were set alight.

'That she was sorry you were dismissed from Kut Madan. That you were very good with the horses—'

Kyntang laughed, it reverberated across the empty hills. He wished the doctor a good evening, heaved the sack up on his back and walked away.

The doctor stood on the road with the wind whipping his face. The light in the west, a knife-stroke of silvery white, was fading slowly, while the sky throbbed with slow and fiery darkness.

It wasn't until six months later, when monsoon clouds gathered murderously over Sohra, that Doctor Wallang was reminded of Lucy. He'd wondered about her, of course—news filtered through to him from Sahib Flynn that in March, with the first flourish of spring, she'd left Sohra for Shillong, then Calcutta, and onward to England. There she would stay with Mrs Smithson's friend and her family, and study to become a nurse like her mother. That summer Sahib Flynn was also leaving, abandoning the failed plantation to go work in the plains where the weather conditions were far more suitable for growing tea. His departure, however, had been delayed by a spell of thunderstorms that broke out in clamorous bursts over the valley. One night, during a particularly heavy downpour, Doctor Wallang thought he heard the drone of an airplane.

'Not in this weather,' he murmured before turning back to his book.

The next morning, a helper from the Smithson household called at the clinic.

'Please, doctor,' he said, out of breath, 'could you come immediately—there has been an accident behind the bungalow.'

'What happened?' he asked as they hurried down the road.

'Last night, something fell out of the sky.'

There was already a large gathering when he got there—people from the village, a cluster of priests in their black habits, and, some distance away, Jonah and his mother. They were all standing at the edge of the forest, pointing and looking over the cliff. Doctor Wallang made his way to the front of the crowd, and found himself next to Flynn.

'What is it?' he asked, although he'd already guessed.

The cliff face was gashed by trails of black scorch marks, which ended in the shrubbery.

'A Dakota,' replied Flynn, 'carrying passengers...bless their souls.'

The aircraft could barely be seen—it had crashed and tumbled further down to a ledge—though metallic fragments were scattered across the rocks like shiny rain. A group of nimble-footed valley men had clambered to the airplane but found no survivors—only burnt, mangled limbs. Now they were carrying back machine parts to sell as scrap.

'Tragic,' said the doctor. 'But to travel in such weather…'

Flynn nodded. 'Insanity. But war forces people to do stupid things.'

'How many were there?'

'Three …two men and a woman. We think.'

The doctor shuddered. He'd seen death in many guises, but this seemed strange and violent and lingered uncleanly in the air. He had a sudden urge to leave Kut Madan. Flynn seemed to feel the same—'Need to head back,' he said abruptly, 'Sonny's on his own.'

The doctor tried to keep it out of his mind, how it must have felt to fall helplessly through the air. Suddenly, he heard a familiar voice: 'I wonder who they were.'

It was Kyntang, who'd appeared as though from nowhere.

'I don't think we'll ever know,' the doctor replied.

There were others around them voicing similar thoughts; exclamations continued to fill the air—'It happened around midnight', 'How much can I sell this for?', 'Any identification?', 'Were they all bilati?', 'Mad to fly in the storm', 'Did anyone see it?'

'I did, I did,' shouted a boy no older than ten. 'From the window…flying across the sky. It looked like…like…'

'A fire bird,' the doctor thought he heard Kyntang say, but when he turned the young man was gone. Behind him were

42

a crowd of unknown faces, while in front, the valley opened up, a hollow green casket cradling a disconsolate wind. Stray strands of fog, exhaled from the earth, would soon envelop Sohra and conceal it from the world.

He walked home slowly, and when he reached, he stopped to look at the 'knupmawiang, whose yellow flowers were just beginning to bloom.

# Echo Words

Often, when I stand at the door of my grocery store, watching the buses offload their passengers, I remember the French lady, and how she arrived in Shillong out of nowhere on an afternoon like any other. She wore a high-waisted navy skirt, a well-cut blazer of the same colour over a crisp white blouse, and a floral-patterned scarf that kept her hair in place. I remember how, after she alighted, she stood for a moment in the sunshine, taking in her surroundings—Kelvin Cinema, the Secretariat building and its sloping, manicured lawns, Mr Biswas's Time House watch shop. Even from that distance I could tell she was exhilarated to be here.

I remember wondering why. I couldn't understand it. Apart from pernicious local drama, nothing of much excitement ever happened in our small, sleepy town. At the time, the British had been gone five years, but Shillong still slumped in post-colonial depression. We missed them; some wouldn't even mind having them back. As Mama Jos would say when he came in to buy tobacco, 'Better the white man than these dkhars.'

'Which ones?' I'd ask.

'All of them.'

It was a useful word, dkhar, clubbing together anyone who came from beyond the hills.

Everyone had watched curiously as she walked briskly towards my shop—Mr Biswas, the market women with their baskets of seasonal vegetables and fruit, Kong Lee who manned a makeshift kwai and cigarette kiosk, Bah Lyngdoh from his jadoh stall nearby. I knew the questions later would be deft and numerous.

The bell tinkled when she entered. She couldn't have been more than thirty-five, on the fringes of youthful beauty. Fair, freckled skin stretched over high cheekbones, and hazel eyes, the colour of our winter trees, were framed by a pair of light spectacles. Beneath the scarf, her hair was pulled back and coiled into a bun. I conjectured silently that she must be here on business of the church; it was the most likely explanation. If that were so, she'd probably be the most attractive sister of mercy we'd seen yet. She greeted me, and said she wished to buy a few things—candles, matches, barley water, a bottle of ink. Her accent was soft, slightly nasal and breathless; I couldn't recognize it even though I was familiar with many others—pukka British that had been around so many years, Italian from the Salesian priests at Don Bosco, the lilting Irish of the Catholic nuns and monks who ran the town's missionary schools, and even German, before the first great war rendered the Salvatorian fathers our enemies.

'Shall I call a taxi for you, madam?' I offered, curious to know where she was going.

'Thank you, I have one waiting already.' She gestured to a blue Chevrolet parked outside my shop.

When she left, I noticed the car headed in the direction of Ward's Lake and assumed she must be lodging at Pine Wood, the grandest hotel in Shillong.

After that, the French lady was sighted regularly on our streets, walking around with a notebook and sheaf of papers.

'Memsahib beit', was the common refrain; most people thought she was clearly crazy, a young woman travelling alone in this remote part of the world. A few others conjectured she was a nurse, a nun, a foreign government official, until Mama Jos in his infinite wisdom and uncanny ability to pick up gossip, told us she was an anthropologist.

The people gathered in my shop remained silent—they furrowed their brows, stared blankly, and blinked. They'd never heard the word before. I busied myself with tidying the canned fruit shelf.

'What in Jesu's name is that?' asked Kong Lee.

Bah Lyngdoh, smoking a beedi at the door, said it sounded like a disease.

'Ni, all of you are such villagers,' pronounced Mama Jos, thoroughly enjoying the bewilderment he'd created.

'Yes, we're all from Jowai.'

That was Mama Jos's hometown.

It took a great deal of cajoling after that to get him to continue.

'Well,' he said finally, 'I heard from Kong Shai'—who was a friend of a cousin of a lady who worked as a cleaner at Pine Wood—'that the memsahib is here to write a book on the Khasis.'

'Why?' said Bah Lyngdoh at once. 'Are we some rare, exotic animal species?'

Kong Lee remarked that he might be but the rest of them were pretty normal.

Mama Jos shrugged. 'Now, why and for what she's doing this, I don't know. The sahibs have strange ideas...but no good will come of this, I can feel it in my bones.'

I suppose you could say I played, however unknowingly, an important part in the drama yet to unfold. The French lady came to the shop one morning to buy ink and mentioned she needed a translator, someone who could speak both English and Khasi. I suggested she meet Malcolm, who lived a few doors away from me on Quinton Road, and taught at one of the convent schools. I'd known him since he was a boy and he'd grown into a good-natured if slightly ineffectual lad with more than a little evidence of Anglo ancestry in his features. I offered to go across to his house that evening and ask him, if he was keen, to get in touch with her at the hotel. Sooner than I expected, it was all fixed up, and the French lady and Malcolm travelled around town together—the fair princess and her knight—swiftly meeting and interviewing people.

Try as we might, there was not much information to be gleaned about her. Some said before this she'd travelled around Cambodia, trekking through jungles and living in remote villages. Others were convinced she'd lost her mind after her husband was killed in the war. 'That's why she wanders the world pulled by some 'suidtynjang.' Mischievous spirits that led travellers astray. Yet as far as I could see, she was quite sane and dedicated to her work. One evening, Kong Lee told us the French lady had stopped at her kwai kiosk, and questioned her about her children (five, all of whom worked in the paddy fields), her husband (a drunken lout), and her livelihood. 'She wrote it all down in a notebook,' she said, trying, and failing, to not sound excited. At Bah Lyngdoh's jadoh stall, the lady was interested in the food being cooked over the big wood fires in the kitchen.

'Asked me about all the damn ingredients,' the owner told us, a trace of gruff pride in his voice. 'What's in the doh jem? How is this called? How do you make doh shiang, doh khleh…she even tried some of the stuff.'

'Did she like it?' I asked.

'Must be. She finished everything on her plate.'

More often than not, she attracted the unwanted attention of our young men, loitering on the roadside.

'Come home with me, I'll give you lots to write about', 'Why don't you write a book on Khasi birds, I'll show you my sim.' And they'd point, unabashedly, to their crotch.

If Malcolm was there, he'd fend them off, describing, in the choicest Khasi words, whose sons they were and which parts of their anatomy should fall off. Else the French lady ignored them, walking past with her skirts bristling.

The stories about the French lady and Malcolm started about a fortnight later, when the schools closed for three-month-long vacations and people spent a large part of their day sunning themselves in short-lived winter sunshine.

'Is she writing about the Khasis or Malcolm?' sniggered Bah Lyngdoh.

'He has a Khasi mother,' replied Kong Lee, 'that's probably enough.'

Bah Jos, however, provided us with more gossip, filched most faithfully from his friend and neighbour Kong Shai. The hotel cleaners had heard them, he said, doing unmentionable things in the middle of the afternoon. It had been unmistakable, the sound of skin slapping against skin, the moans, the murmurs. Afterwards, they'd sat out in the veranda, smoking cigarettes, drinking tea, cool as cucumbers, in front of everyone in the clear light of day. That's what was so surprising, the utter candidness of their affair, with no regard whatsoever for Malcolm's wife.

'Didn't he marry her only for the money?' someone conjectured.

'What else? Have you seen her face?' The people in the shop dissolved into laughter.

It was true Kong Banri couldn't be called a town beauty— she had sweet enough features but was far from being as striking as the French lady. When she and Malcolm got married a year ago, everyone said she was lucky to have snagged herself a good-looking half-sahib.

As the days passed, the stories grew wilder and more extravagant. He'd spent the night with her, leaving for his house rumpled and sleepy in the early hours of the morning. They were at it like dogs, the people in the next room had complained to the receptionist about the noise. Someone said they'd seen them sneaking off like teenagers into the Risa Colony forest, where all sorts of wanton debaucheries were rumoured to take place near the abandoned water tank. Soon, there was talk of Malcolm leaving his wife.

All this while Kong Banri remained impassive—venturing out into the market in the evenings to buy fruit and vegetables, walking to her family home in Polo Grounds, stopping to pick up tailored material from Roopkala. When she dropped into the shop, everyone said her smile, never usually generous, seem more forced than usual.

One afternoon, I was alone when she entered, saying she'd like to buy some flour. I bustled around nervously, but she stood there patiently, looking out of the window, her eyes taking in the pine-forested hills in the distance. I felt sorry for her, but there was little I could do apart from make small talk—the weather, the price of tomatoes, the rumours about the nongshohnoh sightings in town.

'Mostly around Iew Duh,' I prattled, 'but that's not too far from here.'

Stories of the nongshohnoh, or hired kidnappers, sprang up every once in a while—someone went missing or somebody saw a figure skulking around in darkened areas, or worse, dragging away a gunnysack big enough to hold a body.

Kong Banri murmured something suitably perfunctory— 'It's terrible the things one hears about'—and left.

In a small town such as this, word of the nongshohnoh even reached the French lady. She came in one morning, fresh and radiant—her eyes a deeper hazel, her face framed by hair worn long and loose. Her pale russet dress was most becoming, bringing out the warmth of her skin and the slim shape of her figure. As Kong Lee said later, she looked like a woman who'd been getting it good and often.

She asked me what it was all about, the thlen and nongshohnoh, and I explained as best I could.

'A nongshohnoh is paid by thlen keepers to kill people for blood, or he marks his victims by cutting off a bit of their hair or their clothing.'

'Do they drink the blood?'

'No, it's for the thlen...the person who is marked falls ill and dies slowly.'

'Ah! And, of course, the keepers are wealthy families, because the thlen, in return, makes them rich beyond their dreams?'

I nodded.

She played with the plastic plate on the counter, the one on which I kept kwai for my customers. 'You know, they say you never need to put a lid on a basket of crabs.'

I was confused. 'Why?'

'Because if one tries to climb up, the others pull it down.'

I didn't know what to make of it; I felt as though she was mocking me and suddenly I didn't want to answer any more of her questions.

'Will that be all?' I asked, referring to her purchases. She looked up, her face oddly serious. 'And what does it look like, this thlen?'

'Supposedly a snake, a small serpent.'

I hoped she wouldn't ask me anything more, and she didn't. She paid and stepped outside, her hair glinting in the sunlight.

That evening, I shut shop early; for some reason I was weary, and felt a strange sense of foreboding. In the distance, the hills gleamed a darker green, and despite a full radiant moon, it seemed as though there were forces at work that bathed the whole world in shadow. In my dreams, restless as my slumber, I thought I heard the faint beating of drums played on some distant rooftop like a steady heartbeat.

The next day the lovers disappeared.

I mean they weren't seen on the streets together any more. He didn't stop by to place a bet at the thoh teem shops in the morning, and didn't drop in at Bah Lyngdoh's food stall for a quick ja bowl. She wasn't sighted near Ward's Lake where she liked to go for long walks or in the veranda near her room where she read and wrote for hours. The first thing we assumed, of course, was that they'd run away together.

'She's gathered more than enough material for her book.' Kong Lee giggled as she quartered betel nut on her palm.

There was a deliciously thrilling ring to the story; perhaps they'd manage to make their way to Guwahati, or even as far as Calcutta to live in the big city—an unknown, mysterious couple, far from the cloistered confines of Shillong. Some people even said that they admired the pair for their courage and the unbridled surety of their love.

A week passed before Mama Jos wondered aloud whether anything worse had happened.

'Worse? What do you mean worse?' asked Bah Lyngdoh, standing at the door, smoking a beedi as usual.

Mama Jos tapped the tobacco out of his pipe.

'Kong Shai said that the memsahib hardly took any of her things from the hotel room. Isn't that strange?' The word hung heavy in the air, like a coil of thick, dark smoke.

Someone said they should inform the rangbah shnong, the neighbourhood chief, he would know what to do, or even the police. Mama Jos said we should keep an eye on Kong Banri.

I tried to cut short the madness, saying that surely she wasn't that kind of woman, besides she was so small and slight, there was no way she could overpower her husband as well as his lover.

'There are other ways to harm somebody...' said Kong Lee from the corner. We knew she was referring to ancient charms and mantras. Kong Banri came from an old Khasi family, the Rynjahs, still unconverted to the light of Christianity.

'I've heard that's how her mother owns so much property in town, all thlen money,' added a woman who sold vegetables around the corner.

We were still discussing the issue when Kong Banri walked into the shop. Her dark eyes flittered over everyone, and a deep flush crept up her cheeks. Since we all fell silent, looking away in embarrassment, she must have realized that we were talking about her. Yet she forced on a smile and asked for a variety of grocery items.

'Kumno,' said Mama Jos; he was the only one who dared address her.

She nodded in acknowledgement. He asked after her health and then about Malcolm.

'He's gone to Garo Hills,' she replied quietly. 'The memsahib needs a translator for her work there.'

When she left, the room drooped in disappointment, but soon Kong Lee declared that if Kong Banri believed that unlikely story she deserved to be cuckolded. What sort of a stupid wife was she? The vegetable seller whispered that old mantras worked even from great distances; as long as Kong Banri was in possession of something that belonged to the lovers, she could still do them harm.

'What do you mean?' Bah Lyngdoh was now mincing tobacco on his palm.

The lady told us about a family in Laban, the oldest neighbourhood in Shillong, who were originally from Sohra. Very rich, very proud. They probably weren't thlen keepers but they knew mantras which could cause great harm.

'It could be a slow disease,' she elaborated. 'The kind that doctors can't diagnose. Or'—and this she swore she'd seen with her own eyes—'like what happened to poor Bah Passah.'

'What happened to poor Bah Passah?' we asked.

She wrapped her jaiñkyrshah, a checkered cotton apron, closer. 'He'd had an argument with the head of the family, about some property somewhere...and one day, when he walked out of their house, he dropped dead on the road. A healthy man of fifty.'

'That's crazy,' said Bah Lyngdoh.

Bah Jos nodded gravely. 'I'd heard about this...'

'Let's wait and see,' I said feebly, 'I'm sure they'll return soon.'

No one, not even me, I must admit, was convinced.

A fortnight passed by, and then a whole month. There was still no news of the French lady and her translator. The hotel staff had apparently resorted to stowing the memsahib's things in a godown, as they needed the room for other guests. Our small town was inflamed with stories, and people began to take sides in a quiet civil war—those who were convinced that Kong Banri and her family were behind the disappearance of the lovers and those of us who still believed they were travelling through Garo Hills. The latter were fast dwindling in numbers.

Everywhere crept whispers of the Rynjahs being thlen keepers, old stories were dug up of how, in the past, their business rivals left their home with a moora stuck to their backsides, that their greater enemies would suddenly drop dead on the streets.

'I thought that was the family in Laban,' I said.

'The Rynjahs too,' snapped Kong Lee, annoyed at the interruption.

The vegetable seller was telling us that strange drumbeats could be heard on the Rynjahs' roof every night—feverishly playing until dawn. They lived in a large double-storyed bungalow near the racecourse and the busy Polo market.

'Speak to anyone there, they'll tell you' she concluded.

When we asked Kong Banri about her husband, she'd say he was still away, working as a translator for the memsahib. I don't think it would be wrong to say that her words sounded hollow. People started keeping away from her and her family, and soon she moved out of the house on Quinton Road and went to live in Polo Grounds with her parents.

'It's the guilt,' said Kong Lee, 'it's probably driving her mad.'

'Even if she did something,' I interrupted, 'what on earth did she do with the bodies?'

Unfortunately, that set up another hundred rounds of breathless speculation—perhaps they'd been thrown into Ward's Lake, or further away into some river outside Shillong. Maybe they'd been burnt in the Khasi crematorium in Wahingdoh, where bones of the deceased were placed in small stone urns dotted around the hillside. They could have also been buried in the vast barren land behind the Rynjahs' house in Polo Grounds. The last was dismissed unceremoniously until Kong Lee, walking past there one evening, on her way home, came across a dog carrying a bone that looked like a human femur.

The next morning, the police swarmed the place, as did a crowd of onlookers. Everyone willing and able were given shovels. I held mine tight but couldn't bring myself to dig the marshy ground; a great wave of nausea washed over me, I felt betrayed by the earth beneath my feet. A group of feral dogs sniffed and snuffled around us, probably looking for more meat. Some people beat them away with shovels until they yelped. It was impossible, I thought, yet perhaps it was precisely because nothing ever happened in this town that we were willing to believe anything. Rumours had given shape to something tangible. The winds here were trapped by the mountains; our words weren't blown away. Instead, they returned to us in strange, distorted echoes, ferocious reflections of ourselves. On that crisp February day, the cold clawing at our fingers, we dug with mighty fervour, some working harder than they had all their lives. We brought up stone and roots and mud that would turn into thick, endless sludge during the monsoon. We realized that the burial ground, for lack of a better name, was about half a mile further when a young police officer there struck something with his shovel. The crowd moved up like sheep who'd found a greener pasture to graze. Soon, more cries and the sound of ringing metal filled the air. Slowly, we unearthed skeletons, not of humans, but horses, and rusty frames of entire vehicles.

It was a war cemetery, the livestock, ammunition and jeeps that the American and British army buried before leaving Shillong. They were given orders to do so rather than hand over their equipment and other paraphernalia to the locals. Before us spread an absurd assortment of military goods, abandoned and forgotten. The metal curled and twisted, the place stank of mould and old rot. I had a fleeting thought that this was where our words died and decayed. Soon, the dogs went crazy over the animal bones, barking and fighting with each other until they were kicked and chased away with sticks and stones. Scavengers started picking at the vehicles for scrap metal. We left only when evening fell, after we'd finished resurrecting our past.

A few weeks later, just before the schools reopened, Malcolm returned. Banri moved back to their house on Quinton Road. We never saw the French lady again. Once, I asked Malcolm about her, and he gave me a vague answer saying that on their travels she'd fallen mysteriously ill with a fever that seemed to slowly suck away her strength and colour. Instead of coming back to Shillong, she went to Guwahati from where she'd make her way home, and hopefully recover.

People say the night Malcolm came back the drumbeats stopped, but even now I still hear them sometimes, throbbing in the darkness, steady as a heartbeat, old as time.

# Dream of the Golden Mahseer

The elder brother was taken by drink. The younger one by fairies.

The rational explanation for his disappearance was that he suffered diabetic hallucinations and walked off a cliff or into a forest, never to return. But I think that's ridiculous. Mama Kyn was the fittest man I knew. He survived the African Front during the Second World War. Not many people managed to do that.

In those days, when Mama Kyn and his brother were alive, we lived in a large, rambling house in the far west of town, near Iew Duh—the local market that spread like an ancient labyrinth beyond the Mot Phran war monument. It was a house that began life as a room my great-grandparents built. It survived the earthquake of 1897, the one, the old people said, that flattened the landscape as though it were butter and opened up valleys to the core of the earth. Although the room forever carried cracks and lopsided floorboards, it stood resolutely, the strong, steadfast heart of the house. As the family grew so did the building—wings and corridors added on like meandering afterthoughts, resulting in uneven floors and crooked doors and windows. The wooden shutters barely closed, but in those days there was little fear of burglars. Neighbours walked in and out as though it were their own home, friends dropped in at odd hours yet never left without a meal, and stray cats and dogs were welcome to stay long after the rain that had driven them to shelter had stopped.

Around the house, at the edges of its vast and untamed garden, were a tilting row of tin and wood shacks occupied by a motley assortment of people—an old woman called Mena who helped with the cooking and cleaning; Bah Lam, the dwarfish household handyman; and, at the end of the line in two separate yet identical containers, the brothers Mama Heh and Mama Kyn. Within the main house were my grandparents, their eldest daughter Ruth and my young uncle Gordon whose room was closest to the main door so he didn't have to stagger far after a raucously late night. My parents occupied a bedroom towards the back of the house, next to which I slept with my older brother Keith and my sister Stephanie. I was eleven, small for my age, and mostly bullied by everyone. On particularly windy nights, when chestnuts dropped from the tree overhanging our roof, pattering on the tin like rain, Keith would shove me with his foot. 'Ei, go get the soh ot.' If I pretended to be asleep, Stef would join in from the other end of the room. 'Aaron, go, otherwise I'll tell everyone you wet your bed.'

'I do not,' I'd protest.

'But who will believe you?'

I could see the whites of her teeth as she grinned in the darkness. My sister was stocky and strong, and most of the neighbourhood boys were afraid of her. Inevitably, I'd climb down from the bed and tiptoe outside through the bathroom. I met Mama Heh on many nights as I scrambled around trying to collect chestnuts in the cold. The fact that I was outdoors never seemed to surprise him; usually he'd be tottering towards the general direction of his shack, belting out a war song or peeing long and hard against the garden wall.

Or both.

'Mei, why does Mama Heh drink so much?' I once asked my mother.

'Because he's seen two wars.'

Africa in the first and Burma in the second, I found out later.

'So?' I persisted.

She paused at chopping the onions. 'He has many memories to forget.'

'And Mama Kyn? Why doesn't he drink? He was in one war.'

'You ask him that,' she replied and told me to stop bothering her with silly questions.

Uncle Gordon, who spent his few waking hours strumming a guitar in his room, told me Mama Heh had many more reasons to be unhappy.

'He survived the prison camp, you know, but his only son didn't.'

'Did he have a wife?' I asked.

'Yeah, but she ran off with a Scottish soldier or something. He was in the military hospital here in Shillong, and she was a nurse.'

'What about Mama Kyn? Was he married?'

'No. The only love in his life is kha bah.' A type of local fish. Mama Kyn was a keen fisherman.

Our curious patchwork of lives lapped on peacefully—my grandfather left for his car workshop every morning at eleven; my father to the government health department where he was a medical officer; Uncle Gordon made occasional perfunctory stabs at attending college where he was supposedly studying zoology; Aunt Ruth diligently attended to her duties as

English teacher at the Montessori school; my grandmother, a devoted gardener, spent her time coaxing vegetables and flowers out of warm, red earth; and my mother, once she'd packed Keith, Stef, and me off to school, would retire to the kitchen, to her knitting, or walk to Iew Duh to bargain for the day's freshest culinary offerings. This steady routine was interrupted occasionally by childhood illness and local drama—a neighbourhood wedding or funeral—and at other instances by Mama Heh's flamboyant drunken outbursts.

Once, my grandparents threw a birthday party for Uncle Gordon, and while everyone sang love songs around the piano, his voice rose above the clamour, brash, slurred, and angry—'You have never known war,' he shouted to a slightly embarrassed-looking young man next to him. He was the friend of a neighbour's son who was the same age as Uncle Gordon. The music came to an abrupt halt.

'I didn't...' he began but was interrupted by a string of expletives that outlined in rich detail what Mama Heh thought of the young man and his ancestry. 'May you all never know war,' he said, and his words rang through the living room, twining around the cigarette smoke, settling in between the piano keys, turning the alcohol in everyone's mouth a little flat and sour. When the glass slipped from Mama Heh's hand and shattered on the floor, he started openly weeping and my grandmother and Aunt Ruth had to lead him away.

'What did you say?' asked Uncle Gordon later.

The young man, flushed to the tips of his ears, said he'd asked if Mama Heh had any war wounds.

Occasionally, though, when Mama Heh was sober and lucid, he would join in our backyard football games, played between the kids in our house and our neighbours' brood, who'd jump across the wall any chance they got. Two tall bamboo sticks made for a pair of unsteady goalposts, and the ball, regularly flattened by an enthusiastic forward, was usually wrapped in rags. Mama Kyn, who often left for his fishing trips to Um Ïam at dawn, was hardly ever around. So far, Mama Heh was my favourite of the two—especially since we always won whenever he was in our team.

Mama Heh's wish for us all to never know war didn't strictly come true—although our brush with conflict was restricted to wrestling each other for the radio tuner to listen to the evening news. I have hazy memories of the India–Pakistan war of '65. We spent hours pasting newspaper on our windowpanes, blackening our Hillman's headlights, and digging trenches in the garden. All this only to run outside to catch a glimpse of the East Pakistan bombers as they roared across our skies, drowning the wail of the town's warning siren. What's more clear in my mind is that it was the year Mama Heh died. It wasn't long after the war that he took to his bed and refused to leave his room. Within the depths of those pillows and blankets, he aged more than he had in the past fifty years, as though the weight of life had suddenly fallen on him all at once. He became delirious, mixing up his memories, calling out for his runaway wife and long-dead son.

'We ran away together, Jacob and me, from the war camp. In Burma it was very wet and cold. We walked for days and days. He was so tired, my poor boy,' he'd say.

Nobody had the heart to remind him that Jacob had succumbed to his wounds a day after being taken prisoner. Before Mama Heh died, at about four in the morning when the rooster crowed, he smiled. Aunt Ruth, who was watching by his bedside, said he muttered 'He is here'.

I only started spending time with Mama Kyn later that year when my mother discovered I was failing almost every subject in school. This was not, as my teacher pointed out, because I was stupid but because I wasn't even trying. 'Aaron is distracted,' said Mrs Nongrum, peering at us over her spectacles. 'Sometimes he's also very sleepy in class. Your son should go to bed earlier, Kong Jasmine.' I didn't think it worth explaining to them how I spent many nights collecting chestnuts.

On the walk back home, my mother decided our house was filled with too many diversions, that there was always somebody dropping by, and that Uncle Gordon or even my own siblings hardly set me a good example to follow. 'Keith only wants to go to Kelvin Cinema, Stef is better at football than every boy in the locality...you're the only one with brains, Aaron. For studies.' I was dismayed at my mother's ambitions and the hopes she'd pinned on my academic abilities. It was better for her to expect nothing, allowing me to get away with little or no effort at schoolwork. 'You study in Mama Kyn's room,' she declared as we neared our gate, and my heart deflated, much like our football when Stef stepped on it.

For two hours every evening, I was sent across the backyard with textbooks and pencils in hand. It was October and the

Shillong air was soft and mild. Perfect for playing outdoors—seven stones, dodge ball, hide-and-seek, or when we felt particularly imaginative, smugglers and pirates. We'd tie an old pillowcase to a stick and sit atop the Hillman, waving it in the breeze, pretending we were far out at sea. We wouldn't be sailing long before an argument would break out between Keith and Stef over who'd be appointed captain, but it was tremendous fun while it lasted. Those evenings I'd gaze longingly at the others, with only the fear of my mother's anger keeping me glued to my seat. She had a sharp, impatient tongue that we were all used to, but her temper was fiery as sohmynken khnai, tiny 'rat' chillies that could send even my grandfather reeling.

It wouldn't have been as hard if the company I kept was a little more entertaining. Mama Kyn didn't talk much and it was up to me to initiate conversation when the drudgery of math and grammar became unbearable. This wasn't easy. Unlike Mama Heh, who was usually tipsy and voluble, his younger brother cleaned his fishing equipment in silence, rarely taking his eyes off the reel or the fine tangle of angling bait. Finally, despite the fact that I wasn't the least bit interested in the sport, I hazarded a question.

'What was the biggest fish you ever caught, mama?'

He didn't stop polishing the rod. I thought he hadn't heard me and was about to give up and turn back to my books when he replied, 'Bhoroli, 23rd December 1958.'

'Where is Bhoroli, mama?'

'It's a river in Assam, in the Bhalukpung district.'

'Is it bigger than Wah Dieng Doh?' I was referring to the river that hemmed our neighbourhood, where Keith, Stef, and I would sometimes go swimming in the spring.

Mama Kyn snorted, puffing at his pipe furiously. 'Bigger? In the monsoons you cannot see the other side. It's as wide as the sea.'

After that, none of our evenings were spent in silence.

He knew the rivers of the region intimately—both in the plains and the hills—and listed their characteristics like old, familiar lovers. Lai Lad, he said, was unpredictable, always in danger of swelling with swift and brutal flash floods, while Subansiri was complacently calm, perfect to visit for long, unhurried excursions. Ranikor was the wild child, difficult to navigate and tame, yet her waters were home to the golden mahseer, rare as drops of solid sunshine. On the Brahmaputra, mighty and vast, he had travelled and hunted with pirate boatmen, floating on makeshift bamboo melengs in jungle darkness when they'd sing folk songs and drink rice beer.

'What does rice beer taste like, Mama Kyn?'

My grand-uncle shook his head. 'I don't know. Never touched a drop.'

Brave enough now, I asked 'Why?'

He restuffed his pipe, bits of tobacco dropping to the floor like dark snowflakes.

'I was with supplies in Africa...'

I held my breath. Mama Kyn hardly ever spoke of his war days.

'We were in Tripoli, and had faced three days of non-stop shelling. They always went after supplies...the bastards. My friend Bolen and I were taking a walk; it was August, hot, dry, sand everywhere—in our food, our eyes, our socks, it even coated us like a second skin. So much sand. But we walked because we'd had enough of squatting in the trenches. Hipster...this bilati chap...and his gang were sitting on a tank, drinking. "Hey, Bobo...that's what they called Bolen... come join us," they said. We were going to, and any other day we would have, but that afternoon, I said no. I don't know why. They made fun of us, of course, called us women and all sorts of names, but when we were about a hundred metres away, a stray aircraft flew past and dropped more bombs. One hit the tank. They were gone before the dust cleared.'

His pipe had gone out, but Mama Kyn didn't seem to notice. There was a strange look in his eyes. He never spoke to me about the war again.

I spent less time with Mama Kyn when our winter holidays began, and since everyone was busy preparing for Christmas and the annual locality fête, they didn't seem to notice his longer-than-usual disappearances from the house. Whenever I peered into his room, in between playing football and kali het, it was empty—his clothes neatly folded at the foot of his bed. It was only later I realized that his fishing equipment was where it always was, neatly stowed away in the corner near a small tin trunk.

'Mei, where is Mama Kyn?'

My mother was plucking chicken feathers. It looked like a tiny white storm.

'Where he always is kein...at Wah Dieng Doh or Um Ïam.'

'But he's left behind his fishing things.'

'So maybe he's using nets now.' It was a tone that implied I should run along unless I too wanted to suffer a fate similar to the fowl.

71

I searched everywhere—in the main house, in the rooms where he sometimes liked to read or play carrom, in the garden where he often polished his fishing equipment, and for no good reason, even the vegetable patch where my grandmother was tending to a row of large-hearted cauliflowers. After some deliberation, I looked in Mama Heh's room. It had lain empty since his death and a thin film of dust coated the surface of everything. To disturb it, I felt, would be sacrilege. In the afternoon, I ventured further, to my grandfather's car workshop where a mechanic showed me how to test spark plugs; Mama Kyn, though, he said, hadn't set foot in there for months. Later, I walked down to Wah Dieng Doh, just in case my mother was right and he'd found an alternative to fishing rods. But there was no one by the river, and the water, cold and calm, flowed silently past. That night, unable to sleep, I crept out in the wintry darkness to check whether Mama Kyn had returned.

A light burned at his window, and the door was slightly ajar. Low voices wafted out of his room, but the only pair of shoes near the steps belonged to him. This was strange, I thought. As far as I could remember, apart from me, Mama Kyn never had anyone visiting him in his room. I stood shivering in the cold trying to catch the murmured sounds— were they speaking in Khasi? I couldn't pick up any familiar words. Were they speaking at all? At times, I thought I heard soft moans. As I crept closer I tripped over an upturned flower-pot. The voices stopped. The door flew open and Mama Kyn stepped out. 'You!' he shouted, and we stared at each other in silence, until he turned away.

'Mama Kyn,' I called. 'Mama Kyn.' But he didn't turn back.

Bewildered, I returned to bed where I fell into a restless sleep. I dreamt I was standing outside Mama Kyn's door, and when I pushed it open, I found the floor had turned into a pool of deep, swirling water.

The next morning, I ran to his shack, and was relieved to find the place intact. Yet Mama Kyn, once again, was nowhere to be found.

No one paid me any heed until he didn't show up for his meals two days in a row.

'Where could he have gone?' said my mother at dinner. She sounded cross; this was inconvenient. 'How can a grown man just disappear?'

At times like these, a pyrta shnong was set up, a town crier who passed the message around the neighbourhood— that help was needed to look for my grandfather's brother-in-law who had vanished without a trace. In those days, the entire locality got involved, dropping their chores and meals, and hurrying outdoors, combing the streets like a small, diligent army.

The next day, Mama Kyn was found seated on a rock perched precariously by the Wah Dieng Doh waterfall. He didn't seem to notice us beckon to him, his arms drawn around his bent knees, his eyes staring into nothingness.

'Lah kem puri,' I heard people whisper around me, but I didn't know what that meant. 'It'll never stop now,' someone added, and they all shook their heads sadly.

Finally, my father, Bah Lam and a group of men from the locality managed to climb up to the rock and bring Mama Kyn down. He was weak, and didn't put up a fight. When they reached home, he fell into an exhausted asleep.

Later that evening, when the commotion had died down, I was in Uncle Gordon's room watching him smoke a joint.

'What is puri?' I asked.

'Hmmm…supposed to be a water fairy.'

'That's what happened to Mama Kyn? He was taken by a puri?'

I got a face full of foul-smelling smoke.

'Who told you that?'

'I heard from the others mynneh…'

'Puris trap men and take them away to their dwelling places underwater…old people believe in all that…' Holding up the joint, he grinned and added, 'And you will too if you smoke enough of this.'

I learnt more by eavesdropping in the kitchen. 'She must have followed him home from the river. Once that happens, he'll always be under her spell,' said Mena. She was frying kha bah in a large pan; the pieces spluttered in the mustard oil, one was a head with a black, blind eye. 'They're beautiful creatures, these puri. People say they have waist-long hair and skin the colour of moonlight.'

My mother snorted; she had no patience for stories of any kind, especially those that involved lissome fairies. But the old woman continued unperturbed.

'The mischievous ones are alright, they don't do much harm, they tempt and tease and only visit the men at night, you know, to…'

'Yes, we know,' interrupted my mother.

'But the malicious ones, they're very dangerous,' Mena continued. 'They lead men to dangerous places, to cliffs and waterfalls, to whirlpools and deep lakes. I've heard they're persistent, and will do anything to lure them into the water.'

She flipped the pieces of fish over; one side was crisp and shrivelled. The eye, I noticed, had turned white.

'There's only one way to stop the puri,' she continued. 'He must leave a broom upside down outside his door every day. That's the only way she'll leave him alone.'

'Mena, get back to work,' said my mother. 'This is all nonsense.'

A broom was placed by Mama Kyn's door after the fourth time he disappeared. This time for almost a week. I remember the odd stillness in the house. The constant waiting, the careful pretence of normality. With death there is grief, and pain and closure. A disappearance, though, fosters only deep, profound unknowing. Stef, Keith, and I made a game out of it—'Mama Kyn is playing hide-and-seek,' we declared, and searched in all our favourite secret places—the neighbourhood, with its sprawl of low-roofed houses and narrow sloping lanes, was our playground. Yet it became clearer as the days passed by that he wasn't anywhere in the locality.

He was found by a boy hunting birds near Bishop Falls, more than ten miles away from our side of town. Mama Kyn was lying on the ground, facing the stream, too weak to move. He had to be carried on a stretcher that my father brought from the hospital. Back at home, he fell into a fever, and muttered strange names, calling many times for Bolen and Hipster.

'Who are these people?' asked Aunt Ruth.

I held my silence.

While he was convalescing, Mama Kyn would sit outside his shack, sipping tea, and often I would keep him company.

The broom was always stationed by his door like a sentry on duty. As usual, we didn't talk much, this time not even about fishing, but I thought if I were with him, perhaps he wouldn't disappear so often.

One clear afternoon in early spring, we were alone in the backyard; there were no football matches in progress and the air filled only with the fragrance of sweet peas.

'Mama, when you—go away, do you remember anything?' I asked.

A small smile spread over his face. 'I am catching Golden Mahseer. They're all around me, flying through the air, leaping into water. I reach out, one after another…they lie in my hand like pieces of the sun.'

When Mama Kyn vanished for the last time, people in the household spent days blaming each other for removing the broom. 'It must have been Gordon, coming back late at night and thinking it'd be funny.' Aunt Ruth disapproved of her younger brother's lifestyle. 'Maybe Bah Lam,' suggested my mother, 'he's getting a little forgetful these days.' 'One of those neighbourhood kids playing a prank,' said my grandmother, 'they're always jumping in and out of our garden.' Suspicion even fell on us, but Keith, Stef, and I solemnly denied it. For days, accusations flew around like sharp poisoned arrows. Nobody thought of the possibility that he'd done so himself. No one saw how the broom probably didn't keep anything away.

Many years have passed and the rooms at the great old house have gradually emptied. Each generation passing on—Mena, my grandparents, Bah Lam, my mother and father, succumbing to the slow, crushing wheel of time. Others, like me and Keith, moved away to our wives' homes in other parts of town. Only Stef and her family remain. At times, I visit and notice all the changes that have taken place. The shacks at the edge of the garden are now smart cement houses rented out to strangers; the kitchen has lost its open wood fires and soot-blackened walls to gas stoves, melamine and fresh coats of weather-proof paint. Kamra rim, the original room, has been bolstered by hardy new planks. Outside, though, some things remain the same—football is still played in the backyard, albeit with better equipment, and my grandmother's vegetable garden is still tended by someone with careful, loving hands. One afternoon, I landed up to find a stash of things being emptied from the storage room—school books and notepads, a rusty typewriter, a small tin trunk. I picked up a fishing rod with a broken line, it lay cold and heavy in my hands.

'Is that yours?' It was Stef's younger son. He watched me, curious and alert.

'No, not mine.' I told him about Mama Kyn.

'Where did he go?' he asked.

I tried to explain about the spirits that lived in the waters, who followed us home and beckoned us back, the ones that made us fall in love.

The ten-year-old looked incredulous. 'Only old people believe in all that.'

Occasionally, when I go fishing, I sit on the bank, or wade into the water, hoping to catch a glimpse of something wondrous. What does it take, I think, to have faith in things beyond the ordinary? Age? Childlike wonder? Is it right to cling so fiercely to the world? As they absorb my solitude, the silence of the distant hills and the drifting indifference of the clouds, I think of disappearances, the ones that surprise us and those that don't. At first, I am steeped in sadness. Then I notice how the air fills with cicadas, the trees cast their trembling shadows on the water, the reeds bow in steady reverence. I realize that no one is truly ever gone. All voices are heard in a river's murmuring.

If I get lucky, I manage to reel in a kha bah and hold it in my hand, its scales smooth and brittle, glistening like broken rainbows in the sun. I am yet to catch a Golden Mahseer. If I do, I will set it free and hope Mama Kyn will find it.

# Secret Corridors

That morning the world had shrunk to the size of a mole. A small, chestnut-coloured spot to the left of a cupid's bow that dropped elegantly away from a soft and full middle. It was a mouth that made Natalie think of forbidden things, like the forest behind her house, which she wasn't allowed to explore, or the pink roadside ice sticks she'd been expressly instructed not to taste. That morning, the intricacies of chemistry didn't interest her as much as Iba's mouth; and the face to which it belonged, she thought, was just as attractive. Boyish, some said, but not for Natalie. She liked Iba's slanting eyes and the smooth plane of her cheeks. It was a face infinitely more interesting than anything Mrs Chatterjee had to say about centrifugation.

'This machine will rotate rapidly. And then what will happen? The milk and cream will separate. Why this will happen?'

It was the first lesson of the day, and the room, filled with forty-five girls, bristled with restlessness. Sister Josephine, the headmistress, had announced at morning assembly that the school fête would be held next month, and the girls were distracted, silently planning what they would wear, which stalls they would visit. When Iba bent over her textbook, Natalie shifted her attention to the view outside the window. The school was built on a terraced hillside, and their classroom overlooked the playground, which in turn offered a sprawling view of the town swelling across the hills in rambling disarray. Below, rows of eight-year-olds in cloudy grey pinafores moved in aerobic tandem to the PE teacher's drumbeat. The basketball court nearby was overrun by class ten students, two years senior to Natalie. She watched Amanda, a tall girl with cropped hair, execute a perfect lay-up. One, two, three, and shoot. The ball dropped gracefully through the hoop. Amanda sprinted back to her friends, laughing. She had the largest number of 'fans' in school—junior girls who blushed at the sight of her, aching for a glance or a smile, and dropped love notes into her lunch bag or had them sent through a giggling messenger. Beyond the court, a row of jacarandas were on the threshold of bursting into violet blossoms. Spring was in the air, with March winds tugging at their school skirts in a blustery frenzy. For the students at L— Convent, Shillong, it meant three months of winter vacation had come to an end. Natalie's daydreams were interrupted by a nudge in the ribs. Her benchmate Manisha was staring straight ahead at Mrs Chatterjee, who'd asked Natalie a question. The class had dissolved into giggles. Natalie flushed.

'Sorry, miss.'

'Come, sit here.' The teacher rapped the desk in front of her. From there, she wouldn't be able to see Iba; worse, she'd be next to Carmel.

'Sorry, miss, I...'

'Nothing doing. You want to be sent to Sister Josephine?'

Natalie dragged herself over—a few faces flashed small sympathetic smiles—while Carmel ignored the proceedings and filled her pen with ink. Within this classroom, like every other, there were invisible lines of demarcation as strict as in any church or temple. Who it was acceptable to eat lunch with, who you could partner for arts and crafts, who to include in your team for Danish Rounders, and, rising singularly above the rest, who you sat next to in class. Nobody, for instance, would willingly occupy a seat beside Rini, the Mizo with body odour; Paromita, the Bengali whose hair oil smelled peculiar; or Erica, the Jaintia girl who threw up on her desk every other day. Carmel, however, was the worst of them all. She'd joined the previous year—appearing out of nowhere like an odd April shower—and had never quite fit in. Perhaps it had something to do with the rumours that followed her into school. The stories varied, changing shape with every retelling. Parents waiting outside the school gates discussed Carmel's mother. *A string of affairs with some naval officers in Bombay... No, an Israeli, and now he's returned to Jerusalem. That's why she's come back to Shillong.* Within the century-old walls of the school building, teachers in the staff room debated over the possibility of Carmel and her siblings all having different fathers. Rapidly, and as pervasive as pine dust, the rumours filtered to the schoolgirls in strange, contorted forms—*Carmel meets boys after school... She takes them home... She goes with them to the Risa Colony forest to drink alcohol...who knows what they do there.* Here, where the family name was passed down through the mother, the children also had to bear the weight of her weaknesses. It was 'wantonness', that temerarious trait of lust and shame that marked Carmel for its own. *She is sure to turn out just like her mother*, the senior girls hissed. Amanda, sitting amid a cluster of delighted girls, declared Carmel a kynthei dakaid. A bad girl. It was that easy. Her fate was as tightly sealed as Sister Josephine's pursed, disapproving lips.

The other reason the girls disliked Carmel was one they didn't talk about. She was exceedingly pretty. Whoever her parents might have been, that was something no one could deny. They merely punished her for it. For looking like the girls in the British *Woman* magazines that Natalie's grandmother so assiduously collected from second-hand bookshops. Exotic as the things they advertised—Kit Kat chocolates and Yorkshire pudding. Natalie sat at the edge of the chair, as far as possible from her new benchmate.

'Now, who can tell me about the process of distillation? Anyone apart from Swapna.' Mrs Chatterjee beamed at her favourite student—a Marwari girl with a red hairband and enormous kohl-lined eyes.

Natalie sighed. It was going to be a long morning.

During lunch break, a band of girls took over the only sunny corner of the summer house in the playground. It was a rambling wooden structure, coated with a thick, bubbly layer of blue-grey paint. Iba occupied the seat near the window, while the rest arranged themselves around her—Amesha, petite and fairy-like with a pale, heart-shaped face; Doreen, whose dusky skin reddened with every tempestuous outburst; Eve, Iba's cousin, who had thick, dark hair reaching her waist; and Miranda, a skinny teenager who was unusually tall for a Khasi girl. Sitting slightly outside the sacred circle was Natalie, unsure yet whether she was fully part of the gang. She tried joining in the conversation but found it was dominated by Doreen and Miranda jostling like skilled duellers for Iba's attention. At the opposite end of the room, a group of dkhar girls animatedly conversing in Hindi, occasionally erupted into raucous laughter.

'Marwaris,' muttered Doreen. 'My dad says we need to kick them all out of our state.'

Natalie shifted uncomfortably. She didn't dare say anything, but she didn't quite like it when they spoke this way about the others. Her friends in the neighbourhood where she lived, whom she played with in the evenings, were Assamese. Like her, born and brought up here, and who considered Shillong their home. If Doreen knew this she'd call Natalie an ieid-dkhar. A dkhar lover. The thought made her nervous. Was it something that could be sniffed out, as dogs sense fear? Did it show? Could they tell? 'So, Nat–' She looked up in alarm at Iba addressed her. 'What was it like sitting next to Carmel?'

Everyone's attention was suddenly trained on her. This was her chance to say something witty, clever, and impressive.

'She smells,' blurted Natalie.

Iba burst out laughing, and a moment later so did everyone else. A chorus of voices rose—'Tell us, what does she smell of?' Like a ripple in a pond the circle had expanded.

'Old socks and sour milk.'

'Very kinjing!' said Miranda.

'Chee … chee,' said Amesha, pinching her nose.

'I heard,' Iba began conspiratorially, and everyone instinctively drew closer, 'that over New Year, Carmel went to Breeze Dale.'

The girls shuddered in delight. The resort, half an hour out of town, courted a reputation for being a disreputable getaway.

'And,' Iba's eyes widened, 'she didn't go with just *one* boy...'

It was deliciously scandalous. The air hummed with hushed, excited voices, buzzing like a cloud of summer bees. *Which boys? How many? Did she kiss them? Did she do more?* A quarter of an hour later, when the subject had been exhausted, Iba declared she was bored with Carmel, and that they needed to do something exciting to liven up the term.

'There's the fête next month,' offered Natalie.

'Who cares about that?' Miranda had swung her long legs onto the windowsill and looked like a reclining queen.

The girls dismissed it with scorn. It was deemed a dull affair, which, this year, they'd undoubtedly outgrown. Natalie retreated into silence. Doreen stood up to imitate Sister Josephine—she exaggerated the headmistress's slight limp and nasal voice. 'Girls, girls, no running down the corridors. Young ladies must walk. Iba, your skirt can be two fingers above the knee, not an entire arm. Otherwise you'll drive the St Edmund's boys mad.'

'She already drives them mad,' said Miranda and exchanged glances with Iba.

Natalie watched in awestruck wonder. There were universes unfolding before her like crisp white bedsheets. Eager to be the centre of attention again, Doreen added, 'Yes, but that Daniel is too short...Reuben is cuter.'

'I wish we could invite them to the fête,' said Amesha. She was braiding Eve's hair with a length of silky red ribbon.

'Maybe we could let them in secretly.' Miranda giggled. 'Sneak them in somehow.'

The girls laughed at the impossibility of the suggestion—

the nuns would be keeping a hawk-eyed watch over all possible entrances.

'Remember how Sister Mary caught Langkupar last year?' said Doreen. The boy and his friends had tried to sneak into the girls-only dance at the end of the fête.

Miranda nodded. 'She almost whacked him with her walking stick.'

Every year, the fête yielded a new crop of stories—boys run off the school grounds for smoking, for smuggling in alcohol, and worse, for attempting to speak to the girls.

'We'll have to dance with each other.' Doreen turned a dainty pirouette.

'Unless we find the secret passage,' said Natalie.

'What secret passage?' asked Miranda.

Natalie flushed. What she had said suddenly seemed very silly. 'They say there's a secret passage from the summer house in the front lawns that runs all the way to St Edmund's.'

'Nonsense.' Doreen sometimes threw out words like sharp, steely knives.

'My mum told me...she studied here too. She said...' Natalie fumbled, she felt pinned to the wall.

'And no one has ever found it in all these years? What rubbish!' Doreen's voice seethed with scorn.

'I've heard that too...' It was Eve, her voice calm and steady. 'My mother studied here, and she also told me the same thing.'

It was an impasse. Doreen didn't dare treat Iba's cousin with contempt. Natalie didn't dare say anything at all. The girls waited for Iba to react, but they knew she wouldn't belittle Eve.

'Let's go look for it then,' said Iba finally.

As they trooped out of the summer house, swinging their lunch bags, the bell sounded from within the recesses of the school building. It was time for afternoon lessons, so they turned towards their classroom instead. Iba chose to walk beside Natalie while some of the others looked on enviously.

Miss Tina John's gaze swept across the room, at rows of heads in neat twosome columns, and wished she were anywhere but here. It was her second week on the job, her first job, and she was nervous. The girls knew it and spared her no mercy.

'Miss, miss,' a tall girl near the door had piped up earlier. 'What's the meaning of "gay"?'

They were studying Guy de Maupassant's *The Necklace*. Miss John didn't recall coming across that word in the story.

'It means happy,' she'd replied in her most teacher-ly tone.

The girl persisted. 'But, miss, is that the *only* meaning?'

Only when Miss John noticed the stifled giggles did she tell them to get back to their books. They were a tough class at a tough age, Sister Josephine had told her, but she was sure Miss John would manage them. She looked at the textbook in front of her and felt hugely doubtful. A handful of girls seemed to be the main mischief-mongers in the class, and their fretfulness affected the others. Miss John could see she wasn't the only one at the receiving end of their attention. A girl with a ponytail and light, freckled skin was also being troubled, in the most surreptitious of ways. When Miss John had entered the classroom at the beginning of the lesson, the girl was pulling off a piece of paper taped to the back of her sweater. At her desk, it looked like the inkpot had overturned and stained her textbooks. Miss John glanced at her; her head was bent so low she couldn't see her face. The girl next to her had turned round and was signalling to someone sitting at the back.

'I asked everyone to read the chapter quietly,' said Miss John in a tone that surprised even herself. 'You can discuss it with your friends later. Anyone caught talking will be sent to the principal.'

'Sorry, miss,' the girl mumbled, and a wave of quiet washed over the room. No one noticed the small, brief smile that flitted over Miss John's face. Maybe this wouldn't be so difficult after all.

'We'll eat at the tennis courts today,' declared Iba as they hurtled out of class during tiffin break. No one disputed her. On their way down, past the corridor and long flight of dark green stairs, the girls laughed over their morning escapades.

'Did you see her face?'

'She looked like she wanted to jump out of the window.'

'She should have!'

Natalie walked along unsure whether they were referring to Carmel or the new English teacher. Her mind was elsewhere, on their plans for the next hour—a quick lunch and then a stealthy expedition to the front of the school (where students were strictly not allowed), down to the sloping lawns, within which was ensconced an octagonal wooden summer house built on a high brick platform. This was older than the one in the playground, with diamond-shaped window panes and dark Tudor-style beams, surrounded by a tangle of rhododendron bushes and tall pine trees.

'We had our singing lessons there,' Natalie's mother had told her on their way to school that morning. 'With Sister Catherine. This huge Irish nun with a voice as loud as a trumpet.'

'Did you ever look for the secret passage?'

Her mother laughed. 'Many times. All of us liked some St Edmund's boy or the other.'

'But did you find it?'

'Find it? Nat, I'm not sure it even exists!'

That had made Natalie nervous. Doreen would never let her forget it. She glanced at the girl walking ahead with Amesha. Something told her Doreen was still smarting from yesterday's incident. She didn't seem like the kind of person to forgive, or forget, easily. To make things worse, Iba linked her arm through Natalie's.

'This is so exciting,' she sang. Today, her hair was pinned up with red bow-shaped clips. Even in school uniform—a dull grey pleated skirt and plain white shirt—Iba stood out from all the rest. Even Carmel, Natalie thought. She could feel everyone's eyes on her, burning as much as the touch of Iba's skin.

After lunch, Miranda acted as a lookout while the rest scrambled past the auditorium and into the garden. Sunlight patch-worked the short, tough grass and the wind, a trifle gentler today, rustled the leaves around them. They made their way undiscovered to the summer house and when they reached, sat on the ground, leaning their backs against the brick platform. No one spoke as they caught their breath.

'Is it open?' whispered Iba, turning to Natalie.

'What?'

'The door, you beid.'

Natalie winced at being called an idiot and scampered to the entrance. The lock, rusty and unused, broke in her hand. Inside, sunlight filtered through the windowpanes and made a pattern on the floor. Swirls of golden dust rose lazily as they entered.

'So, where is it?' asked Doreen.

Natalie thought it a silly question, but didn't say so. Instead she got down on her knees and peered under the seat that ran the length of the room. The others followed. They pressed their fingers along the wooden planks, tapped the walls, squirmed into corners, and soon the silence was broken by giggles and proclamations that this was a waste of time. Doreen complained the loudest, while Amesha, Eve and Miranda treated it as a joke. Natalie sat in a corner, watching the others. She longed to wipe the streaks of dirt from Iba's cheek, to tuck a stray curl behind her ear. Iba was exuberant, her hair wild and undone, her eyes shining with delight.

'Look at me, I'm a little dog,' she squealed, scampering around on all fours. She pretended to nip at Miranda's hand, then stopped in front of Natalie and brushed the tip of her tongue against Natalie's cheek. It was an electric shock; Natalie's stomach fluttered, something inside her constricted like a coiled snake. Then a long shadow fell across the floor. There was someone at the door.

'Good afternoon, Sister,' everyone mumbled when they saw who it was.

Sister Josephine remained silent. It wasn't a good sign. The girls scrambled to their feet, nervously dusting their hands and skirts.

'Your parents shall be informed of this,' said the headmistress and stepped aside to indicate that they were to file out quietly.

When they were back in the school building and out of Sister Josephine's earshot, Natalie began to apologize—'I'm sorry, I didn't mean to get my friends in trouble...'

'Friends?' spat Iba. 'Don't you dare call us that.' She was flanked by Miranda and Doreen who stared down at Natalie like a pair of avenging angels.

'Keep away from us, beid.'

Natalie's words died in her mouth as she watched them stride off. When they were gone, she ducked into the nearest doorway. She didn't want anyone to see her cry. She leaned against the wall and swallowed her grief in great, empty mouthfuls. Only when she'd steadied herself did she notice where she was—the abandoned bathroom near the library. In front of her hung a cracked, dirty mirror and, against the wall was a row of broken, bone-dry washbasins. The doors to the toilet cubicles hung awkwardly on their hinges. Natalie stared at her warped reflection—*beid, beid, beid.*

From a faraway place came the clanking of the bell. It was time for afternoon lessons. If she didn't go, she'd be in more trouble, yet how could she face them? As she stood undecided, and the clatter of footsteps in the corridor outside faded, she thought she heard a sound. A low, muted sobbing. Yet that couldn't be. There was no one else around. Suddenly, stories she'd heard of L— Convent being haunted came flooding back. The white lady on the staircase. The old nun near the chapel. The boarder who'd died in the days when this was a residential school. The sobbing continued, hollow and consistent. It seemed to be coming from somewhere near the toilets, from behind a door she hadn't noticed before, the wood blending with the dirty wall. It was ajar.

Ghosts don't leave doors open, Natalie told herself. She stepped into a long rectangular room lined on one side with wrought-iron beds. There were white bedpans and trays stacked in a corner and thin mattresses piled against the windows, blocking out the light. On the floor, leaning against a tall almirah was a girl with a ponytail and pale, freckled skin. She was crying, her head between her hands. A pang shot through Natalie.

'Carmel,' she said softly.

The girl looked up with startled red-rimmed eyes. Then she hid her face again and continued weeping quietly. Natalie made her way to her, bumping her knee against a bed in the dimness, and sat down. She didn't know what to say so she waited until Carmel's sobs subsided. She'd lied the other day—her benchmate didn't stink of old socks and sour milk; in fact she smelled quite nice, of fresh linen and talcum powder. Natalie dug into her pocket for a handkerchief. Carmel accepted it with a mumble of thanks.

'What's this place?' asked Natalie.

'Don't you know?' Carmel dabbed at her face. She looked like a girl out of a magazine despite the sore, red nose. Natalie shook her head.

'It's the old hostel dormitory.'

'Why's all of that here?' Natalie pointed to the bedpans.

'They used this as a military hospital during the Second World War.'

Natalie's mother had told her about this once, but she'd never quite believed her. On another day, she might have explored the room, its drawers and containers, but this afternoon, Natalie wanted to leave. It was a place of illness and pain and death.

'My grandmother met my granddad here. She was a nurse,' Carmel continued. 'He was a British soldier. A Major-General.' There was a flicker of pride in her voice. After a moment's silence she handed the handkerchief back. Their fingers brushed. Carmel's eyes met hers. Her lashes were wet and dark. 'You're kind.'

Natalie didn't know what to say; she had the grace to blush.

'Not like the others.'

Carmel put her hand on Natalie's knee. Her fingers felt hot against her skin. She leaned in closer, her hair undone, framing her face. Natalie closed her eyes before their lips met. It was nothing like she'd ever felt before. A low roar filled her ears, as though she was listening to a shell and could hear the sea. Something inside her unravelled, it uncoiled to the floor, and filled the room, every inch of its dusty corners. The world, with its scorn and derision, receded, and she was left with Carmel's mouth, which was soft and warm and tasted of tears. For a moment, the ghosts around them, and within, fell silent.

19/87

———•◦•———

Kite warriors wage a faceless war. In the city, on rooftops and terraces and small open car parks, the enemy is hidden, concealed at the other end of the string, probing the sky with slim, curving weapons. Hardened troopers like Suleiman, however, come to know their rivals well, their style of play and combat, even though they wouldn't recognize them on the streets of Shillong. Amid the carousing flutter of kites during the season, usually deployed by kids after school, there were a few to watch out for, the ones that swirled and snuck around, their string dipped in shards of powdered glass. Most of the expert fighters, down towards Umsohsun and up the hill in Mawkhar, flew small, insidious, single line kites. They were all good at the 'pull'—when a kite is flown ahead of the others and then tugged quickly, cutting all the lines in its path. Suleiman preferred to fly a larger kite, one with a pastiche of tissue paper that he pasted together with great care. When he was a boy, he would hold the spool for his father, learning to release just the right amount of line. Later their roles were reversed. And now, well, he hadn't flown many kites since his father died three years ago. Most of the time he didn't feel like it; it brought back too many memories. The last few evenings, though, Suleiman had noticed a new rival in the neighbourhood. Someone who flew a kite as large as his, and who seemed, Suleiman admitted grudgingly, to be almost as good. He itched to find out if it was true.

This afternoon, he looked repeatedly out of the window, past the guava tree, beyond the line of low tin roofs, at the sky. There were more kites than usual this August, perhaps because of all the trouble in town. Weeks of curfew forced everyone to stay home, and there wasn't much to do on these long autumn evenings. At least a kite was free to travel, over electric wires and telephone cables and treetops. The large kite was there, swimming invitingly above the rest. So far it had beaten the ones who'd challenged it to a fight. 'All confident now, saala,' muttered Suleiman. He was annoyed. Even if he did make a kite that evening, he had no one to hold the spool for him. A few times, he'd called Usman, a young boy from across the courtyard wall, to be his charkha gir. Trying not to lose patience when he released the line too quickly, or not at all, forcing the string to snap. 'I'm sorry,' Usman would say, sounding rather miserable, as they stood watching Suleiman's kite sail untethered, swooping lower and lower until it dropped out of sight. 'I'll be better next time.' But there couldn't be a next time any more for Usman's family had packed up and left a week ago. He'd hopped over the wall to say goodbye, and explained, 'My father says it's getting too dangerous to live in Shillong.' It wasn't an uncommon refrain; Suleiman's father had told him he'd heard the same from the time Meghalaya was carved out of the expanse of Assam in '72. After that, many locals in town, frustrated with having 'outsiders' running the state and controlling banks and businesses, organized themselves into various insurgent groups—the Khasi Students Union (KSU) and the Hynniewtrep National Liberation Council (HNLC)—and waged a civil war against the government and the ethnicities they saw as most threatening. The ones who had taken their jobs, their resources, their women. Now, around him

Suleiman heard 'It was the Nepalis in '79, the Bengalis in '81, then the Marwaris...who knows when it'll be our turn. We are what they call dkhars too.' The cluster of Muslim families living in the area rapidly grew smaller.

Suleiman watched the large kite fly unchallenged, and decided it was all a frivolous waste of time. He needed to get back to work. Soon, the room filled with the click and hum of the sewing machine, and he hunched over the cloth, engrossed in the intricate play of line and thread. Fortunate that he was the most skilled, and reasonably priced, tailor in the neighbourhood. Fortunate too that even in times of unrest, buttons came undone, trouser pockets inexplicably tore, and shirts mysteriously snagged on washing lines. Despite the small town he lived in ripping itself apart, people, outsiders or not, still dropped by to have things mended.

Although that was all they did. Especially the Khasis.

Where once they'd chat idly about the weather, share neighbourhood gossip and discuss how close they were to betting the correct thoh teem numbers, now they hurried away, as though he had the plague or terrible body odour. Or worse that his being dkhar was somehow contagious and that others less forgiving and tolerant would know they'd visited him.

'Khublei, dorji,' they'd mumble their thanks and shuffle out of the door.

Others from his community were almost as reluctant to stay on. Although from the newspapers they sometimes left behind, he could see why. The pages were filled with reports of disturbances and violence—shoot-outs in Iew Duh and riots in Police Bazaar. A few months ago, he'd read that the central government in Delhi had sent the Central Reserve Police Force (CRPF) to Shillong to 'help maintain law and order.' Suleiman didn't think it had helped much, the presence of the CRPF. In fact, the town seemed more inflamed and enraged. Try as he did to not let it affect him, to cocoon himself against the drama, it had changed his life in subtle ways. He no longer cycled around dropping off tailored and mended clothes to his clients. They were to come pick them up. The skullcap he usually wore had lain untouched under his pillow for weeks.

Today, though, rather than fear, Suleiman felt a deep and profound annoyance. He was tempted to walk up to a member of the KSU and say, 'I've been in Shillong for a long time. I'm thirty-four years old and I came here before some of you were even born.' He snapped a line of thread between his teeth. All he wanted to do was fly a kite. He glanced out of the window. At the row of houses beyond the courtyard wall. He'd known some of his neighbours for almost two decades—old Bah Swer was sitting outside, dozing as usual, there was Kong Belinda whose jaiñsem he was mending. These traditional two-piece costumes, that women wore pinned over their shoulders, were often sent to him to be hemmed. He knew Kong Belinda liked green, her jaiñsems were usually that colour. At the moment she was hanging up the washing; her daughter Christine, unfortunately, was nowhere in sight. He thought her especially handsome; with a face like a soft full moon and a sheet of slippery dark hair that reached her waist. Her gold earrings, decorated with pink diamond stones, glinted whenever she opened the door and flirted with him, if her mother and brothers weren't around.

'Have you brought my clothes?' she'd say with a smile. 'The ones I left in your room.'

Suleiman adjusted the jaiñsem material under the sewing needle. It was no good. He ought to get Christine off his mind. He'd be accused of stealing Khasi women away from their men. And who knew what might happen then. At the moment, it was manageable, leaving his house only if he had to, stocking up on food for weeks at a stretch. Often at night, though, there were stones thrown on his roof, shouts resounding in the street—'Dkhar liah, mih na Shillong.' You bastard outsider, get out of Shillong. These were the things, thought Suleiman, that weren't reported in newspapers.

From his window, he could see the path that wound through the courtyard, leading on one end to the main road and the other to the cluster of houses behind his, accessible only by a flight of steep stone steps. He thought that was where the young man was headed, the one who swaggered by, wearing a red chequered shirt and light denim jeans. Instead, a knocking sounded on the door, sharp and persistent. Suleiman looked up from his sewing.

'Who is it?'

There was no answer. The knocking didn't stop.

He pushed himself away from the sewing machine. It was best to open the door.

After he undid the latch, the young man walked in without invitation.

'Ei, dorji, mend this.'

He thrust a black leather jacket into Suleiman's arms. Across the elbow was a jagged rip.

'Can you do it quickly?'

The young man cast a glance at the mirror on the wall, and then around the room. Suleiman saw him take in the small kitchen space in the corner with its shelf of pots and pans and stout cooking stove. The tailored shirts and dresses hanging on a clothes horse, the large ironing table, the scraps of cloth on the floor, and finally the rihal holding the Holy Book and the rolled-up prayer mat. The tailor retreated to his workstation, where he fumbled with needle and thread. The young man stood by the door and lit a cigarette; the smell of cheap tobacco quickly filled the room.

'How long will you take? I have to go to work.'

'Five minutes.'

'Good.'

The boy seemed unused to standing still. He shuffled in his place, then crossed to the ironing table, rifled through a pile of clothes, and picked up a large heavy pair of scissors. They made a sharp rasping sound as he snipped the air. Suleiman watched from the corner of his eye. He was about twenty-five, small, like a bird, with their restless energy rather than their grace. His eyes were black and bright, but heavy-lidded, giving him the appearance of being sleep deprived. Or having just woken up from a long nap. Wrapped around the scissors, his fingers were short and rough, and with a line of black grime under the nails.

The cigarette was soon dropped to the floor, and stubbed by an unpolished black boot.

Suleiman sewed quickly and carefully. The garment in his hands carried the faint odour of old sweat and tobacco; the leather was faded yet tough. When he finished, he made a neat knot and snapped the thread.

'How much?' asked the young man.

'Five rupees.'

'I'll give you three, okay…' He placed the coins on the table and snatched up the jacket. Standing in front of the mirror, the young man continued talking. 'I just lost first round at thoh teem… I can't afford to pay you so much.' He was referring to the numbers that the gambling houses released in the morning. It was a lottery of sorts, calculated by an archery game held in an open field at Polo Grounds; there was another one in the afternoon to determine the 'second round' numbers in the evening. The young man settled his hair and then held up his elbow. The mended rip was barely visible. His tone became friendlier. 'Are you a betting man, dorji?'

'Sometimes.'

'Me too…almost got the second round last week…I bet three and four came. Keep missing it by a few…' He listed his various gambling exploits. Evidently, it was something he enjoyed, even if he wasn't very lucky.

'I won both rounds a few years ago,' said Suleiman. 'Clean sweep.'

The young man stared, his eyes wide in disbelief. 'How did you manage that?'

The tailor smiled. 'It came to me in a dream.'

'Aah…I've heard about that…calculating numbers from dreams. My granny used to do it…I should have asked her. She's dead now. Never understood how it's done.' He glanced at Suleiman, and added, 'Do you…know?'

'Which number came up this morning?' asked Suleiman.

'Two.'

'You can try eight, for the second round.'

The young man laughed. 'How do you know? You're a tailor.'

With that, he left the room, slamming the door behind him. Suleiman put away the scissors. He'd rather not have them lying around.

Later, the town settled into the quiet of the evening, its shops shuttered and streets emptied by the curfew. Looking out of their windows, people would say, 'Not a soul outside, not even a dog.' The uneasy silence deepened with the blackout at six o'clock. It had been announced over a loudspeaker on a KSU van driving through Shillong that it was mandatory to switch off the lights, to paste newspaper over window-panes so even the glow of a candle would be subdued. It was a sign of protest, the KSU declared, but they didn't mention it also helped turn entire neighbourhoods into battlegrounds where rebels and the police alike were offered shelter by the darkness. For the people who stayed indoors, this was a time to huddle around coal fires, take out a well-thumbed pack of cards, or set out the carrom board. Otherwise, there was little to while away the hours. Suleiman usually ate his dinner early and lay on his bed until he fell asleep. This evening, though, he was making a kite. The radio crackled softly in the corner, playing a programme called 'Songs of India' that attempted, through a selection of folk music, to invoke patriotic camaraderie among its listeners. He left it on mostly to keep the silence at bay. Else, he would only hear the wind outside, swooping over the hills. The guava tree near the window tapped on the roof. In the distance there were shouts of a fight or a call for dinner; it was hard to tell. He'd cut out the tissue paper earlier before daylight faded, and now was carefully pasting them together with gluey rice.

The smaller the pieces, the better. The kite would resist tears and could be easily mended. It was going to be a large one; the bamboo slivers lay waiting to be bound together into a frame. He was almost done when the first stone hit the roof. And then another. They rolled off and fell to the ground in dull, solid thuds. Tonight he hadn't been called any names, but in alarm, he'd pulled at the tissue paper, and it lay on the floor torn and ruined.

The next afternoon, as Suleiman expected, the young man reappeared. This time he waved amiably at the tailor as he walked across the courtyard. He knocked once.

'It's open.'

He entered and shut the door carefully behind him.

'Kumno dorji.'

'I'm busy.'

'Yes, of course.'

Suleiman was measuring fabric on the ironing table. The young man stood behind him.

'Kwai?' he offered, holding out betel nut and paan wrapped in a torn scrap of newspaper.

'No, it's alright.' The tailor straightened up. 'What can I do for you?'

'Banri. My name's Banri.'

Suleiman moved to the sewing machine. The young man followed.

'I was hoping...you could help me...'

'Do you need something mended?'

The boy hesitated. 'It's not really about that...'

'Which number came up yesterday? In the second round.'

The young man rushed forward in excitement. 'See, that's the thing…eight. Just like you said.'

Suleiman bent over the machine, stringing up new thread, hiding a smile.

Banri pulled up a moora and sat close to him.

'Can you tell me what will come today?'

'It depends.'

'On what?'

'Do you remember your dream?'

He shook his head. 'That's the thing, I never remember my dreams. But Don, he's a mechanic I work with, he told me his dream this morning. Will that do?' He looked hopeful.

Suleiman shrugged.

'Don said he dreamed he was in a boat, you know in Ward's Lake, there was no one else around. Just him in this boat, and he didn't know how to get back to the bank. He had no oars, nothing. Suddenly these two huge fish jumped into his lap. Two live fish. What do you think that means?'

Carefully, the tailor arranged Kong Belinda's jaiñsem under the needle, in a neat, straight line. He picked up a piece of chalk and made a few illegible marks on the fabric.

'Try five and nine.'

'Five and nine…okay.'

Banri was about to light a cigarette when he stopped. 'You don't mind me smoking here? No? Alright, khublei.' He settled himself comfortably on the moora. 'Dorji, how do you do it?'

'How do I do what?'

'These dreams and numbers.'

Suleiman stopped working the machine. He straightened the cloth. 'Everything in the world runs on calculations.'

'But...' Banri laughed. 'I get it, you're like a magician, who doesn't reveal his tricks.'

'Go make your bet and then tell me if you think this is trickery.'

'Hey, relax, I was only joking.'

The young man didn't wait to finish his cigarette, he offered Suleiman more kwai, and then hurried out. The closest thoh teem shops were up the hill in Mawkhar, and the tailor assumed that was where Banri was headed. He put away the jaiñsem and smoked a beedi by the window. In the sky, he could see two kites engaged in a fight, each desperately trying to cut the other's manja. They danced around each other like birds performing an ancient, ritualistic dance, until one slowly swung low and dropped out of sight.

In Mawkhar, thoh teem shops sprouted in tiny nooks and crevices, in side rooms and makeshift tin stalls and spaces under stairs. The warren of alleyways in Iew Duh spilled into the Mawkhar neighbourhood, and its streets were packed with small local shops. Bakeries sold Khasi sweets on white melamine counters—piles of long, twisted deep fried dough coated in sugar, warm, sticky slabs of rice putharo, and deep bowls of lal mohan swimming in syrup. There were shops that sold clothes and wool by the kilo, while some were lined with shelves of cheap, fake leather shoes. Further away from this, after the spread of residential houses, along the road leading out of town, began the rows of car workshops, each with their own graveyard of abandoned parts and automobiles. Somewhere in the middle, no less grimy and greasy than the others, was Bah Heh's workshop where Banri worked.

As he could be found on most afternoons, Bah Heh was lounging in a chair, lazily strumming a guitar.

'How many roads must a man walk down...' he sang, 'before you can call him a man...' Having forgotten the rest of the lyrics, he made do with tuneful humming. The day was unusually warm and humid, and Bah Heh roused himself by shouting at the mechanics in his workshop. They went about doing their jobs paying him no attention; they were accustomed to his attempts at feeling important.

'All of you buggers, hungover from last night, I know it.'

'What else to do but drink when there's curfew in the evening?' said Don, walking past with a bucket of dirty, soapy water.

'You only need some excuse, useless bastards.'

'Actually even when there's no curfew I drink every evening,' mumbled Khraw as he hunched over an engine, and tinkered with the battery.

'And where's that idiot Banri? Has he found himself a woman or what?'

'No, a tailor,' said Don, and Khraw sniggered.

'She's a tailor?'

'No, some dkhar guy he's become friends with. He's been visiting him every day now...for at least a week.'

'See here, I don't want any trouble in my workshop. Who's this dkhar?'

'You can ask him yourself,' said Khraw pointing to the gate. Banri was strolling in with a plastic bag in his hand.

'Time-out mo, Bah Heh,' he announced as he approached.

'Time-out? Where do you think you are? A basketball court?'

'I have momos for everyone.' From the plastic bag he drew out a banana leaf packet tied in string.

Khraw and Don crowded around.

'What's the treat for, bro?'

'You and the tailor getting married?'

Even Bah Heh joined in the laughter.

Banri ignored them; he undid the small plastic packet of virulent red chilli sauce and poured it over the dumplings.

'I won, only the first round. But still...'

'Again? At thoh teem? But you never win...' Don sounded justifiably incredulous.

'What jadoo-mantar has this tailor been doing?' Khraw bit into a momo, the pork and onion filling, shiny with oil and fat, oozed out of its floury skin.

'Nothing,' said Banri quickly. He hadn't explained in too much detail how Suleiman could interpret dreams, or as the tailor said mysteriously, 'calculate the value of symbols.' 'Anyway, never mind all that. The important thing is I won.'

Bah Heh reached for the plumpest dumpling in the pile. 'Okay, everybody hurry up and eat...plenty of work to be done.'

Half an hour later, there was another interruption—a group of young men walked in through the gate. Banri recognized some faces—they were from lower Wahingdoh and Umsohsun. They went up to Bah Heh and instructed him, politely and firmly, to keep the workshop shut the next day.

'For the rally,' said the one who was evidently the leader of the pack. He had a smooth, clean-shaven head and face. 'We hope all of you will be attending? Yes? Good. Good. We need our youth to support us. After all, this is for your future benefit only.' His eyes glinted as he looked them over; they rested on Banri who was wiping his greasy hands on an even greasier rag. 'This rally will be big; the government must listen to us this time. Remember,' he ended with practised ease, 'it all depends on your support.' They trooped out like a small, determined army, and headed to the next workshop.

'Great,' said Khraw. 'Holiday tomorrow.'

'Which means you do extra hours today and the day after. Now get back to work, scumbags.'

Don disappeared beneath the stout, rounded frame of an Ambassador, Khraw continued tinkering with the engine. Banri wet a sponge and soaped the vehicle. Something in the air had changed, it hung clenched and heavy above them, tight as a fist. There was no teasing and chatter, the workshop was quiet. They worked without saying a word. Bah Heh strummed the guitar for a while and then put it away.

Later that evening, Suleiman applied the finishing touches to his new kite after he returned from a quick shopping trip to the market. It had a bold red body with a neat collage of multicoloured paper in the middle and indigo blue seams pasted on the slim bamboo frame. He held it up by the string, and let it swing gently in front of him. Its shadow swayed across the floor. It seemed well balanced and strong, and would make a good fighter, he was sure. Maybe tomorrow, if the wind was right, he'd test it and find out. As he put the kite away, a shout from the street startled him. He was nervous today, more than usually on edge after he returned from the market. A group of Khasi youth had followed him, or so he thought. Or they could have been going somewhere the same way. It was hard to tell. He'd walked a convoluted route back home, and eventually lost them in the crowd. It wasn't getting easier, he thought. How much longer could he... Suddenly, someone rapped softly on the door.

'Ei, dorji...let me in.'

Suleiman didn't move.

'Hurry, it's cold out here.'

He undid the latch, not opening the door very wide.

'Why are you here?'

'Let me in.'

He stepped aside; Banri entered the room with a brown paper bag under his arm.

'Why are you here?' he repeated.

'Well, I thought, you know, it's been a good week...I won at thoh teem a few times. Even today, you were right. Well, you were half right. I won the first round. I thought we should celebrate...' He drew out a bottle of rum.

'No, no.' Suleiman moved swiftly to the stove where a pot of rice bubbled gently. 'I'm cooking dinner now.' Banri pulled up a stool and sat next to him.

'Come on, we must celebrate.'

'I don't feel like drinking.'

'Nonsense.'

'No, really...'

'Just a little, no harm.' Banri was brazenly cheerful. Suleiman detected the faint odour of alcohol on his breath; this wasn't his first drink of the evening. His uninvited guest plucked two tumblers from the shelf and turned on the radio. It crackled to life with the local news:

'...the shoot-out at Laban last week. There have been minor cases of unrest throughout the town, and encounters between the KSU and CRPF continue. Bah Lyngdoh, the Superintendent of Police, says security will be tight, especially with the KSU rally planned for tomorrow...'

'Let's find some music,' said Banri. He fiddled with the tuner, but failed to coax out anything more tuneful than static and fragments of the news.

'I'll do it,' said the tailor. 'You pour the drinks.'

'That's an old radio.' Banri measured out generous amounts of dark rum.

'It belonged to my father.' He turned the tuner gently, and finally, it caught a station playing Hindi music. 'He brought it with him when we came to Shillong in '55.'

'From where did you come?'

'Lucknow...in Uttar Pradesh. You know where that is?'

'Yes, of course. Near Bihar. Now drink.' Banri slugged his alcohol like most other hardened drinkers in town. A few quick, neat gulps.

Suleiman followed, albeit slower.

'You came so long ago...why didn't you go back?'

'My father didn't want to. He said our old hometown was filled with sad memories, and this was a fresh, new start.' He took a sip. 'My mother died when I was born.'

'Ei, sorry to hear that.'

Suleiman shrugged. 'I didn't know her at all. I didn't even miss her.'

'You've been around here longer than me.' Banri poured himself a refill.

'That might be true but it makes no difference; people still throw stones at my house.' Suleiman gulped his drink. His eyes were slightly glazed. 'They call me all sorts of names... bastard outsider.'

'Don't worry, they throw stones at me too, dorji.'

'No, they don't, you lie,' he said with sudden vehemence. 'Only at mine and others like me.'

'What I meant was... Here, calm down. I'm sorry...'

The candle spluttered and crackled, it was beginning to burn low. Banri handed the tailor a replenished tumbler. 'Tell me about your father.'

Suleiman stirred the rice; it was dry and almost done. 'He was a radio operator with All India Radio; he worked for them most of his life.'

'And now...?'

'He passed away three years ago. In a way I'm thankful... before this trouble got bad.'

Banri swirled his glass, watching the alcohol catch the candlelight. 'I never knew my father. He died when I was three. Too much drinking.'

'You shouldn't be drinking so much then.'

'What else to do in this god-awful town?' He knocked back his drink. 'Especially if you have no woman around. How come you live alone, dorji?'

Suleiman thought of Christine, her plump arms, the dimple on her left cheek, and muttered something about not having found the right person.

'Right person, wrong person...who knows until you try.'

'Maybe you're right,' said Suleiman, and then added that, anyway, he probably wouldn't be in Shillong for much longer.

'Even I want to get out, sometimes, you know, see a bit of other places.' Banri hesitated. 'Earlier today these KSU guys came to the workshop, to tell us about the rally, and he was talking about the future. You know, how they needed our support and it all depended on us...all the stuff I've heard before many times. Is the future built on these things?'

Suleiman remained silent, an unlit beedi in his hand.

'People keep asking me why I don't join KSU...that it's a cause for our tribe. They think...I see it in their eyes when they look at me...they think if I don't then somehow I'm not a real Khasi, you know?' He shrugged. 'I mean I see their point and all—we don't own any businesses here, or hold important government positions...but I don't know,'—he struggled with his words—'if this is the right way...fighting, beh dkhar...chasing outsiders out of Shillong.' He pointed his glass at Suleiman. 'Where will you go? Anyway, even if I join them who will look after my mother and my sisters? With my dad gone...we're on our own, you know.' He laughed. 'Maybe I'll go where you go, dorji.'

The tailor struck a match and lit his beedi. 'That's the problem. I don't really have anywhere to go. I was two when we came to Shillong. I thought it was the most beautiful place on earth.'

'It is.'

For a while they sat in silence and smoked. Then Suleiman took the rice off the stove. The coal glowed warm and bright, filling the room with a little more light, dispersing the meditative mood.

'Ei, dorji, how do you do it? You know, calculate these numbers...'

'I told you I see them in dreams.'

'That makes no sense. If you decide to leave town, just make sure you teach me first.'

The night settled around them in a shadowy haze; it was quiet now with few shouts in the street, and no patter of running feet. No stones pelted at Suleiman's roof either. Perhaps for now the trouble had moved elsewhere. If anyone were taking a walk, they'd catch the smell of coal fires, and draw their shawls around them closer, for it was always cold in the hills. They'd pass darkened windows where candlelight bled around the edges, and the faces inside might be wary and fearful, not holding a glance, wondering why there was someone outside at this hour. In some rooms children may be listening to grandparents telling stories of a time that was simpler and kinder. From one house might come the sound of raucous, drunken laughter, drowning the music from an old radio. Yet this was not the occasion to be curious, it was safer to move on.

Suleiman hung out the washing the next morning, and buried his face in a crisp white kurta. It lay wet, and cool and fresh against his face. His head throbbed, a restless demon trapped inside it, and razor-edge pain sliced across his forehead each time he moved. His face was still wrapped in the kurta when a voice called out behind him.

'Ei, dorji.'

Suleiman didn't move.

'Ei, dorji.'

'What do you want now? You only went home a few hours ago.'

'Yes, but, dorji…'

If it was any consolation, Banri looked worse—his eyes bloodshot and dark-circled. But there was something more than ragged tiredness that weighed on his face.

'I had a strange dream.'

'You don't remember any of your dreams.'

'But this one, I do.' His hands shook as he lit a cigarette.

Suleiman moved to the shade of the guava tree and leaned against the trunk. The sunlight hurt his eyes. 'What did you see?'

Banri paced in front of him. 'I was walking in a field, like a rice field I think, and ahead of me I see my grandfather. He died long ago; I barely remember him. But he was calling me, so I followed. And you were there too, dorji, on a cycle, I don't know why. You cycled next to me. And suddenly I saw it wasn't my grandfather but my father. So I followed him, into this forest, and you disappeared, and I think I was lost. Then in a clearing, I saw them all…'

'Who?'

'My granny, my grandfather, my father, my uncles and aunts, all dead and gone. Dorji,' he clutched the tailor's arm, 'it was like they were waiting for me.'

'My friend, it was just a dream. Sometimes, I see my…'

'But isn't it bad? They say it's bad to see the dead.'

'No, it's lucky,' said Suleiman softly. 'Your loved ones come to visit you through your dreams.'

Banri dragged on his cigarette. 'I don't know. It scared me. I woke up, and I couldn't go back to sleep.'

'If it makes you feel better, I can give you numbers.'

Banri looked troubled. 'I don't know, dorji...maybe for this...'

'The worst thing that'll happen is you'll lose...which you're used to anyway.'

The young man managed a small smile.

'Do you want numbers?'

'Alright, why not?'


It was a cool, clear evening, the wind was just right—neither strong nor slack—and Suleiman's kite barely lifted off the ground. He tried repeatedly, but it was difficult to keep the line steady whilst releasing the spool.

He remembered something his father had once told him, that the kite held the soul of the person who flew it. 'What does that mean, abba?' he'd asked, and his father had replied, 'What you feel flows through the string.'

'Bah...' said Suleiman in disgust as the line dropped yet again. If what his father said was true, it also didn't help that his head, though better than in the morning, still throbbed with a dull, persistent ache. He sat down and silently cursed Banri, and himself. The air was hazy with the smoke of evening fires, and a light mist rolled down the hills in the distance. From his vantage point on the roof, he could see the town spread out before him, with its red tin-roofed buildings, dark pine treetops and tangles of wires and kite strings stitching the sky. On another afternoon, he would have headed to the gentle open spaces of the golf course, and walked along the edges of the forest until he felt soothed and better. Now, though, he was confined to this square piece of ground while kites prowled above him like birds of prey. He'd give it one last try, he thought. And this time, helped by a nifty breeze, the kite lifted. Soon, it was swooping through the air like a delighted bird. He laughed. Perhaps this is what his father had meant—that the kite mimicked his gladness. It flew higher, leaving the rest behind. Some of the smaller kites challenged him to a duel, but the battles didn't last more than a few minutes. He was invincible. Finally, a large kite rose in the air and swirled around his.

'Here's the bastard,' muttered Suleiman. At first he allowed his kite to be trailed, followed like prey; they swayed in the sky, their lines crossing but not breaking. He waited for the fighter to get impatient, make a mistake, move too soon. But he didn't. He was as careful as Suleiman. Soon, in turn, his kite was the stalker, the string strained against his hands as he tried to steady the line. And then for a moment the kites were so still they seemed to have stopped moving, the clouds behind them ringed with the dying edges of sunlight. It continued for a while, this mid-air game, blown in the wind. Suleiman didn't know how much longer he'd be able to keep it up. All at once, though, and, with some luck, he pulled and a line snapped, the other kite dropped, floating lower and lower until it disappeared into a cluster of treetops. Suleiman managed to hold the line steady long enough to bring the kite down. It lay in his hands, fluttering like a breathless bird. Around him, the town looked coy and peaceful, hiding behind long shadows, a few lights flickering on the hills.

From the courtyard down below came the sound of running footsteps. It was Banri.

'Dorji,' he shouted into the tailor's empty room.

'I'm here.'

Banri looked up, his face round and bright as a newly minted coin.

'I won! Clean sweep! Both rounds.'

Suleiman smiled.

'What are you doing on the roof?'

'Nothing.'

'Let's go drink. My treat...'

'Allah! No, I told you, never again...'

'Okay, we'll go eat. There's a good Muslim restaurant in Mawlong Haat.'

'Near Iew Duh?'

'Yes.'

'But...' He stopped himself from reminding Banri about the rally. Surely, by now it must be over. How long could it go on? And this evening, for some reason, he felt as though the town was his own.

'Alright, let's go.'

He was ready, even in the smallest possible way, to reclaim it.

That night, before going to bed, Suleiman once again climbed to the roof. Without his kite. It probably wasn't safe to be there at that hour, so he'd only stay for the length of a beedi. The time it took from the first puff to the last. In the vast and infinite darkness, he could barely see the town that sprawled around him. Somewhere, within its sloping streets, he'd hear narrated on the radio tomorrow, a rally had been held that slid out of control, that pockets of violence had left many dead and wounded, outsiders and Khasis alike. He would once again consider moving away.

Now, though, he was thinking of the evening. They'd walked to Iew Duh, and wandered its crowded alleyways lined by makeshift stalls that looked as though they'd been built and rebuilt by many hands through the years. They picked early winter oranges from a fruit seller's basket, and coated them in salt and chilli. He bought a packet of freshly roasted peanuts, still warm and sandy to the touch. At Naz Hotel, they ordered mounds of steaming rice, buttery korma and heaps of kebabs sizzling in a bed of raw onions and lime. They even asked for dessert, bowlfuls of rich, creamy kheer speckled with almonds and raisins. He told Banri this was the best food he'd eaten in a long time. They'd walked back slowly, sluggish from a full stomach, emptying silvery packets of Pan Parag into their mouths.

He was nearing the end of his beedi. A strong, brief wind rustled the leaves of the guava tree, somewhere echoed the empty clank of a loose tin sheet. Another day, he thought, another day is what the future is built on. He looked up. The sky, emptied of kites and wires, had unravelled and was full of stars.

# Laitlum

Every other day, the world ended. Often within our house rather than on the streets of Shillong. Out there it was a riot between the Outsiders and the Locals. Yet what troubled my parents through the early '90s, more than the antics of the KSU, the HNLC, the CRPF, and the government (both central and state), were the shenanigans of my elder sister, Grace. She was seventeen, and as unfathomable to them, and to me, as the stars.

Looking back now, I'd say those were my generation's glory days—of perpetually shut schools and closed colleges, of curfew-emptied roads where we played endless games of cricket, of blackout evenings filled with grandfather tales of bears and ghosts, and long afternoons in the sun dipping into bowls of soh khleh, pomelo and orange tossed with chilli and mustard oil. The grown-ups have remembrances of their own, of course—entire colonies burnt to the ground because their inhabitants happened to come from across the border, random shoot-outs in the night that killed so many weary innocent, the rush to buy food at six o'clock before shops ran out of bread and milk and eggs. Yet who cared, if you were young and life suddenly seemed like infinite summer.

I was twelve, gawky, awkward, and dreaming of the day I'd perhaps turn out like Grace—effortlessly beautiful, so infinitely comfortable within her own skin, so shockingly bold. 'I loathe you,' was her standard response to any rules my parents enforced, which, to be fair, covered an alarmingly wide number of things—no late nights, no parties, no boys coming over, no alcohol, no going over to boys' houses, no smoking, no torn jeans, no hanging around on the streets of Laitumkhrah, and so on.

Grace casually flouted them all. Some at the same time.

I suppose our parents were like any other in Shillong—aghast about how suddenly and irrevocably rebellious the youth were—but since they both worked as doctors at private clinics, they were more worried than most about what 'other people would think'. The activity they hated most, for instance, was what I liked to term the 'languid lounger'.

'Standing on the roadside all day...as though you're homeless,' our mother would say, 'and in those—' she'd point to Grace's ripped stonewashed jeans. 'What will people think?'

'They don't care. They're too busy chasing dkhars.'

And then, as these scenes usually ended, she'd be sent to her room.

Sometimes, for no fault of mine, they'd involve me. I'd usually be within earshot, pretending to read a book.

'Why can't you be more like your sister?'

I'd look up and feign surprise, as though I didn't know what the conversation was about.

'Because,' said Grace, 'she's boring.'

And hurt as I would be, I knew it was the truth. I liked reading, wore my hair cropped short, couldn't tell, or care, what clothes looked nice on me, and unlike her, I didn't have any glamorous, aspiring rock star companions. Instead, I hung out with Anku, a plump kid from next door who was my age, wore spectacles, and liked to play cricket. He was Assamese, and since the situation in Shillong didn't seem to be getting any better, I was in constant danger of losing my only friend. The thing that saved his family, he told me in one of our many over-the-hedge conversations, was that his businessman father had arranged benami with many Khasis.

'What's benami?' I asked.

His dad, he explained, paid the locals handsomely to set up shops in their names instead of his own, and thus far, nobody had dared lay a finger on him.

Apart from Anku, I didn't really get along with the other colony children, who played frightening physically demanding games and scaled pine trees as though they were nothing more than flights of stairs. I could hear them sometimes, rushing down the road, stealing sour red soh lia from our trees, shouting out rude nicknames in Khasi, returning slippery-slick from swimming at the old abandoned water tank in the forest. My sister's friends, on the other hand, were all the popular kids—the athletic basketball stars, and cool, pretty girls, the ones invited to all the parties, who played guitar and smoked real cigarettes—not the sweet Phantom ones Anku and I puffed on cold winter evenings and then exhaled pretending our foggy breath was smoke. Her friends streamed in and out of the house like a colourful, exotic parade, and I kept out of their way, while desperately longing to be included. My sister's closest friend was Sarah—a rather dopey-faced girl with a definite smattering of Anglo genes somewhere in her recent ancestry. She had impossibly light hazel eyes, a glossy tangle of almost-blonde hair and a spray of attractive freckles on her nose. She'd also kissed every boy in town, mostly in our house, and I'd often encountered these passionate embraces at the bottom of the stairs and at the top, in the loo and on the roof, in my sister's room and mine.

While Sarah's fleeting suitors came and went, there was a steady group of boys that waltzed through our doors much to my parents' mounting chagrin. A long-limbed Manipuri guitarist and a couple of Anglo-Khasi boys with boyish charm, bold, loud voices, and lips stained scarlet with betel nut juice. The handsomest of them all was Sarah's brother Mike, who had perfectly gelled hair and wore immaculate white T-shirts, tight, skinny jeans and polished black boots.

'Hiya, kid,' he'd say, making my young heart leap into my mouth, and my stomach flutter in the most curious manner. For him, I could easily enough scale those skyscraper pine trees. Or jump into an icy cold water tank. Sometimes, he'd sit himself down on the sofa, close enough for me to smell his hair gel and Old Spice, and wrench a book out of my hand.

'Whatchya reading?'

My mouth would go dry, and I'd stutter. 'N-Nancy Drew.'

'Hmmmm…' He'd glance at the cover. 'Cute chick. Just like you.'

I fell madly in love.

In those days, my sister's parties ('better at home where we can keep an eye on her than anywhere else where we can't,' was how my parents relented) were held during the afternoon. The curtains drawn to create the illusion of night, Shakin' Stevens booming out of tinny Philips speakers, and Gold Spot and Thums Up slugged out of dusty glass bottles. If the drinks were spiked, which I'm sure they were, it was done with the utmost discretion. I wasn't allowed into the room, but wandered in from time to time with messages from my mother regarding the volume of the music, or the lateness of the hour. Nobody seemed to notice I was there, lost as they were in each other's arms, floating around to Air Supply. Once, I saw Mike and Grace kissing, and ran out with tears in my eyes. Anku, clueless when it came to matters of the heart, didn't quite know how to help.

'They were kissing? That's gross.'

After that I encountered them everywhere. Draped across the sofa, walking hand in hand in Laitumkhrah, or giggling at the gate where they spent a million light years saying goodbye and goodnight. But it was bound to have happened. Don't beautiful people gravitate towards each other? Like proverbial moths to a flame? And don't the less attractive have to make do with leftovers? Mine, I decided, wasn't going to be a happy life. Grace and Mike were in love. I was left with Anku and my books. Suddenly they too seemed irrelevant and dissatisfying, the worlds I conjured up while reading. Even my mother's secret stash of Barbara Cartlands, that I found in a drawer and devoured, could hardly appease my discontent. There wasn't much to choose from, I decided, between this life and the one imagined. Until, that is, the Manipuri guitarist brought Chris over to our house one evening.

Chris belonged to Shillong's oldest, wealthiest Chinese family who'd immigrated to the hills from Calcutta in the '60s. They owned a string of restaurants and shoe shops in Laitumkhrah and Police Bazaar, and lived in a sprawling bungalow in Laban. Chris, the elder son, had been studying in Bangalore all this while, but was back now, in these troubled days, to help with the family business. The first time I saw him, he roared up on a Yamaha, helmet in hand, leather jacket in the other, and I thought he was the hippest person I'd ever laid eyes on. On his back was a hardback guitar case, casually slung across as though it weighed no more than a feather. I saw my sister's face when she was introduced to him; I don't know how to describe it, except I'd never seen her look that way at Mike.

'I'm a guitarist in a band,' he said, flicking back his dark, spiky hair. 'I'm on lead, my brother Melvin is on drums.'

Melvin was a shorter, stockier version of Chris, with none of his sharp, angular features and charm. He stood silently at the back; clearly he was used to his brother taking charge. When they entered our living room, I heard Chris rifle through Grace's cassettes and say, 'Air Supply. Foreigner. Roxette. You listen to rubbish. Have you heard Hendrix?'

That evening all that drifted through the door was the electrified twang of a guitar and a husky voice singing songs I didn't know. It was music I'd never heard before—angry, raspy sounds that emerged from inexplicable rage.

The brothers didn't leave until almost midnight, when my parents protested and they were bundled out of the room like a pile of laundry.

'It's not safe to be outside so late...' my mother warned them. 'Things are getting worse...'

The brothers were respectfully silent while gathering their things. At the door, though, I heard Chris mutter to my sister—'We know everyone who's roaming the streets...'

From that evening on, my sister and Chris were inseparable. I'm not sure what happened to Mike—although there was a time he stormed in, threatened to beat Chris, and then stormed out not to be seen again. I watched him from the window, strutting down the garden path and to the gate where a couple of his friends were waiting. He gestured to them and then to the house; I wondered what story he was making up to explain my sister's sudden change in affections. One afternoon, Sarah too left my sister's room in tears, saying how she'd hoped some day they'd be sisters-in-law, and that Grace had treated her brother most unkindly. I don't think my sister cared.

We didn't see her for hours on end. She was usually at Chris's house in Laban, doing, as my mother said, 'God knows what'. If Mike was what she called a 'khynnah dakaid'—a bad boy—it was highly unlikely she approved of Chris. This town, according to my parents, with its constant unrest and wanton youth, was headed for nothing but disaster. They couldn't understand it, where had it gone? The peaceful little place they'd grown up in, with its quaint British ways and pretty bungalows, its safe streets and pine-dappled innocence. They'd watched it transform before their eyes. My sister and Chris tore around on his motorbike, paying little heed to reports of trouble, growing ever since the government had refused to meet with the KSU for talks. There were rumours that curfew would be enforced again, harsher this time, with anyone seen outside threatened to be stoned or assaulted. On certain evenings, the news on the radio would be drowned out by Chris's guitar, as he played for Grace in the living room—on occasion their bassist would also join him, while Melvin sat in a corner tapping his drumsticks on the table. I don't know if my parents noticed but Grace changed in those months—she dressed differently, in darker, more grown-up clothes, she let her hair hang loose and tangled. She took down the posters of Debbie Gibson and Jason Donovan in her room, and replaced them with the ones Chris gave her—Hendrix, Led Zeppelin, The Who, Jethro Tull, The Beatles.

'What's happened to you?' my mother once asked in exasperation.

My sister smiled. 'I discovered rock 'n' roll.'

'What's rock 'n' roll?' asked Anku.

'It's a type of music,' I said wisely.

'What type of music?'

'Oh you know, electric guitars, cool drums.'

Anku looked doubtful and decidedly unimpressed, so one afternoon, I snuck him into the house. I allowed him to peer into Grace's room. He stared around in awe. I think, secretly, like everyone else in the world, he had a crush on my sister.

'This is...amazing,' he whispered. 'Like being allowed into the inner sanctum of a temple you'd only worshipped from afar.' I told him to stop being idiotically melodramatic and pulled him to the living room.

Since I hardly knew what rock 'n' roll was about, I randomly picked a cassette from an untidy pile lying on the floor. It was a Led Zeppelin album, I've forgotten which, and although we didn't catch, or understand, most of the lyrics, Anku and I listened transfixed.

*To seek the man whose pointing hand/The giant step unfolds*

*With guidance from the curving path/That churns up into stone*

I hadn't turned the volume up high, but we still didn't hear my sister and Chris walk in.

'What the hell are you doing?' my sister yelled.

We were too frightened to reply. 'I'm sorry,' I blurted, 'I was just...'

'Hey, relax,' said Chris. 'They're listening to music.' He sat cross-legged next to us. 'Do you like Zeppelin?'

Anku and I nodded.

'See, they have better taste than you.' He grinned at my sister who threw a cushion at him.

'If you like this,' he said, pressing the red STOP button, 'you'll love these guys.'

He fished a cassette out of his pocket; the cover had a baby on it, swimming in water. I thought that seemed quite bizarre, but didn't say so. I was grateful to Chris for diverting my sister's anger.

'This is what I wanted you to listen to, Grace...' he said, pressing PLAY. Then he turned to my sister and pulled her close to him. They seemed not to care that Anku and I were there, and halfway through the song, amid a mad crashing of percussion and guitar, and the voice of a truly anguished soul, we left the room.

After that day, I didn't see Chris or Anku for a while. There'd been trouble in town—a massive shoot-out between the CRPF and the KSU—and an endless bandh had been called. 'You go out and get killed, we won't even be able to hold your a funeral,' my parents told Grace, and even she couldn't help but obey this time. We were stuck indoors for days, and while I amused myself by penning down entries in my diary, Grace fared much worse. Either she listened to music at the highest possible volume—as though to say to our parents 'if you make me stay in *this* is what you'll have to put up with'—or prowled around the house like a caged animal. I must admit, though, by the end of the week, I was also restless. Looking out of the window, I could see the colony curiously still and quiet; the roads emptied of cars and pedestrians. There seemed no end to this 'trouble'. When would life go back to being what it had been? Right now, I wasn't sure if that could ever happen.

Later in the month, when curfew hours were shortened, people were still cautioned about being outdoors. So while Chris and Melvin often dropped by, my sister was warned against leaving the house. The worst news came from over the hedge when Anku told me that there was talk in his home of his family leaving Shillong.

'But why?' I cried, even though the answer was obvious.

My friend looked miserable. 'It's my mother,' he explained. 'She says she's had enough, that she wants to be with her own people. She said to abba it was either her or Shillong.'

There was an air of disquiet that hung about our town and our house. It was only relieved sometimes when Chris and his band were jamming in the living room. One afternoon, I almost bumped into Chris while coming down the stairs.

'Sorry,' I mumbled.

'It's not your fault.' Chris put his hand on my shoulder. 'Don't say sorry when it's not your fault.'

'You guys sound good,' I blurted.

He looked pleased, even though I thought my opinion could hardly count.

'Thank you. While cooped up at home these days we worked on some songs; we're thinking of putting an album together.'

'Wow.' More than anything else, I felt tremendously important that Chris was telling me this. 'What's the name of your band?' I asked, a little bolder now.

'Empty Ceremony.'

I looked impressed.

'Next time we rehearse, come check us out.'

I nodded.

He winked at me before vanishing through the door to my sister's room.

The clearest memory I have of Chris and his brother is when we all went to Laitlum. It was a quiet Sunday afternoon and our parents had gone to visit an ailing relative at Nazareth Hospital. As usual, we'd been cautioned to stay home.

'Anywhere,' I could hear my sister say to Chris. 'I don't care. I'm so tired of these four walls.'

He and his brother had come over on their bikes; I'd heard them roar up to the gate.

'Alright,' said Chris, 'let's go for a drive.'

In those days, when Shillong had no fancy cafés, restaurants, gaming parlours, or shopping malls, 'drive' was a magical word. It offered time away, however briefly, from a small town filled with people you knew or who knew your parents. 'Drives' were an escape. And on that particular afternoon, against our parents' orders. Grace shrieked in delight. I could hear them gathering their things. I had never been on a drive, or been invited to one either; it would have been pointless to ask if I could go along. Perhaps, I thought gloomily, I could blackmail Grace. 'I'll tell mei and papa if you don't take me.' And she'd probably laugh and toss her long, black hair over her shoulder, saying she didn't care.

'Let's take her.'

I looked up. They were on their way out and Chris was gesturing at me.

'What? No,' said my sister immediately.

'Come on...'

I held my breath.

'...she's been stuck at home too.'

There was little she could say no to when it came to Chris.

'She can ride with Mel,' she said grudgingly.

'Really?' I found it almost impossible to believe. 'But papa and mei...'

'Will get home and find us not there,' Grace interrupted, 'and we'll get into trouble. Do you want to come or not?'

I nodded.

'Put something warm on or you'll freeze your ass off.'

I ran up to my room, two steps at a time, before they could change their minds.

They say you don't ever forget your first love, your first kiss. I don't know it if applies to your first motorbike ride. It didn't change my life. But it gave me the first tremulous hint of how things could be different. Yes, that there were other ways of experiencing the world. So far, for me, that had been from the security of being on the inside—a car, a book, the judicious guidance of my parents. Cocooned in plastic and metal, in parched pages, within the arms of a suffocating love. And everything goes by, scenery and life, unfurling at a safe and careful distance, a flat democratic haze. Being outside is a step away from safety. On a motorbike, the world rushes up at you from all sides, so do the wind and the colours of the trees and the sky. You are exposed. The sunshine hits your back, your face, the air flies down your throat, and you are nothing but a single, glorious movement.

We wove our way out of our neighbourhood and into Laitumkhrah, usually a busy area with people bustling around the shops and large meat and vegetable bazaar. Today, the streets were almost empty, and we raced through them, weaving around traffic cones and a few clusters of pedestrians. I clung to Melvin madly, laughing out loud. We passed children playing games of football and cricket on the road, and grown-ups who looked at us with the greatest disdain. 'Khynnah dkaid,' I could almost hear them say and it thrilled me. This was better than any book, I thought. It was real. The roads were more desolate as we hit the outskirts of the town. I held on tight to Melvin's leather jacket, trying not to let slip that, for me, this was as scary as it was exciting. I couldn't wait to tell Anku; and then I remembered that the house next door lay empty. Suddenly, I wanted Melvin to go faster, and for the world to turn into a dazzling blur. In front of us, I could see Chris and Grace; her hair streaming in the wind, she leaned in to whisper in his ear. Then she half stood up and raised her arms in the air like an angel. She had her eyes closed. I would have liked to do the same but was afraid I'd fall off. Soon, we were far out of town, driving through rough, barren countryside marked with slabs of dark, layered rock. There were stretches of harvested fields and rows of thatched huts from where children would run to the side of the road and wave at us. I had no idea where we were headed, but it didn't seem to matter. We were away from the disquiet that hung over Shillong, away from the confines of home and the watchful eyes of parents. All these years later, I look back on that day and know it was the afternoon I grew up.

Finally, the road narrowed and changed to a dirt track flanked on either side by tall, graceful bamboo. We took a sharp turn and stopped by an iron gate.

'What's this place?' my sister asked.

'You'll see,' Chris replied.

We walked to the top of the slope and when we reached, my sister and I gasped.

'Welcome to Laitlum,' said Chris and gestured melodramatically to the view.

We were standing on a field at the head of a valley, flanked by rows of jagged mountains that seemed to multiply themselves, growing higher and more distant, layering each other in shades of deep blue and green. The sight stretched far and endless, as though beyond lay mountains and nothing more of the world. It was quiet here too but, I noticed, this was different. The air was light and filled with late afternoon sunshine; it carried no heaviness nor remorse.

Grace laughed out loud. I hadn't seen my sister this happy in a long time.

We walked to the edge of the field, which dropped sharply into the valley. A wind swirled up, tugging at us with invisible hands. Around us were scattered large boulders the colour of wet sand, and a small track wound between them down the slope to the village below, on a ledge halfway to the valley. A small voice in my mind reminded me that our parents might be back home by now...I imagined them walking in and finding our note saying we were going for a walk to Laitumkhrah.

They'd worry, and pace the floor waiting for us to get back. Suddenly, the wind stung my skin in little pangs of guilt.

'Shall we...' I began.

'Sit here?' completed my sister, pointing to a large, flat stone nearby.

They made themselves comfortable and I had no choice but to join them. I wondered how long we'd stay out... Melvin lit a cigarette and pulled out a bottle of rum from his jacket pocket. He twisted off the cap and took a swig before passing it to me; I could smell the alcohol, strong and sweet. I hesitated.

'Go on, take a sip, it gets pretty cold here,' said Chris.

I looked at my sister but she was lighting a cigarette.

'And,' Chris added, 'we're celebrating.'

The rum burned my throat and, though I tried my hardest not to, I spluttered. Soon, a silver prickle travelled down my chest, and I was enveloped by warmth. I took a few more small quick gulps before passing on the bottle. I felt a growing tingle, a delicious exhilaration. I suddenly wanted to stand up and shout, 'This is our right. To be happy.' Around me, conversation was a distant murmur. They spoke of the album, I think, the artwork on the cover, the sequence of songs, and how it would be quite unlike anything anyone in Shillong had ever created before. As the shadows stretched long across the slopes, everyone fell quiet. From behind us came the sound of quick footsteps; it was an elderly man, carrying a khoh on his back.

'Kumno, mama,' called out Melvin. The old man nodded in acknowledgement, his face, though elderly, was smooth and unlined, his eyes sharp and bright like small river stones.

We watched him walk carefully down the path to the village in the valley. He rounded a bend and then vanished behind a boulder.

'Why is this place called Laitlum?' asked Melvin suddenly.

'It means where the hills are set free,' answered Grace.

'Yes, but why? Don't you Khasis have a story for everything?'

'I'm sure there is, something about a cruel giant, or evil serpent, or some person caught by spirits and water fairies. But who cares?' she said, 'Folk stories are rubbish.'

Chris sipped the rum. 'Why?'

'Because they have nothing to do with the world we live in, they're not real.'

'They might not be real to you, but...'

'Look at what's going on,' she interrupted. 'Is there time for folk tales when people are shooting each other across their own town roads?'

'Perhaps that's when they need them most.'

My sister shook her head. 'Maybe once they taught people something about life, and how to live it but not any more. Now you figure things out for yourself, you can't depend on anyone else to get you out of shit.'

We sat a long while in silence, listening to the wind, watching the way rising mist changed shape through the trees. It looked like faces, the ones you pass every day on the street, that turn their eyes away because everyone is a stranger in a town of careless bullets. At times, the mist fragmented like light on water, opening trails and doors and windows, settling into the bulky shapes of houses. It swirled like our feathered dancers holding swords and lamenting about an ancient tribal war; it tiptoed like women on the fringes, moving in slow, graceful lines. The mist was our history.

On the other side of the valley, the sun had shredded the sky and fallen behind the mountains. We watched the clouds bleed.

'When you're sitting here,' said Chris finally, 'all the shit in life seems far away.'

Melvin said he'd build a hut here, a stone cabin to keep out the wind and rain, where he could set up his drum kit... 'And we'll come live with you.' My sister laughed. 'We can play music all day...'

'And drink,' added Chris, holding up the near-empty bottle.

'No one would bother us,' Grace concluded. 'It would be our own place.'

We stayed until light had almost completely faded, and deep shadows lengthened into the valley. The wind had turned cold and we rode back subdued, the bike lights barely dispersing the darkness.


The next year was a time of many changes. Anku came to see me once, when his father travelled to Shillong to take care of some unfinished business. They lived in Dibrugarh now, in the southern part of Assam. When I asked him what it was like, he said it was alright, that the good thing was he had many more people with whom he could play cricket. Since this was years before the Internet, and despite the exchange of a few letters, I never saw my friend again. We also got cable television—and I realized, while blearily watching MTV until the wee hours of the morning, that the song Chris had made Anku and I listen to on that faraway afternoon was Nirvana's 'Smells like Teen Spirit'. It felt like the beginning and the end of an era.

Chris and my sister never broke up. But neither were they together. A few months after our drive to Laitlum, Chris and Melvin's grandmother died. True to Khasi tradition, one they'd adopted as part of having lived in Shillong for many generations, the family gathered to 'said jain', to wash household clothes at Dwar Ksuid. As it usually happens in cases like these, accounts of the accident vary, but it was likely that Chris lost his balance on wet, mossy rock and slipped into the river. Despite being a good swimmer, he was caught in a strong current that pulled him under. His brother jumped in to try and save him, and for a moment it looked like he might succeed. He dragged Chris while trying to make for the bank, but it proved too far. They were both drowned. At midday, the time at which, they say, the water fairies call from the water. My sister didn't emerge from her room for weeks, listening over and over to the album the band had released merely a week earlier. I'd sit outside my sister's door, clutching a book, unable to understand how they could be gone.

The album received a small, enthusiastic response, but mostly people didn't understand why their music didn't revolve around love. Instead it sounded angry, speaking out against the world, and condemning it for its failures.

*Such a stupid life.*
Chris sang.
*Such a stupid life.*

My sister took the music to heart. After the accident, she refused to attend church, saying she'd been confused before, but now she was sure there wasn't a god. My parents were at a loss, this time not knowing how to argue with her. Her friends, though sympathetic at the beginning, stopped dropping by. The parade diminished to a trickle. Mike made an appearance once or twice, but was desultorily sent away. Things did not improve for Chris and Melvin's family. One by one, their businesses packed up and closed—the extortion demands from militant groups in the state were getting larger and bolder. It was unsustainable to keep their shops and restaurants open. Finally, my mother told me, they all left Shillong, probably for Calcutta, or Canada, nobody really knew. Laitlum, I heard, was eventually closed to the public—people drank there and got into fights despite the 'Commit No Nuisance Here' signboard nailed to the gate. Unlike the hills and mist, for us freedom doesn't last a lifetime; it comes and goes on unexpected afternoons.

# Sky Graves

It was mostly at funerals that people told stories. On the three night-long watches kept by the ieng iap briew—the household of the dead—when windows and doors stayed open for the spirit of the deceased. Sometimes a stool would tip over, a wooden shutter suddenly rattle or a tumbler fall to the floor. These were indications of a ghostly visit, some believed, mysterious signs that the one who'd passed away was making peace with the world they were leaving behind. On these nights, people whiled away the hours playing cards or carrom; in the kitchen women would splice betel nut and fold tobacco leaves for the next day's visitors, they would talk quietly of the bereaved and the inconsolable. In a separate room, in a musty corner, a group of men would huddle around the chula, giving off warmth and light like a familiar, benevolent mistress. There were funny stories of drunks who wandered into empty churches and talked to stoic ceramic saints, of animal hunts that went heroically right, and sometimes tragically wrong, tales of journeys through jungles and wilderness involving characters they'd never met but who'd become real and intimate through years of retelling. Stories are told at festive, joyful gatherings, but the ones narrated at funerals are special because they reaffirm existence, of the listeners and the narrators. They are times of remembrance that haul the past into the present, and keep people alive even when they're gone.

It wasn't often that Bah Hem told stories. He would sit in silence, listening to the others, his eyes fixed on the glowing coal. On nights that were a trifle colder and quieter, though, he could be persuaded. If he'd had a drink—smoky rice beer or a sharp stinging glass of clear kiad—someone would ask for a story about love, and he'd speak of the man who came from the place where birds go to die. And like at the beginning of so many stories, the room would transform, assembled anew with words.

'He showed up one late September morning,' he'd begin, 'when memories of monsoon rain were fading with the mild autumn sunshine. He walked into my workshop, silent as a hunter.'

The stranger was greeted with no small surprise—this was the rough 'wild west' part of town, an area of strict local laws and devout churchgoers. Not a place for outsiders.

'I'm from Jatinga.' His tone was soft, foreign, not of these hills.

'You came all this way?' Bah Khraw, assistant at the workshop, sounded as rough as the sandpaper in his hand. He'd worked there thirteen years, almost as long as the place had been open, and felt he'd earned the right to choose the people he wanted to be agreeable to. The young man, tall, thin, with the dusky complexion of the people from the plains, remained silent. He was no more than twenty, but his eyes, quietly pensive, looked much older. The weapon in his hand was a solid 10 gauge double-barrel shotgun, much used and badly in need of polish.

'That's because Bah Hem is the best. Number one gunman.' This came from a gentleman in the corner; a group of them huddled like crows around a bottle of Royal Tusk whisky and pinched tobacco into dust between their fingers.

'And marksman also,' somebody added. 'Four in one hole.' He was referring to a recent shooting competition held in town where Bah Hem had shot four bullets through the same hole on a target. The trophy stood on a shelf in the workshop, next to many others, which could be dated by the layers of grime they'd gathered. The older ones were of darkest black.

'Four in one hole.' The bottle was raised to a slurry chorus of approval.

Bah Hem was seated at a table, writing. He paid them no attention. A cigarette smouldered between his fingers. Eventually, he looked up at the stranger.

'Where did you get that?'

'My father bought it from Haflong.'

Bah Hem examined the weapon in silence. He ran a finger over the barrel, unloaded it in a few brisk movements and aimed outside the only window in the room. 'There's a problem with the viewfinder...'

'That's what my father said,' interrupted the young man.

'Oh, and who is he? The gun specialist in Jatinga?' Bah Khraw bent over the vise machine, tightening it around a small metal plate; the men in the corner sniggered.

The young stranger flushed but didn't retort; in his eyes a small anger glowed like embers in a winter chula.

'Ignore him; Khraw has the manners of a pig.' Bah Hem stubbed the cigarette out on the desk.

His assistant scowled.

'And sometimes the face of one too.'

The men exploded into laughter. They found everything he said funny out of courtesy for permitting them to carouse freely in his workshop. Bah Hem stepped outside with the gun and the stranger followed. From next door, the sound of the dentist's drill shattered the quiet mid-morning air. In front of them, the main road lay pale and empty.

'So where did you get the gun from?'

The boy looked down and stayed silent for a long while. 'My grandfather used to work as a chowkidar in a dak bangla in the Cachar district. Once, this bilati officer came to stay, he was very ill with kala-azar...he didn't last the week. My grandfather didn't take anything else, only this.' He placed a hand on the rifle.

The drill whined to a stop. Bah Hem lit a cigarette.

The young man asked, 'How did you know?'

'There's never been much of an arms market in Haflong. Everything comes from Bangladesh.' Bah Hem didn't add that a person's initials (G.D. Bradbury) were carved on the handle; it was likely the boy and his family couldn't read.

'My grandfather never took anything else.'

'I know people who have taken more, and you still can't call them thieves.' Bah Hem added that the gun would be ready in four or five days.

The boy took his leave. He said he needed to start on his journey immediately, otherwise, with all the army checks along the way, he wouldn't make it home before midnight.

A week later he was back. This time, Bah Khraw ignored him as did the group in the corner, today diminished to a trio resolutely playing cards.

'Have something,' Bah Hem offered when the tea lady appeared at the door with a basket of jing bam—soft, sticky 'putharo, golden brown 'pukhlien and sticks of hard, honeyed 'pusyep. The boy ate and drank quickly like a watchful animal.

'Your gun is ready.' Bah Hem waved to a row of gleaming weapons lining the wall behind his desk.

'How much?'

Bah Hem told him. The boy drew out a cloth pouch tied around his waist, and carefully counted out the notes as though it were some sacred, ancient ritual.

'We'll be here all day,' muttered Bah Khraw, picking at a metal spring.

The boy handed over the money and walked out.

'That's the last we'll see of him, I hope,' said Bah Khraw.

A shout from the corner caught their attention.

'Lah bowww...'

Someone had a particularly good hand; there was a hundred and fifty rupees at stake. The boy was forgotten.

That night, though, while lying in bed in a silently dreaming house, Bah Hem thought of Nathaniel, his eldest son who'd died two summers ago. He was nineteen then, and consumed by a disease they couldn't understand.

It had started with him feeling nauseous and fatigued, his brow burning with a low, steady fever, his throat sore and painful. What they'd written off as a seasonal flu didn't improve over the next few months. He lost an alarming amount of weight. His wife and him took Nathaniel to a hospital in south India, where they placed their trust in a man with a kindly manner and an accent they found difficult to decipher. He told them the name of the disease, it sounded long and terrifying, unfurling like a snake on their tongue. 'The white blood cells multiply at an abnormally rapid rate,' the doctor tried explaining, 'his body can't produce enough healthy blood cells...' They understood him well enough though when he said the condition was acute and that they needed to start treatment immediately. The young man who'd walked into his workshop today reminded Bah Hem of Nathaniel before the radiotherapy. Before the machines, those large metallic monsters, slowly blasted out all life from his son. What was it about him? His eyes? The shape of his jawline perhaps; the same shadows filled the contours of his face. His careful silence? Bah Hem wasn't sure. If he could only find some way, he thought, to see him again.

It was late; the dentist's clinic had shut, and the neighbourhood emptied as the cold settled into its nooks and crannies. In the quiet of the evening, Bah Hem sat alone in the workshop, cleaning a flintlock pistol. He liked to do these himself. They were beautiful weapons; he liked the way the light glinted off the intricate metalwork, the way the barrel lay slim and smooth against his palm. Around him the workshop was left in casual, greasy disarray. Opposite his desk stood a large table he'd salvaged from the town jail when it was being relocated. Many years worth of equipment and spare parts had built on it a jagged landscape of metal, grime, and dust. The smell of machine oil hung in the air. Just as he was giving the flintlock one last careful buff, there came a hurried knocking at the door. On the steps outside, he found the young stranger, shivering in the cool evening air.

'Please, we need help.'

Bah Hem stepped aside to allow him in.

'There's no time...'

'You're cold,' said Bah Hem calmly. 'Come inside...there's no point in falling ill and making things worse.'

The boy's shoulders drooped and he consented. Bah Hem rummaged under the bench and drew out a half-bottle of Old Monk. He poured a large shot and handed it to him. Then he threw more coal into the chula and pulled it closer.

'What's happened?'

'I–we need you to shoot some...an animal for us.'

'What animal?'

The boy looked down. 'A tiger.'

'A man-eater?'

He hesitated. 'We think it's dangerous. And we've tried to bait it and hunt it down...and failed. They say you...'

Bah Hem lit a cigarette; it glowed in the dim bare-bulb light. 'What's your name?'

'Kasa.'

'Kasa, I'll help you only if you tell me the truth.'

The boy finished the rum in a single gulp and grimaced. There was a little more colour in his face, but he still looked troubled.

'The army people in the area wounded it...it will turn into a man-eater sooner or later. My father—' and here he halted, 'is unwell, otherwise he would have taken care of this himself. He was...is a very good marksman. They say you are too...'

Bah Hem spoke only after he'd finished the cigarette. 'Alright, I'll go with you...' and he raised a hand to stop Kasa from speaking, 'but we will leave tomorrow morning. Tonight you stay in Shillong.'

Since Kasa knew no one in town he could ask for such a favour, and it wasn't particularly safe for a dkhar to stay on his own in a hotel, Bah Hem invited him to his house. He and his family lived in Umsohsun, close to a bridge over a large stream, in a lime-washed house built on a sloping hillside and accessed by a line of crooked stone steps. As they climbed, both of them bathed in moonlight, Bah Hem thought how it could have been him and Nathaniel returning home. Esther, Bah Hem's wife, made up a bed for their visitor, downstairs in a cot in the living room, surprisingly without question. Usually, like most locals in Shillong, she was wary of outsiders and, what they considered, their strange language and habits. Their other children—a son and two daughters—treated Kasa as a curiosity, something their father had picked up from one of the locality melas he was so fond of attending.

'Patlun lyngkot,' giggled one of them, pointing at Kasa's shorts.

Esther told them sharply to behave themselves, especially at the dining table, and spooned out more stew on their visitor's plate.

Only late at night, in a silently dreaming house, did Esther say to her husband, 'He has Nathaniel's eyes.'

Bah Hem said he thought so too.

Before Nathaniel grew too weak to stay awake and spent most of his days lying in bed, dehydrated, with his hair falling out in clumps. By then he also threw up most of what he ate, everything made him nauseous. The fever had been replaced by headaches, a perpetual throbbing at no particular spot in his head. 'It doesn't look like he's getting better,' Esther would whisper while their son slept, clutching her husband's hand in terror. Yet when they asked the doctor, he said there was not much more he could do. They needed to be patient.

On some afternoons, while Esther rested in the hotel, Bah Hem would sit in Nathaniel's room, narrating stories, not the ones he'd told him when he was a child, but of what they'd do when Nathaniel grew older. He'd take him fly-fishing to the Bhoroli, hunting in Garo Hills, perhaps they could get Nathaniel that drum kit he'd always wanted. Even with his wife they'd only speak of the past or the future. There was nothing in between. The present didn't exist; it was a black hole they all stood over. He'd always hated hospitals, and this one with its sterile whiteness seemed to suck away all the colour off Nathaniel's face. How could he take it away? Why was this happening to his son? There were no answers. Apart from a slant of sunlight that caught Nathaniel's cheek, now hollow and wasted, the vase of wilted flowers, and the beep of a machine that mechanically monitored his heart.

The next day, they set off early, catching the first bus out of town before the sun's rays brushed the mist-shrouded hills of Shillong. Bah Hem had wanted to drive his jeep, but Kasa said it was safer travelling in a group.

'It takes time for the army to check all the passengers, but it's better than being caught alone by militants.'

They hit the dirt track around midday although the landscape around them had long given way to paddy fields the colour of sand. Soon this too would change to the perpetually lush hills of North Cachar. The army, Kasa explained, had been sent in by the central government two years ago to quell separatist movements in the state. Their presence was less around this area, though, and their numbers mainly concentrated in the other more troubled parts of Assam such as Lakhimpur and Sibsagar. These were the main strongholds of the United Liberation Front of Assam, a group who claimed to be fighting for sovereignty and independence.

'I don't know which is worse,' said Kasa. 'The ULFA…or the army who trouble us and call us militant dogs.'

Along the way there were seven checkpoint stops—each time they were made to get off while the interior of the bus and its luggage carrier were inspected. Bah Hem had heard of how people were robbed on night journeys—his Mizo neighbour's niece had hidden her money in the hem of the bus window curtains; the only place that hadn't been searched. Their rifles were stashed at the bottom of a canvas bag that Bah Hem had packed the night before; stowed under Kasa's seat. It went unnoticed.

They were dropped off at the outskirts of the boy's village, from where they had to walk. The gulmohar-lined road was empty apart from a boy herding cows. It was strangely quiet. Soon, the settlement came into view, perched on the edge of a ridge, ringed by sloping hills criss-crossed by dusty yellow footpaths. It was late afternoon and the sun was slowly dragging light away to the west; a thickening curtain of mist hung above the ground. They stopped outside a thatch-roof house slightly bigger than all the others in the line. Faces appeared and disappeared at doorways and windows yet no one approached them. A boy, no older than ten, stood shyly in the compound, peering at them with large, dark eyes. A cat the colour of night twined itself around his ankles.

'Noru, ask Maina to make tea.'

The boy and creature vanished.

After a quick wash at a garden tap, Kasa ushered Bah Hem to the kitchen, where a girl of about seventeen tended to a kettle on a wood fire.

'My sister,' said Kasa.

Maina nodded at their visitor, her long hair falling over her shoulders. She was dressed in a cotton mekhla the colour of mustard, and it made her seem older, as though she'd stepped into someone else's clothes, and someone else's role. Bah Hem wondered what had happened to their mother, why she wasn't here. As Maina bustled around with cups and cutlery, he noticed there was something restless and fluttering about her. Like a caged bird. Noru, though playing with the cat in the corner, kept a careful watch on them all. Kasa and Bah Hem sat at a low-lying table, and an old man shuffled in like a ghost through the door. His age was impossible to reckon; he could have been anywhere between sixty and hundred— immensely thin with a pale chador wrapped around him like a shroud. His eyes, though, were sharp and bright as any youngster's, glinting with wisdom and wariness.

He introduced himself as Kasa's grandfather. 'Thank you,' he said in a voice that sounded like dry, raspy leaves. 'We are very grateful for your help.'

'You should wait to thank me until after I've killed the tiger,' said Bah Hem. To his surprise, the jest was met with solemn silence.

The grandfather joined them at the table and Maina served them tea and a plate of coconut sweets.

'How's your father?' asked Bah Hem.

Maina and Kasa exchanged a look.

Their grandfather answered, 'He's keeping poorly; we can only hope for the best.'

The nearest medical clinic, he explained, was over an hour away in Haflong. They had brought medicine for him, but it didn't seem to have helped.

'When do you think you can start the hunt?' asked Kasa.

Bah Hem felt four pairs of eyes boring into him, even the cat seemed to be waiting for an answer.

'Whenever you like.'

'There's no need for our guest to stay up tonight,' interrupted the old man. 'He has had a long journey, let him rest.'

That night Bah Hem might as well have kept watch. Despite being a sound sleeper in mostly any circumstances—knobbly forest floors, dank circuit house beds, cramped train berths—he was kept awake by a feeling that something was amiss and unnatural. His room was bare yet comfortable, and he lay there staring into the darkness, with a peculiar heaviness in his chest. It didn't help that close to midnight strange noises echoed from the other end of the house. Whimpering that changed to low moans of pain and then to cries of great distress. It must be Kasa's father, he thought. Except sometimes, the sounds seemed inhuman. Finally, exhausted and wide awake, Bah Hem crept out of the room to investigate. A pair of glassy green eyes stared at him in the corridor—it was the cat. If Noru wasn't asleep, he wouldn't be far behind. At the end of a narrow corridor, the door to the invalid's room was slightly ajar, just enough for him to peer through into murky lantern-lit dimness. He could see the edge of a thin mattress next to which sat Maina and her grandfather. The girl was crying softly while the old man had his hand out, muttering under his breath. Bah Hem couldn't see the suffering man, but he could hear him. As the cries rose to a dreadful shriek, a touch on his elbow startled him. He looked down at Noru, cradling the cat in his arms.

'Father is wounded.' It was the first time Bah Hem had heard the boy speak. Before Bah Hem could ask who had wounded him, Noru walked away to the kitchen where the wood fire lay low and dying.

The next morning, Bah Hem arose after a few hours of sleep, unrefreshed and restless. Despite warm sunshine bathing the small village and lapping over the paddy fields below, he was still uneasy. He would prefer to leave soon, he thought, as he ate breakfast, a plate of small puffy puris and spicy potato. After his meal, determined to carry out his mission, he asked Kasa to show him around the village, and the outskirts where the tiger had been sighted. It didn't take them long to walk through the settlement; women sat in front of their huts cleaning rice or spreading thick red chillies out to dry. Children ran up and stopped at a distance, staring at them curiously, pointing to Bah Hem and whispering among themselves. At the foot of the hill, on the other side, a dense forest began—'That's where the army camp is...' pointed out Kasa. The people of the village would gladly have stayed away from them if it weren't for a path running through the forest to Malangpa, a neighbouring market village. 'We can't stop using the road...how would we survive without the bazaar?' said Kasa. 'They're vile creatures. Our women aren't safe. My sister...' he began and then stopped. Bah Hem could see why the people here kept a wary distance from him. Their distrust of outsiders had only deepened with the army's presence. Kasa also showed him where the tiger had been sighted—drinking water at a pond near the paddy fields, in the bamboo thickets near the village, and mostly pacing near the edge of the forest.

'We'll keep watch from seven-thirty this evening,' said Bah Hem. Kasa agreed but added, 'I must warn you, at that time it's difficult to see in the mist.'

Bah Hem said he'd been on shoots in far more difficult conditions.

'I'm sure...but you don't know the Jatinga mist. Even birds get disoriented. They fly into our torches and die. Or sometimes, they lie on the ground waiting for us to kill them.'

'Why?'

'We believe it's a mercy.'

'Don't you leave the birds to fly away?'

'It's not what they would want us to do.'

After that they both fell silent; Kasa polished his shotgun with a rag, while Bah Hem paced and smoked a cigarette.

That evening, after quick cups of strong black tea, Bah Hem and Kasa stepped out with their rifles slung over their shoulders. In this half-light, with the moon and cloudy shadows, Kasa reminded him more than ever of his eldest son. The slope of his jaw, the way his mouth was set, and the look in his eyes, like Nathaniel just before he played a football match or while he wrestled with a catch on his fishing line. Bah Hem remembered the stories he'd told Nathaniel on his sickbed—a pang shot through him sharper than the thorns of the jara tenga his hand accidentally brushed against.

'Those birds you told me about,' asked Bah Hem, 'when do they fly to Jatinga?'

'During these months,' the boy answered, 'up until November.'

'Do they come every year?'

Kasa nodded. 'Every year since even my grandfather can remember.'

Bah Hem hesitated. 'Have you killed any?'

'Yes. Many. I told you,' the boy stopped and looked at the older man, 'it's a mercy.'

They had almost reached the edge of the settlement, the mist lying thick and vast before them like the sea, blurring the lights of the village.

'You stay here.' Bah Hem indicated a cluster of flowering hibiscus bushes. 'I'll move further down the slope...closer to the forest.'

Bah Hem stowed himself behind a clump of soil and tufty undergrowth—it could be a long wait. The stillness of the evening around him was broken only by the dismal howling of dogs, and the shrill chirping of crickets. He brushed away a spider that crawled over his hand. Somewhere, he could hear a rustle—of leaves, wings? he couldn't tell—and he thought about the birds that lay waiting to die. He remembered an afternoon three weeks before Nathaniel's death; his son had had a particularly bad night and was almost unrecognizable as the nineteen-year-old who'd left Shillong only six months earlier. The doctor had broken the news to them as gently as he could—that there wasn't much hope, that the chemotherapy wasn't working. The disease was rapidly spreading to the nervous system, after which...

'It would be best to take him home,' the doctor suggested, 'make him as comfortable as possible.' Bah Hem had refused; he would stay here as long as it would take for his son to get better. There was no other way. That afternoon, standing by the window, watching his son sleep, he tried to will the doctor's words out of his head.

Then Nathaniel awoke. 'Papa,' he called quietly.

Bah Hem had rushed to his side. Was there anything he needed? Was he comfortable enough? Should he call the nurse?

His son shook his head. It was an effort for him to move. Infections, small and insidious, had wracked his body to shreds. 'I had a dream, papa. Of where I would go after this…'

'You mustn't speak of…'

Nathaniel tried to lift his hand. 'I can feel it. This immense warmth and light. But something won't let me go…'

He drifted away and fell asleep, exhausted from the effort. The next day Bah Hem asked the doctor if they could take Nathaniel home. It was, he hoped, as Kasa had said, an act of mercy.

Somewhere in the darkness a chorus of drunken cries rang out, a party of soldiers were staggering back to the camp. Bah Hem's eyes burned from the strain—it was difficult to see in the fog—and his shoulders ached from the weight of the gun. They'd been waiting two hours. If the tiger didn't show up tonight, he would have to stay longer in this place. He felt weary and dispirited. It didn't bode well, it wasn't the right mood for a hunt.

Yet when he heard a short, sharp hiss from Kasa, his thoughts cleared, and the ache was forgotten. The creature had been sighted. Bah Hem shifted his position and trained his eyes towards the clearing before the forest.

It was barely a shadow, a dark form in the mist, but it moved, treading carefully, its grace defeated by a terrible limp. It paced restlessly, head hung low, moving in and out of the dull moonlight. If he wanted a clear shot, he would have to get closer. Kasa was behind him, breathing heavily, his eyes burning with a strange light. They crept down the slope, taking care to keep the creature in sight. The tiger was resting now, licking its wounded paw. For a moment it looked up and let out a low growl. Finally, Bah Hem settled to take a shot. He unclasped the safety catch, waited for a moment's breath, and pulled the trigger. In a second, the animal crumpled to the ground, roaring in pain.

'Got it,' said Bah Hem and glanced at his companion.

Kasa's face was wet with tears.

They left the creature where it was—'our people will clear it in the morning'—checking only to see that it was dead. Its eyes stared sightless, curiously human eyes filled with pain that hadn't left even in death. They walked back to the hut in silence. Bah Hem was exhausted. It hadn't been a good hunt. He was left with none of the heady exhilaration that accompanied a kill.

Back at the house, the grandfather was standing at the door.

Kasa uttered one word. 'Father?'

The old man shook his head.

Kasa melted into the shadows inside.

Bah Hem put away his gun and warmed himself by the kitchen fire. Maina and Noru were nowhere in sight. The warmth and tiredness closed in on him; he must have dozed.

It was a strangely dreamless sleep, as though his mind had completely shut out the world. When he opened his eyes, the grandfather was sitting nearby wrapped in his chador, his shadow long and limbless against the wall.

'Where's Kasa?' asked Bah Hem.

'He is resting.'

'I'm sorry about your son.'

The fire was sinking but neither made an attempt to revive it.

The grandfather's voice was low and toneless. 'Five evenings ago, when Maina was walking back from Malangpa, a group of army men started harassing her in the forest. This had happened before, but this time there were more men teasing her, frightening her. Suddenly, she said, out of nowhere a tiger flung itself on them...it gave her time to run away. She heard shots but she didn't look back. That same evening my son fell ill.' He paused before asking, 'Do you find that strange?'

Without waiting for an answer, the old man continued. 'They say all over this region—in Sohra and Jirang and other far-flung corners—there are what people call shape-shifters, men whose souls can inhabit animals...' He left the sentence dangling like a broken fishing line.

'If what you're saying is true, then I killed your son.'

The old man shook his head. 'No, you didn't. His spirit was wounded. You only set it free.'

For some inexplicable reason, Bah Hem wanted to laugh so it would swallow his grief.

'How would men change into animals? Do they utter some mantra? Or drink some magic potion that gives them fur and a tail? Or...or is it hereditary? A family secret passed on from father to son.' He sounded hysterical.

The old man looked at him with pity. 'It can only be done out of love.'

When he left the room, Bah Hem was still seated by the fire, watching it glow resolutely, a dull core of heat undying at the centre, the wood releasing all its tender memories of the earth.

# Pilgrimage

*You who has kept us alive, sustained us, and enabled
us to reach this season*
                                    —Shehecheyanu blessing

When he wasn't looking, Barisha slipped rice into his bag. A small plastic container of red-husked uncooked grain that he probably wouldn't notice on his travels. If there was nothing she could do to keep him from leaving, perhaps this would somehow bring him back. Every time she left Shillong, her mother would do the same—'to always bring you home safely'. It was what the Khasis believed, that rice, commonplace and ordinary, carried the power of the earth where it was grown, and would lead you back to where you belonged.

He, whom she had loved so deep and for so long, was leaving in search of something they both couldn't quite put a finger on. He was an Ashkenazim Jew who'd grown up, like her, in Shillong, brought up by parents who'd long forsaken their quest for a distant promised homeland. Their ancestors had fled Germany with many others and reached Calcutta; from there a group of them made their way to the hills of Assam. His parents didn't want to leave. 'Not yet,' they said, 'perhaps some day.' But they weren't serious. Their life and friends were in Shillong, built from scratch. They were comfortable. For him, though, it was different. Barisha had known it all along, through their many years together. There had never been a departure so foretold. He was leaving—'for a year or two, I'll see what I can find'—and there was no question really of her going along. Wordlessly, she understood this was one of those things he needed to do alone, his own personal aisha. It was too heavy for him to disregard, the weight of the history of the world.

After he left, she found herself standing on the balcony in the evenings, watching life move on. The South Delhi neighbourhood they lived in was peppered with outsiders like them who'd come to the city from states like Nagaland and Meghalaya. Perpetual pilgrims, she thought, always journeying elsewhere. When the silence in the flat grew too great to bear, Barisha decided to journey home.

She arrived in Shillong after a four-hour drive from Guwahati, up a winding road clogged with smoke-belching trucks and crusty yellow Sumos overladen with passengers and luggage. It was mid-October, and a fine grey drizzle, the diminished end of a long monsoon, started falling as they drove into town. Shillong sprawled before her in all its unplanned ugliness. This was where she'd grown up; she knew the place intimately like one knows an old lover, its familiarity lay in its imperfections.

'Look at you, Barisha!' Her mother cupped her face in her hands, gently, as though it were a candle flame threatening to flicker out. 'So pale, like garlic, your mei-iad would have said.' She sat her down at the dining table in the kitchen, made her a cup of tea, pressed small rice cakes into her hand and talked about trivial things like the weather—how the evenings were beginning to grow chilly already, and the new neighbours from Nagaland—'A few pet cats and dogs have disappeared from the colony...you know how they eat everything.' Her father, she explained, was in the Bhoi district helping a friend set up a turmeric farm. 'He likes all these odd jobs. Keeps him busy after retirement.' She began to say something else, but looking at her daughter's face, fell silent.

Later, in her room, Barisha listened for the sounds of her childhood—the frogs in the abandoned water tank, the cicadas in the forest bordering the house—and for a long while she watched the lights flickering in the distant hills. Every time she returned home, they'd increase in number, filling up the blank, dark spaces in between. She lay awake within the familiar confines of her narrow single bed, and before she could cry, she fell asleep.

The next day, she stayed in bed.

On the second day, she ventured into the kitchen, where her mother had left syrwa—a stew of pork and potatoes—and rice on the counter. For the first time in months, she ate two helpings. On the third day, she followed her mother around the garden. The roses weren't doing well this year after a virulent attack of aphids—particularly potent in these hills—but the azalea shrub, dotted with tiny white buds, promised to be spectacular.

'We'll use these for All Souls' Day,' her mother decided, and Barisha wished she hadn't said so. She felt the flowers, like her, were now marked by melancholy.

After the drizzle on the day she arrived, the showers petered out, and the days, though shorter—it was dark by five—were filled with clear autumn sunshine. The guava tree dropped plump, softened fruit to the ground and their bitter-sweet scent hung in the air, clinging to her hair and clothing. Slowly, she began to feel stronger. At the end of the week, her mother led her to the storage room next to the garage, where she said she had something very important for Barisha to do. She pointed to a stack of boxes.

'I didn't know what to keep and what to throw away. You said you needed to sort things out...well, you can start here.'

Barisha knew what those boxes contained—the contents of her room, packed up by her mother when her visits from Delhi grew increasingly infrequent over the years. They'd finally whittled down to once, usually at Christmas. She folded her sleeves, squatted on the dusty floor and got started with a sense of gritty determination. If he was on a quest for the past, she must be ready to leave it behind.

The first carton held an assortment of schoolgirl notes passed surreptitiously in class, old journals filled with the achings of adolescence, Christmas cards from names whose faces she couldn't recall, and shiny sweet wrappers she'd carefully folded and stored for reasons she could no longer fathom. The second, smaller box contained cassettes, most of them without covers, some tangled in their own glittering, undone spools. In the third carton, however, she found among other things an empty chocolate tin, rusty around the edges. Inside, was a yellow envelope with a card flamboyantly signed, 'Love you forever...Vivek.' She turned it over in her hand, carefully as though it were a rare jewel, struck by its candid simplicity. Had things ever really been so uncomplicated? There were a pile of things she cleared out of the cartons, but she took the card upstairs to her room.

She hadn't thought of Vivek in a long time—over a decade, in fact. He'd been what they demurely called in her household a 'special' friend. Barisha laughed softly into the darkness of her room. They were fifteen or sixteen and their relationship had consisted of chance meetings on their way home after school, shy smiles as they crossed paths and vast amounts of daydreaming about each other—until he'd finally gathered enough courage to say hello on a wet June evening. She was struggling to hold up her umbrella against lashings of wind and rain, and when it fell he'd picked it up. It was momentous. After that, he'd wait at the red postbox next to the bus stand close to her school, where they'd exchange little snatches of conversation rehearsed through the day in their heads—'How was your day?; I did so badly in my math test; When do your exams start?' They spoke about music; he liked Elvis and golden oldies—songs like 'Peggy Sue' and 'How Sweet It Is (to Be Loved By You)'. He said he'd make her a mixed tape. One day, he held out his hand and she wasn't sure what to do, so she shook it. All the way home, her palm tingled at his touch.

That night, with the card placed on her bedside table, for the first time in a while Barisha didn't dream about the man who'd left her for Israel.

The next day, she was back in the storage room, rummaging through more boxes. Among a batch of fungus-ridden videotapes, she found a plastic-bound address book, one of those that shops in town handed out free along with a calendar in the New Year. Into its lined pages—with no allotment for email or cellphone numbers—she'd painstakingly copied out the names and details of friends and family. Vivek's entry was alphabetically last—Assam Cottage, Upper Lachumiere, Shillong, 793003—followed by a landline number. Barisha slipped it into her pocket.

The scrap of paper where he'd written out the same details

171

was either lost or tucked away into one of her diaries. Even after all this time, she remembered that cold November evening particularly well. She was walking home from school and had almost given up on seeing him when he called out to her from across the road. He'd been stuck in an extra class at school, but he'd hurried out as fast as he could.

'Can I call you?' His usually neatly parted hair was tousled from his run.

'Okay.'

'Will you give me your phone number?'

She'd written it down on textbook paper and he'd done the same, and they'd exchanged the scraps as solemnly as wedding vows. Back home, she could barely concentrate on her homework. Later, she'd waited nervously near the telephone pretending to read a textbook, worried about what her parents might say—the instrument wasn't used for social calls, it was too new and sacred for that. He rang just before eight while her family readied for dinner.

'Hello.'

'Hello...may I speak to Barisha, please.'

'Speaking.'

Since they weren't face to face, and as they quickly ran out of pre-planned conversation, they'd improvised and talked of new things—what their plans were for the winter holidays, how much they both loved rivers, how, sometimes, they felt nobody understood them at all. They said goodbye only when mei-iad, Barisha's grandmother, then still alive, complained about how the telephone was for emergencies only—and god only knows how anyone could call them if their line was engaged for twenty minutes.

'Shillong could be burning and we wouldn't know.'

'Why would Shillong be burning?' Barisha toyed sullenly with the vegetables on her plate.

'Because of the rallies, child.' Mei-iad was hushed by her father, who asked for another helping of rice.

That night, after her mother had gone to bed, Barisha slipped downstairs to the foyer where the landline was kept in a corner like an old relic. Her Delhi cellphone lay in her bag, unused and out of battery. She stood in the dark, the floor cold under her bare feet, lifted the receiver and dialled. A sprightly automated voice told her to check the number. Then she realized she hadn't added the extra 2s at the beginning. She dialled again. At the other end, the tone rang out loud, rich and full of promise. She waited until it cut off and tried again. This time, as well, nobody answered. Perhaps they were all asleep. Or out. The important thing was that the number still existed. She went to bed stringing together make-believe dialogue—'What have you been doing all these years?; Me? I'm a copyeditor with a magazine in Delhi; No, I'm not married; Yes, it would be nice to meet up...' Her laugh would be light, airy, unpractised.

The following afternoon, her mother, on her way to attend a women's organization meeting in the colony, asked anxiously whether Barisha was alright being left alone at home.

'Unless you want to come with me?'

'And listen to how our colony pets are being eaten by the new Naga neighbours? No, mei...'

Her mother, relieved at Barisha's attempt at a joke, was reassured.

For a while, Barisha sat in the kitchen drinking a cup of

tea; the radio was on. Names of people and places tripped off the newscaster's tongue—a robbery in New Colony, water shortage in Polo, a school sports function later that week, electric cables stolen in Laban. It was oddly comforting, this sudden downsizing of the world. Later, she stood outside near the gate—toying with an idea in her mind, playing with it like the March winds tossed the leaves. She could go now. Lachumiere was a mere fifteen-minute walk away—nothing was too far in this town—and she'd probably be back even before her mother returned.

She set off down the colony hill, passing a couple of boys with catapults aimed at a street light, and a group of workmen constructing a wall.

This was going to be a casual enquiry, she told herself. Like most others in this town who never moved away, his family—and Vivek—might still be living there. She'd like to take a look; she needn't go in, just a brisk walk past, a quick glance to check the name on the mailbox. The sun streamed through the pine trees and lay dappled on the road; above her the sky was a clear, breathless blue. Everything around her seemed tense—who knew what the afternoon held in store? This was the most amount of anticipation she'd felt in months. To anticipate was to feel alive.

She tried to recall the last time she and Vivek had met, before he went off to Calcutta for—engineering? medicine? It was sometime in May, that crystal-clear month before the monsoon set in. He'd come to her house, and stood at the door while her grandmother, suspicious of all dkhars, interrogated him:

Whose son are you?

Where do you stay?

What does your father do?

He'd answered her patiently and politely, standing at attention with his hands behind his back. Mollified, mei-iad had allowed them to go for a walk. They strolled up to the border of the Risa Colony forest, down to the foot of the hill and finally to a deserted car park that overlooked orchards dotted with pale late-blossoming peach trees.

'I have something for you.' He unwrapped a plastic bag he'd been clutching all this while. His cheeks flushed as he handed the chocolates over. 'And read this later.' It was a card in a yellow envelope.

They'd stayed out late that evening, sitting on a low cement wall that ran the length of the parking lot, holding hands, talking about the future. She had another year in school, perhaps she'd study in Calcutta after so they could be together. Barisha wasn't sure what she wanted to do, what her parents had in mind. They watched the sky change colour, streaks of silvery-gold that magically turned blue and purple, darkening until the stars were out.

'Do you see that light on the hill?' he said pointing.

Barisha nodded. There were several, but she presumed it was the one burning brightest on its own.

'No matter what happens, and where we land up, just like that light, I will always be there, and I will always return.'

It was the most romantic thing Barisha had ever heard; she hoped he would kiss her but since he didn't she lay her head on his shoulder and thought she might burst with happiness. Before them, the world and all its possibilities stretched out far beyond the distant horizon.

When she returned home, her left cheek burning with his chaste goodbye kiss, her grandmother and father were waiting at the door. She was too young to understand why they were worried and angry—after all, she and Vivek had been just down the road, not far from the house—but she heard mutterings of 'dkhar boy', 'not safe'. She remembered that in the news a few days later, there was a report about a Bihari man burnt alive on his way home from the market.

On this warm afternoon, though, it was difficult to picture that kind of violence taking place in Shillong. It lay sweetly dreaming in the sunshine like a passive, benevolent cat. Barisha passed the fruit canning centre belching out white smoke, and reached the main road, which bustled with traffic. Past Dhanketi junction where traffic lights, put up a year ago to great excitement, stood unblinking and unused, and a row of shops to which there'd been many recent additions. She made her way up the Lachumiere slope; on her right stood Loreto Convent, one of the town's biggest schools, overhung with bare jacarandas. She hoped to meet someone she could ask for directions. The mailboxes, tied to the gate or hung by the front door, carried many names—Diengdoh, Swer, Richmond, Shadap, Goswami—but not the one she was looking for. The road then ended abruptly, at an Assam-style cottage with freshly painted white walls and highly polished wooden beams. A dog ran into the lawn and barked and wagged its tail. A woman, hanging out clothes, looked up.

'Kong...where is Assam Cottage?'

The woman apologized saying she didn't know, that she'd started working here only a few weeks ago. Barisha walked back down the street, wondering whether she'd missed a turning or a nameplate. Eventually after two rounds of the area, she stopped at a small cigarette and kwai kiosk. The shopkeeper, a gentleman well into his sixties, was splitting betel nut into quarters.

'Bhaisaab…where is Assam Cottage?'

He stopped, knife poised in mid-air. 'There's no house by that name around here.'

'The Hazarikas…they live—they used to live there.' The excitement had settled at the bottom of her stomach like a lump of lead.

'Kong, this used to be Assam, many Hazarikas used to live here. After the…after '87, they're mostly gone. There is no Assam Cottage.'

'Are you sure?'

He put down the knife and took off his spectacles, squeezing the bridge of his nose. 'Kong, I've been here thirty-two years and…'

'Oi, kumno mama.' It was a young man in jeans and a football jersey; he seemed unconcerned about the interruption.

The shopkeeper greeted him politely.

'Ai san kyntein kwai.'

The packet of betel nut and paan were obligingly placed on the counter. The young man picked it up, fished out a crumpled five-rupee note and walked off, shouting out his thanks.

In the silence that followed, Barisha could feel the man watching her before she spoke.

'Bhaisaab, you were saying?'

'I was saying that the past is sometimes better left alone. People move on. They must.'

She was about to thank him and leave when he added, 'But you? You are on a pilgrimage of the past.'

'Aren't we all?' She laughed.

His eyes betrayed interest rather than humour.

'But yes, I suppose you could say that...'

He resumed splicing betel nut. 'I had a Muslim neighbour once who did the Hajj. He went to Mecca, did the whole route—Mina, Arafah, seven times around the Kaabah, of course, and prayers at the masjid. You know what he told me was the best part? Coming home.'

The man placed the kwai on the counter.

'And that's what pilgrimages are for, really. To think about the places and people you leave behind.'

Barisha made her way back slowly. Dusk hovered over the treetops; the sun had set without much fuss or fury. A group of schoolchildren overtook her, laughing and shouting. They were dressed in sports gear, flushed from exercise. Cars rushed past in a noisy hurry, and pedestrians swirled on the pavements like awkward dancers. She waited at the junction to cross, a water tank passed by, somewhere people were waiting for rain. We move, she thought, across the surface of the earth, steady as the pattern of the winds. She had a few more days in Shillong, and then she would head back, to her flat in the noisy South Delhi neighbourhood, cooking meals, reading, sleeping. Being grateful for reaching this season, she thought, remembering the words of a Jewish prayer he'd once taught her.

When she walked in through the gate, her mother, waiting outside, asked her where she'd been. She smiled. 'Here all the while.'

# Boats on Land

I can measure our days together by the number of times we went to the river. Ten in fourteen days. Which by most accounts is not long, yet a dragonfly, you told me, may live for only twenty-four hours, and if we were dragonflies we would have spent ten lifetimes together.

When we went to the river that winter you said it wasn't half as wide as during the monsoon, when the water stretched out vast and splendid as the sea. Instead we had miles of sandy banks to write on with our footprints, or to sit and watch the Kaziranga forest on the opposite side darken as the light faded. Those were sun-tempered, smoke-hazy days that lengthened with the evening shadows until the nights seemed endless and intimately ours. You smoked cigarettes in secret. The ones you rolled burned like slender torches, pinpricks of light in a dark and unknown universe. You conjured them quickly, like a magician.

'Years of practice,' you said.

You were nineteen then; three years older than me.

We met because my parents and I went on holiday to Chandbari, a tea estate in Assam, one of many sprawling plantations of neatly trimmed bushes that spread for miles like a dense green carpet. I'd only ever driven past them, on family trips to Potasali and Nameri, and they seemed far removed from the countryside's lush wildness—ponds overflowing with hyacinth, thick clusters of swaying bamboo, and gulmohar that burst into a rage of orange and yellow blossoms. I'd always wondered what they were like inside, beyond the gated and guarded entrance. Our fathers, who had been in school together, friends, met at an Old Boys' dinner, and yours invited us over for a fortnight in January. For my parents, it was tempting; Shillong, where we lived, was crippled by winter and cloaked in dull, monotonous grey.

'Is it alright to stay that long?' my mother asked, sounding a little doubtful.

My father laughed. 'They have a battalion of household help at the bungalow. I don't think we'll be much trouble...'

While they looked forward to the break, I wasn't keen to go. All my school friends were in Shillong, and during the winter vacation we had plans to visit each others' houses and make trips to Police Bazaar to eat momos at Peking Restaurant and cream buns at Floury's. More than the culinary delights, though, it was a chance to meet boys, walk past them as though we didn't care they were watching, be approached and asked if we'd like to go to Ward's Lake for a boat ride, or to Udipi Hotel for a coffee. There was a whole world waiting to be explored now that we weren't confined mainly to the grounds of our all-girls' convent school. One boy in particular filled my waking hours with lucid daydreams. His name I'd recently discovered was Jason; he had longish brown hair that fell over his eyes, and wore a striped flannel scarf with élan. This love affair, of secret smiles and glances, however, would have to wait.

'If your brother were here, you could have stayed behind, but we're not leaving you alone at home,' my mother told me, and no amount of sulking would change her mind. My elder brother was studying law in Pune; my plans, also laid out clear and simple, were to do medicine at Lady Hardinge in Delhi. Our parents gently nudged us towards our choices: these were respectable, lucrative careers.

'And you'll have company there,' she added. 'The Hazarikas have a daughter your age...or maybe a little older.'

So I packed my dresses, made my friends promise to fill me in when I returned on all that had happened, and said a silent, aching prayer that Jason wouldn't find somebody else to love.

Chandbari was eight hours away, and my father drove there in our trusty grey Ambassador. We soon left the pine-tree slopes and winding roads of Shillong behind, and from about halfway at Jorabad, the highway widened and flattened, flanked by vast stretches of paddy fields lying crisp and harvested in the sun. We passed dusty hamlets that my father described as 'immigrant Bangladeshi towns', and great sandy lengths of rivers that only came to life in the summer. I drifted in and out of sleep, sometimes catching snatches of conversation—something about my brother's upcoming exams, an ailing distant relative, a neighbour's new-born baby. Halfway we stopped by the roadside to eat packed sandwiches for lunch. It was warmer in the plains, and the sunshine, pleasant and welcoming. When we resumed our journey my father told us his friend Ranjit Hazarika came from an old, wealthy Assamese family who'd owned many successful businesses in Shillong, all of which folded during the trouble in the '80s when the locals turned against the outsiders. The Hazarikas then bought plantations in the Bishwanath district and with the tea boom in the '90s had done exceedingly well. 'They're one of those families marked by tragedy though,' he added, dropping his voice. 'First they had to leave their hometown, then his first wife Mamuni killed herself...' The loud, dragging roar of the engine drowned out the rest of his words. At that age, though, the fear of death, my own or others', hadn't yet clutched me, and instead I found myself thinking about you and whether we'd get along, and become friends. Perhaps, I dreamed, we'd be like sisters.

I awoke much later when we turned into a side road with a gate held open by a uniformed guard. It was late evening and somewhere the sun had set leaving behind orange gashes in the sky. We were on an avenue of tall birch whose silver-grey bark glinted in the twilight. The bungalow stood at the end of a long driveway; it was white, open and airy, and our entire house back in Shillong could have probably fit into the veranda.

Your parents were there, having tea that had been brought out on a trolley. Your father was tall and well built, dressed in crisp khaki trousers and a spotless white shirt. His skin was evenly tanned, and his hair stylishly grey at the edges. He shook hands with my father, and gave my mother a quick, neat hug. Your mother was a tribal Mising lady, with chic shoulder-length hair and flawless skin. She was dressed in a floral-patterned kurti and dark green pyjamas. I wished my mother was in something more appealing than a crumpled jaiñsem. Our luggage was deftly handled by two silent liveried bearers and we were shown to our rooms to freshen up. My parents were given the main guest room, and I had a smaller place in an annex joined to the bungalow by an open corridor overhung with coils of flowering thunbergia. Your mother had apologized for my room—'It's small but we hope you'll be comfortable'—yet I found it more than spacious and, with its light walls and large, creamy bed, utterly delightful. There was a table with magazines, and a wardrobe large enough for me to hide in. I slipped off my shoes and walked across the carpet, thick and spongy under my feet. There were no signs of you. I thought it extremely rude you hadn't emerged to greet your guests.

Instead, when I entered the bathroom, you were there, in the bathtub, fully clothed, smoking a cigarette. The window above your head was wide open.

'Oh,' I said, 'I'm sorry.'

You laughed. 'For what? I'm not taking a bath.' It was true, the tub was dry. You hoisted yourself up—'And technically this is your bathroom for now'—and taking a last drag, flung the cigarette out of the window. Your T-shirt barely touched the top of your jeans. You were taller than me, and thinner, and even though your clothes were crumpled and your hair uncombed, it was I who felt inelegant and scruffy. Your movements were slow and unstartled, as though I wasn't there.

You washed your hands at the basin and rinsed your mouth. 'Don't tell anyone about the smoking. Poor Shambu mali will get into trouble again.'

Why would that happen, I asked.

'Because he brings me the local stuff.' When you saw my incomprehension, you added, 'Tobacco. The stuff inside cigarettes.'

Only after you left the room did I realize you hadn't apologized for being in the bathtub. Or asked me my name. Or said hello.

For the next two days you kept out of our way, emerging from your room only at mealtimes. And even then, you sat there, silent, eating small, finicky platefuls. Often, you disappeared for hours on end. Your parents seemed embarrassed by your behaviour but didn't appear to know how to deal with you. In a way, I was relieved you weren't around, to watch me clumsily adjust to a way of life I'd hardly been aware of—where morning tea was brought to us on trays, beds made and rooms cleaned by invisible hands while we were at breakfast, towels were changed twice a day, dirty laundry magically reappeared in a neatly folded, ironed pile, meals and fresh fruit juice ordered at the touch of a bell. During the day, the bungalow could be cool as a cave, its high ceiling soaring above us, its corridors deep and endless. I waited for the evenings in the veranda outside, and watched the countryside darkness close in over the trees and felt the sun-warmed air turn chilly and brittle. Later, we'd emerge from our rooms, showered and changed, and gather in the living room, where the fireplace was lit, the ice bucket filled, and bowls of roasted cashewnuts were placed on the side tables. Your father would bustle around the bar, mixing whiskies and opening bottles of homemade wine, of which I was given a small glass. Even though I'd usually sit alone in a corner, looking through picture books from the shelf, it was a life entirely new and enthralling.

Your father and mine talked a lot about Shillong—their escapades at school, and where various classmates had ended up. They spoke of midnight shows at Kelvin Cinema and parties where they danced to The Beatles and The Monkees. The town, they agreed, had changed almost beyond recognition from what it was in the '60s. Or what they referred to nostalgically as 'the good old days' when it was safer, less crowded, and the roads clean and empty. After a fair number of whiskies were downed, they'd speak of the trouble, and how it changed and took away everything they had known and cherished.

'One evening,' your father said, 'Mamuni was coming back from the market, and this Khasi guy stopped her and slapped her, in the middle of the road... I remember when she got home and told me, I was so angry, but she only seemed surprised that he'd called her an outsider. She kept saying, "I've lived here all my life." That was it though...I'd tried to put it off for as long as I could, but I knew we had to leave...'

Then a long silence would settle, troubled only by the crackle of firewood and the faraway hoot of an owl.

Your mother and mine would join in their conversation sometimes, or carry on with their own intimate talk. I overheard your mother say you were studying psychology at Loreto College, Calcutta, but there'd been some 'trouble' and you were sent home early. 'We thought it would help to have someone close to her age around,' she said, unaware that I was listening, 'but she can be just like her father...headstrong and difficult.' Mostly, though, they would exchange notes on recipes and gardening. Your mother called it a quiet life here, with not much to do or many people to meet, and said sometimes she'd fall into a restlessness that no amount of painting, cooking, or stitching could absolve. She tried to visit her family village often but it was difficult with you around. It was nice, she said, that my mother ran a bakery; she too had always wanted to do something on her own.

There were traces of you littered all over the bungalow as though you were a visiting ghost. Occasionally, I'd catch the lingering smell of cigarette smoke even though you were nowhere around. Once, I found your slippers on the veranda, discarded under a chair. Your T-shirt slipped by mistake into my pile of washed and ironed laundry. At times, I had a feeling you watched us from afar, sullen and undecided.

One afternoon, we all went to the planters' club. Even you, though you sat by the window in the car, next to my mother who was in the middle, and stared out without saying a word. When we got there, we headed to the tennis courts, where matches were in progress. You, I noticed, were not with us any more. My parents were introduced to everyone by your father as 'old friends', visitors from his hometown, Shillong. The afternoon was filled with chatter, the monosyllabic thud of tennis balls, and shouts of support and laughter.

At some point, a chubby girl in shorts, clutching a racquet, dropped herself into the white wicker chair next to mine.

'Hi. I'm Radhika,' she said. 'You're staying at Chandbari?'

I introduced myself and said yes, I was.

'How's the depressed damsel?'

I asked if she meant you.

'Who else?' she laughed. 'She has a soul too tormented to play tennis.'

I wanted to defend you but didn't know how.

Radhika looked about twenty-five, and had the friendly, bossy air of some of my seniors at school. Her black eyes were set within a round, plump-cheeked face that reminded me of an owl I'd seen outside my window the past few nights.

'Be careful of that one,' she said.

Again, I asked if she meant you.

She nodded. 'People say she's...'

Someone beckoned from the courts. 'Coming,' she replied. 'I'll catch you later.'

Yet that didn't happen. I didn't see Radhika again because, after a while, I wandered off for a walk.

'I won't be long,' I whispered to my mother and made off in the direction of the golf course, the only open space I could find. I soon discovered why no one else was on the grounds—the place was littered with pats of dried and fresh cow dung—yet I trampled on, aiming for a distant hillock which had a trickling stream curled around its base. To my far left, bordering the course, stood a row of thatch shacks hazily covered in light rising mist. A few children, almost naked, ran after each other laughing and screaming. Further away, a boy was herding cows and their lowing, along with the chirrup of roosting birds, filled the air. On winter evenings, Assam dissolved into a careful watercolour of flat shimmering horizons and low, languorous clouds. So different from Shillong where the skyline loomed with pine-shielded hills.

You were standing by the water, smoking, watching a pair of dragonflies dance on the surface. You'd rolled up your trouser ends and, despite the winter chill, you wore only a light half-sleeved T-shirt. You looked up in alarm.

'Sorry,' I said, 'I didn't mean to startle you.'

'Do you always begin every conversation with an apology?' You laughed at the look on my face. 'No one usually takes the trouble to walk across this golf course—immaculately maintained as it is.'

I scraped off bits of dung from my shoe against a stone. You sat on a spot of dry grassy bank. When I finished, I stood awkward and unsure, undecided whether I should stay or leave. Perhaps you preferred to be alone.

'Do you know,' you said, 'that dragonflies sometimes live only for a day?' The ones you were watching now hovered over a clump of fluff-tipped reeds.

'That's sad.'

'Why?'

I flushed. You made me nervous. More nervous than even being around boys or Jason.

'Why is that sad?' you repeated.

'B-because that's such a short time…to be alive.'

'But the dragonfly doesn't know that.'

I said that was probably a good thing. I remember how you looked at me then, sharp and searching.

You stubbed out the cigarette. 'Come.'

We walked along the stream until it meandered into a marshy pond choked with blooming water hyacinth; we'd left the golf course far behind.

'Why aren't you playing tennis?' you asked suddenly.

I too have a tormented soul, I wanted to joke, but instead admitted that I didn't know how to; I mentioned my brother was the one fond of sports. That he'd wanted to be a football player.

'What does he do?'

I told you.

'And you? What will you do after school?' You stopped, and stood face to face with me. I could smell the cigarette on your breath, and something sweet like cloves.

Again, I told you.

'Is that your greatest dream? To be a nurse?' You picked up

a stone and tried to skim it on the water, but it hit a lavender blossom instead.

I said I'd never really thought about it...that it seemed alright.

'Alright.' You turned the word over in your mouth slowly like something precious.

Encouraged by your rare, sudden verbosity, I asked, 'What do you want to do?'

You dusted your hands and stood up. 'I want to follow rivers.'

That night you shook me awake.

'Come with me,' you whispered.

'Where?' In reply you took my hand and led me outside. The lawn was bathed in shadows from tall edging trees, and even the flower beds disappeared into inky darkness. It was chilly and I shivered in my nightdress; you didn't give me time to grab a sweater. You were in the same clothes as earlier, but slippers, a few sizes too large, slapped against your feet. We headed to the far right of the garden, behind the annex, through a gated gap in the bamboo hedge, where the path opened onto a wide overgrown airfield. Years before, your father had explained, when the Chinese attacked in '62, it was used to drop off food and weapons. Now it lay there benignly as a venue for evening walks, remarkable for its early morning views of the Himalayas. At night, the field could have been a shimmering body of water, the way the grass rippled silver in the pale moonlight. The countryside silence was pierced only by the steady chirrup of crickets. We lay in the field, undiscovered in our kingdom of weeds.

You asked me to look at the sky. The stars were numberless.

'Don't ask me about constellations,' you added. 'I only know that's Orion's Belt.'

I said I had Orion's Belt on my neck.

You pushed yourself up on your elbow; for the first time since we'd arrived there was a look on your face I hadn't seen before—interest.

'Show me.'

I turned my face away from you, and pointed to a mole just below my left earlobe. 'That's one.'

Another lower, near the centre of my throat.

'That's two.'

I undid the buttons of my nightdress. The last one was far below the hollow of my neck. 'That's three.'

You traced a line over them all. You were smiling.

The next day, you were thoroughly charming. Not just to me, but even to my parents whom until now you'd largely ignored. You accompanied my mother and yours on their walk around the large backyard vegetable garden; offered to show my father, since he was a professor of history, a collection of old journals your grandfather had written, and at lunch, which we ate at a table laid out in the lawn under a garden umbrella, you were an impeccable little hostess. You talked about where the cook acquired the freshest fish; how the nearest town Bishwanath Chariali was merely a small cluster of shops—'Blink and you'll miss it'; you queried my mother about the bakery and asked if she could make us some lemon tarts. Your parents, I noticed, looked delighted.

'What are you girls up to today?' your father asked.

You looked at me and smiled. 'I was thinking we could go for a walk...'

Everyone said it was a good idea...the plantation was dotted with historical landmarks from the days of the Ahom kings. We could go see the Vishnu temple, your father added, or the water tank that apparently dated back to the fourteenth century.

I waited, impatient and excited, as everyone retired for their customary afternoon nap—even my parents had given in to this rare indulgence. When you emerged from your room, sulky with sleep, I was sitting on the wooden swing on the veranda, swaying over the cool sea-green floor. I jumped off it quickly feeling as though you'd caught me doing something childish.

A little while later we set off. By then though, your energy had waned, and you'd retreated back into your brooding, reclusive self. As we walked, rather than making conversation, you rolled cigarettes. On both sides of the dirt road were miles of low-lying tea bushes, interspersed by tall silver oak, grown for protective shade.

I asked where we were going.

'Nearby.'

We didn't go far; in fact we didn't even leave the borders of Chandbari. You took me to a pukhuri, a large pond bordered on all sides by raised red-soil ground and rows of birch. In one corner stood a gnarled old banyan under which we sat, brushing away stinging red ants and fat black beetles. You lit a cigarette and let it smoulder between your fingers. Your hair clung to your neck in dark, sweaty streaks. Again, I wasn't sure whether you'd prefer to be alone.

'Are you alright?'

You looked at me as though no one had asked you that in a long time.

'Someone I know,' you said, 'tried to kill herself.'

'Oh.' I wasn't sure whether to ask if she'd succeeded.

'It was one in a long line of unfinished projects. The end of life.'

In the stillness of the evening, your words skimmed over the water and sank without a trace. You told me how she didn't want a decisive relinquishment—a once-and-for-all hanging, or fatal leap or bullet through the brain. She only had an inexplicable urge to extinguish herself and flicker back like a trick candle. She wanted, for instance, to throw herself in the path of oncoming buses, or fall down a steep flight of stairs, or constantly push the number of sleeping tablets she could take. Just enough to sink into a deep and dreamless sleep, where she didn't have to be rushed to hospital and stomach-pumped and forced to open her eyes in a nasty little room blindingly white and sanitized.

'That's what it was,' you finished, 'this duality she wrestled with for months.'

'And how is she now?'

'Still gathering courage.'

'To live or die?'

'Both.'

You stubbed out your cigarette and stood up, extending your hand. 'Let's go for a swim.' Then you pulled me down the slope, rough and strong, running faster and faster. I could see the edge of the lake, oozing mulch, and the water deep and dark, littered with leaves.

'Stop,' I shouted. 'Stop.'

You gripped my hand tighter, and carried on, your shoes crunching grass and stone.

'Let me go,' I screamed and yanked myself away. 'I don't know how to swim. If you push me in, I'll drown.'

The water lapped at our feet. It seeped into the edges of my sandals. I didn't realize it then but my eyes were wet with tears. Of fright mainly, and anger. We walked back to the bungalow in silence.

That night you offered a wordless apology.

I was in bed when you walked in and went straight through to the bathroom. I could hear the sound of running water. I thought you'd come to smoke. I didn't ask because I was still angry with you. Then you called me over.

'Why?'

'Please.'

The bathtub was almost full, and steam rose thickly clouding the mirror, the windows. You stood behind me and started unbuttoning my nightdress. I began to protest but caught a glimpse of our image in the mirror, and in there I was someone else. Held by a stare, by your hands, quick and cold through the fabric. When it dropped to the ground you asked me to step into the tub.

I did. The water was scathing. In a moment you were out of your T-shirt and jeans. We fit snugly, like twins. Then you soaped my back, my shoulders, my hair.

I did the same for you.

And despite the steam I saw how you looked nothing like the woman I thought was your mother. That you came from elsewhere, a life cut unnaturally short, and that even though you were only nineteen you were filled with an old sadness. I noticed the delicate slope of your shoulders, the plane of your back like a smooth river stone, the tiny red beauty spots speckled on your skin, your neck thin and long, swerving up in a tense line, your fingers pale and white. When you turned around and faced me, your eyes were closed, and drops of water glistened on your cheeks, hollow like emptied lakes. We lay there, perfectly still, until the water cooled.

The next day, the world was washed anew.

The flick of a page, a sip from a glass, one leg crossing over the other. Sometimes your hand trailed over mine, your shoulder grazed my arm, or you'd stand close behind me, your breath on my neck. Every gesture, I thought, was significant, and added something unforgettable to our lives.

You never took me back to the pukhuri; instead we walked to the river that bordered Chandbari, that lay beyond a line of railroad tracks, at the end of a dusty, lonely road. We strolled down to the water, which spilled endlessly before us mirroring a vast, empty sky. All along the bank burned small lanterns, and in their golden glow fishermen sat and untangled their nets. Their boats were moored on land, long, narrow vessels that looked like elegant paper cut-outs.

'During the monsoon,' you said, 'the river is as wide as the sea.'

Before I left, we walked there every afternoon; sitting on the bank for hours, doodling on the sand. You told me your mother used to write in journals, filling them out year after year, and that after she died you looked for them. They became the most important thing in the world, except you couldn't find them and you thought perhaps she had walked here one day and drowned them in the river. Sometimes, we clambered around the bank like lost children, climbing large, rough boulders and dipping our feet into the pools that formed between them, crystal-clear mirrors that reflected our faces and the sky. Once, we went much further than usual and came across a temple on a cliff, filling up for the evening puja. The worshippers were mostly women from the nearby villages, with solemn, earnest faces framed by their cotton saris. We stayed a while and listened to the chanting, watched the offering of lights. Nearby stood a large slab of rock, marked with strange lines, squares and squiggles. A woman from the village, who happened to pass by, told us, 'It's the place where the gods play dice.' Another time, we found a stretch of stones that looked like pale, bleached bones. We tread on them gently; it could have been the graveyard of a herd of prehistoric animals. Close to where the fishermen sat, we climbed a hill from where we could see the dry sandy stretch of an old river.

'Don't you feel,' you asked, 'as though you are elsewhere?'

I knew what you meant; in the midst of Assam's lush landscape it was a sudden desert hollowed by dips and dunes. When we were close to the dry river, you threw off your slippers and walked in, I followed. The sand was warm and slippery, shaping itself fluidly under our feet. It was hard to imagine that once where we were standing, a river flowed, swift and spirited. We found perfectly smooth stones that fit the palm of our hands, and strange, contorted driftwood, some large enough to cradle us like boats.

On some evenings, when the light seemed to last longer, we'd hire a boat and a fisherman would row us out on the

Brahmaputra. Mostly you'd ask him to go upstream and then allow us to drift, stopping before the current swept us too far out. We'd sit on the plank in the middle; it smelled of fish, and a certain wet wood dampness, like a forest, I thought, that grew in caves. You looked happiest then, when we floated past the world, gently rocked by lapping water. On some evenings, dusk fell around us, and we were guided only by lanterns and the fisherman's song.

Every night we'd curl around each other in the bathtub, like river reeds, the water deep and warm around us. Sometimes, down my neck, you traced the stars. Sometimes you spoke about your mother.

'Why did she do it?'

You shrugged, the water rippling over your shoulders, the steam quivering off your skin. 'I know why even though I can't explain it.'

Sometimes you tried; you sat up, smoking, feverishly talking. 'Don't you feel that way? This awkwardness, with your place in the world. You know, when I put my head under water I hear nothing, I see much clearer…' And you'd plunge into the tub, grazing against my stomach, my thighs.

The morning we left, you were nowhere to be found.

'I do apologize,' your father said. 'Ever since her mother… you know, ever since it happened, she's been like this, a bit difficult.'

My parents, ever gracious, said they understood, that there was no need for him to be sorry, that they'd had a wonderful time. In turn, they invited your parents to Shillong, and although they promised to come, you and your family have not made a visit.

On our way back I was mostly silent, watching the landscape outside the window flash past. Everything seemed unreal—the low-roofed houses, the swathes of paddy land, the endless stretch of bridges—changing, I felt, on a screen at a distance. Soon, we were climbing, the engine moaned, and the valleys deepened. We passed the sweeping blue waters of Barapani, shimmering coldly in the sunlight, and I felt a great sense of emptiness—as though it had been drained and all the world lay hollow like the lake.

The Shillong we drove into was as cold and dispirited as we'd left it. I found it hard to believe we'd been away. Nothing, and everything, had changed. That evening, Sarah, one of my close friends, called, as she'd promised, to fill me in on events I'd missed. She had a crush on twin boys, but couldn't tell one from the other; someone else had been kissed behind the shelter of an umbrella at Ward's Lake. Jason, she giggled, was eagerly awaiting my return.

'And you?' she asked breathlessly. 'How was your holiday?'

I thought of you, your hands, your face. And folded them up, our secret lives.

*I went to a lake and drowned.*

'Nothing special.'

When I think of you now, it's the feel of wet sand and long grass that comes to me, the smell of cigarettes, and cloves and creatures that live close to water. The stench of your old sadness. I imagine you waiting, like when I first found you, for someone to lead you out to where all rivers end, to the sea.

# Embassy

It was a corpse-cold evening in mid-December when Josephine broke his heart. The sky was the colour of razor blades, lying flat and square outside the window and slivered delicately between the branches of bare trees. The air both numbed and sharpened his senses, froze and shaped his breath. In his ears was the echo of her silence when he asked about Ashley, the Anglo boy from the neighbourhood next to theirs, the boy with the blue-grey eyes who played the guitar like Slash.

'Lal said he saw you with him last week, and yesterday. Just tell me the truth, Jo...'

And in her own way, he supposed she had. First she laughed about it and treated it all as a joke. Then she denied ever being with Ashley in the chai shop—or maybe she'd joined him once, but it didn't mean anything, and surely Tei would not be the sort to begrudge her a cup of tea with an acquaintance. Finally, she lapsed into sullen silence, as though it were all his fault for bringing this up. That things were otherwise alright, and he'd gone and disturbed the peace.

'Just tell me the truth...' he pleaded.

'I don't know,' she snapped at one point. 'What truth? Whose truth?'

It was very simple, he said, did she want to be with Ashley or with him?

And when she kept quiet, he knew.

He walked aimlessly for a while, pacing the sloping streets of his locality until he reached the bustle of Laitumkhrah. The pavements were crowded with evening shoppers and local vegetable sellers stocked with sheaves of mustard leaves. A crowd of youngsters buzzed around the aloo-muri man at Police Point; they stood with banana-leaf bowls, laughing loudly and eyeing each other with interest. Further down the main road, he saw a group of friends turn into a jadoh stall for chai and conversation. Any other evening, he would have joined them, but today he walked swiftly past. Only when he reached Don Bosco Square did he realize what he wanted was a drink. He debated over taking a taxi—the roads were clogged to bursting with traffic—and decided to walk to Police Bazaar instead. Maybe it would warm him up. Perhaps it would clear the pain, and stop thoughts of Josephine running through his head like a madly looped tape. Also, he would save on taxi fare. That twenty bucks would buy him an extra drink. It would keep him warmer than the arms he'd never find himself in again.

After he navigated Jacob's Ladder, a long flight of narrow, slippery stairs that led to the bottom of Don Bosco Hill, he walked briskly by Ward's Lake and the main post office building. Eventually, he strode down the sloping So So Tham Road towards Khyndai Lad junction, a pulsating heart of people and traffic. From here, spreading out in long, grasping fingers, were seedy, unlit streets, each an accomplished specialist in various nocturnal offerings, from the medically urgent to the dubious and debauched. Keating Road on the left came to life after the liquor stores in town had closed. It was lined with makeshift stalls that sold alcohol 'in black' alongside perfectly legal yet deleterious deep-fried prawns packed in greasy newspaper. On the right was Jail

Road whose genteel bakeries and music shops gave way to a dkhar vegetable market and rows of sweet shops that smelled perpetually of rose water and ghee. Running parallel to this was Quinton Road whose one major landmark was the blue-and-white Eight Sisters Hotel—a name which, as everyone joked, referred less to the states in Northeast India than the number of whores you could pay to have in your bed at the same time. Along Glory's Plaza Road, where Tei was now walking, these working women stood outside Payal Cinema, their bodies carefully preened and positioned. 'Come-hither' their hips and hands beckoned, while their eyes darted through the crowd, sharp and knowing. The men they smiled at were the ones they picked as potentials; they could tell, even from a distance, those who were the slightest bit interested or intrigued. Even though he hadn't ever paid for a woman before, for a moment Tei was tempted—an image flashed in his mind of Josephine and Ashley, together, doing the things she'd allowed him to do to her, on her bed, on his sofa, on their long drives to the countryside of Kyrdemkulai. The world roared in his ears. He wanted to be with someone as revenge, as redressal for betrayal. Maybe all he needed to get Josephine off his mind was a good, hard fuck.

Something must have shown on his face—if not the keen edge of desire then something lonely and desperate—for a woman smiled at him and moved closer. She was wearing a silky, shiny blue top and a long black skirt; over this she'd draped a red-and-white jaiñkyrshah.

'Want a good time?' she asked in Khasi. Unlike most of the others, her mouth wasn't stained scarlet by kwai or khaini, and her lips were full and plump. She had a roundness that he

205

suddenly felt a lust for—voluptuous arms and thighs that he imagined entwined around him, his fingers sinking into her flesh.

'How much?' he asked, his voice raspy in nervousness. If anyone he knew, or someone who knew his parents, saw him...

Her smile widened. He could see the tip of her plump red tongue, its infinite wetness.

'Depends on what you want...but why don't we decide on that later.' She reached for his hand—he could see her bitten fingernails, the braceleted wrist—and at the touch of her skin, something like a splash of icy water hit him at the back of his head. What was he doing? It had vanished, his nerve, his bravado, the inkling of lust, and all that remained was a wretched emptiness.

'Next time,' he said, feeling embarrassed, but she already knew, and had already lost interest, her eyes once again searching the crowd.

He walked briskly on, awash with self-reproach, and, in an attempt to assuage the guilt, stopped to drop a coin for the blind duitara player on the sidewalk. The narrow street was lined with food sellers and their shaky wooden carts strung with gas lamps and burners that shed dusty, hazy pools of light into the evening. It all looked appealing—chillies stuffed with potato and mint, brinjal fried in gram flour batter, noodles tossed in fatty pork bits, boiled eggs halved and sprinkled with pepper and fresh coriander—but he was in a hurry. His thirst was stronger now.

Bisesh, the chiselled-face Nepali chap at the counter, nodded as Tei walked in. Everyone knew Bisesh only spoke to regulars. Most of the time he behaved as though he owned this place. He didn't; some Marwari man did, but he wasn't usually at the bar. Shillong was safe now for outsiders to own businesses, but not that safe. Merely twenty years ago streets rang with the cries of 'beh dkhar'. Memories, in cases like these, were long and warily forgiving. It was best to keep behind the scenes like an elusive puppeteer. Hence, even if Embassy had changed hands a hundred times, from one dkhar to another, nobody inside knew; most, of course, were in no state to care. The place looked the same as it had when it first opened in the mid-'60s—two rectangular rooms that echoed like empty tombs, joined by short, stubby steps, filled with rows of wooden tables, and on the ceiling, long-stemmed fans that blossomed like tragic flowers. Here, people drenched their grief in alcohol, and stashed their dreams behind the familiar, flimsy darkness that smelled faintly dank and sour, the odour of defeat.

Tei looked around, over the crowd of heads, and for a moment his intention wavered—he'd come for a drink, but there wasn't a single table free. He stood undecided for a moment, he didn't know of another place he could go to in Police Bazaar—the bar in the fancy hotel on the main road was excruciatingly expensive, and all the cheap alcohol joints near his neighbourhood in Laitumkhrah had been closed by order of the Seng Kynthei, a local woman's organization aiming to eliminate (what they considered) vice and immorality in town. Damn them, he cursed silently. There was always the option, he supposed, of buying a bottle and drinking it on the sidewalk, like so many others did. Then again, there was the danger of someone he knew walking by...his musing was interrupted by a rumble of slurry voices calling him over. The drinkers were in an amiable mood tonight, and more than that, could recognize a thirsting, despairing soul. Hey, bro, they beckoned, join us. Ei, shong hangne. And from a dark corner, a single word—'Teiskem'—someone who knew his name.

From that distance, Tei couldn't make out the man's face. It might have been anyone. Yet, even as he approached the table, he couldn't place him. It was a face that wasn't uncommon, marked by the singular weariness that settled over everyone's features in a town landlocked by more than towering mountains. Somewhere, the light shifted, a shadow moved, Tei caught the highlight of his nose, the familiar eyes, and a name snapped into place like a cocked gun.

'Mama Lang?' he asked to be sure.

The man replied by lifting his glass and knocking back the remaining liquor. Then he waved Tei to an empty chair. His large hands were knotted and gnarled, rough as tree bark, inflicted by a steady tremor. He probably wouldn't be swift and nimble enough to make kites like he used to, thought Tei. Mama Lang's kites flew the highest in the locality, and his mynja, string dipped in shards of powdered glass, was the toughest to cut in a mid-air fight.

'Thank you,' said Tei taking a seat.

'You look the same,' said Mama Lang, pouring out two generous measures of whisky. Tei couldn't possibly say that about him. A decade ago, Lang was good-looking, in his mid-twenties, but now he was an old man. His eyes settled on nothing in particular and flickered like dark moths around a bare bulb, his skin, puffy and pale, hung on his face like a cheap wrinkled suit.

'What brings you here?' he slurred; the smell of stale alcohol clung to his breath, pungent and strong.

Tei drew back, a little uncomfortable, a little repulsed. He couldn't believe this was the same person he'd looked up to as a kid. The one who taught him how to win at marbles, construct a sturdy kali het to joy-ride down the neighbourhood slopes, to fly kites with a quick, confident hand.

'Still staying in Laban?' Mama Lang peered at him over the rim of his glass. The golden liquid sparkled in the dim light.

Tei shook his head. 'We moved...ten years ago. To Nongrim.'

*To a better part of town, less rough, less poor. Away from the riff-raff as his mother used to say.*

'That's why I don't see you any more.' Mama Lang chuckled good-naturedly. The drinks were going down particularly well this evening.

'And you still fly kites?' Mama Lang scrambled on the table for the matchbox. Tei pushed it across with a finger.

'I work.' In the agriculture department...as a special rural development officer. His parents were particularly proud. It was so difficult to get a government job these days. At least without a decent number of contacts in all the right places, and they'd only been in touch with a distant cousin who said he would help but it all depended on how Tei conducted himself at the interview.

'Where?'

Tei told him.

Mama Lang tilted his head and howled like a wolf at the moon. Tei almost spilled his whisky in alarm. A few of the other drinkers turned around and told him to shut up or they'd have him thrown out. He stopped and said, 'Good, good. That's what we fought for. To give our Khasi youth employment and opportunity.' He hiccuped and gulped his drink to subdue it.

Tei shifted uncomfortably in his seat. He didn't want Mama Lang to bring up the KSU days. The days when Mama Lang and the others fought and rallied and lived as outlaws. He'd heard it all before. Over and over again. From friends and relatives and neighbours. He'd come here to think about Josephine and her brown eyes and her full pink lips that he'd never kiss again. He watched his companion struggle to light a match, the cigarette dangling from the corner of his mouth like an embarrassing dribble. The murmur in the room was louder now, the air sticky and warm, the number of figures seemed to have grown silently like a damp patch on the wall.

'What brings you here?' asked Mama Lang again. Maybe he remembered Tei hadn't answered the first time, maybe he forgot he'd already asked the question. With the alcohol snug in his throat, Tei began, 'There's this girl...'

'The most beautiful girl in the world,' finished Mama Lang. 'And she left? Dumped you like a used condom?'

Tei felt a spray of spittle on his face. He wiped it off and nodded.

'Was her name Angela?' Mama Lang had managed to light the cigarette by now and dragged on it deeply.

Tei shook his head. He had a feeling he wouldn't be able to tell his story. But what was there to tell? He loved her, and she'd said she loved him. But she didn't really. And how could he compete with Ashley, with his slick Yamaha bike, his trendy haircut, the shiniest leather jacket in town, and a multitude of talents he was sure extended beyond playing the guitar like a rock star. Tei finished his drink and poured out another.

'My girl's name was Angela, you know. She was…,' Mama Lang struggled to find the words.

'Like an angel,' finished a small, supremely intoxicated man from the next table.

'Or the devil in disguise,' added his equally inebriated companion.

'Don't make fun of her, Rit.' Mama Lang lurched forward. His hands slammed the table. Tei steadied the whisky bottle before it toppled over.

'Let me pour you a drink,' he said hurriedly. 'What happened to her?'

'Kai khlaw,' Mama Lang muttered as he settled back into his chair.

After he was suitably appeased, he began—it happened, he said, in the mid-'80s.

Those days, Mama Lang was in the KSU, running from the CRPF, the central government police force that was sent by the droves to this hill-station town in the middle of nowhere. He and his 'brothers' hid in the jungles (plenty at that time, not like now), ate wild animals, and camped wherever they could find a dry patch in the undergrowth. But he went to see her every day.

Mama Lang shook a finger at nothing in particular. 'Every day,' he repeated.

She lived in Malki and he'd tramp through the adjoining

Risa Colony forest just for a glimpse of her long, black hair and her smooth, amber skin.

Just like my Josephine, thought Tei.

Angela was beautiful but poor. Her father, a modestly successful tailor, had died of tuberculosis when she was nine, and her mother was wilting under the same disease. She had five siblings to look after and bring up on her own.

'I couldn't help,' said Mama Lang, clutching his glass so tight Tei thought it might break. 'Running for my life, living in the wild. I didn't have any money to call my own. How could I help?'

Angela tried to make ends meet by working as a tea lady in a bank and in as many households as she could manage after work hours. But it wasn't enough. What with her mother's medicines and her siblings' school fees and food to feed so many hungry mouths. In desperation, she approached the manager of the bank for a loan.

'He'll give it to me,' she told Mama Lang, her eyes shining like the fireflies he watched in the jungle at night. 'He said he'll give me the money.'

Try as he might, Mama Lang couldn't believe a dkhar— 'and that too a lazy, filthy Akhomia'—would be willing to help. But she was happy and relieved and he kept his reservations to himself. Weeks passed, and every time he asked about the money, she'd clam up...he knew she was hiding something from him.

'What? What was she hiding?' asked Tei.

Mama Lang held up his little finger, said he needed to piss, and shuffled out to the loo.

'Ei, ei.' Rit was leaning back on his chair and miraculously not falling over. 'Ask him if he's sure she wasn't a puri. Lots of them in Risa forest.'

'They were so stoned most of the time they wouldn't know a real woman from a ghost,' added his companion.

Rit laughed and choked on his drink. His friend thumped him on the back.

'They say if you sleep with a water spirit, you're done for,' he continued. 'And look what's happened to Lang—lost all the screws in his head, and taken to drink.'

Tei was tempted to ask if that was the reason why they'd hit the bottle as well, but decided against it. Who knew how far their alcohol-induced good humour would stretch.

'But they say there was some girl...' said Rit's companion.

'Bah,' his friend spat, 'there's always some girl. There's always some girl and there's always some money, and there's always love that wasn't enough or true.'

At that moment, a waiter brought a bottle of whisky to Tei's table.

'Bah Lang ordered,' he said.

'To Angela,' chanted the two drunks behind him, lifting their glasses.

'Or whatever he's calling her today,' Rit added.

When Mama Lang returned he asked, 'What happened?'

Tei hesitated. 'Nothing. The waiter brought another bottle of whisky. Why don't you continue your story?'

One afternoon, Mama Lang began, he and his friend Bantei (killed in a police shoot-out during that year's monsoon) went to the Risa stream to bathe and wash clothes. It was a pretty spot where lovers usually lingered, but with all the trouble in town, nobody visited any more. When they reached, they noticed that two people were sitting by the stream just before it tumbled and vanished deep into the forest.

'Can you imagine my surprise when I saw Angela? Sitting there in her best Sunday dress with a ribbon and all in her hair. And next to her, this dkhar man with a thick moustache and lecherous eyes. My mother is unwell, Angela was trying to say, we really need the money…please…

'I will give you the money,' he said, 'but what can you give me? The bank calls it collateral…' He laughed and put his hand on her knee. Then he tried to force himself on her, his black moustache scratching her skin.

'What did you do?' asked Tei.

'I–I was paralysed.' Mama Lang's head drooped, the grip on his glass loosened.

Only when the man took out a pair of scissors to threaten Angela did something snap inside him and Mama Lang charged at them…but it was too late.

'Too late for what?' Tei leaned forward. The whisky buzzed in his head, he clenched his fists.

She jumped.

Mama Lang tipped his glass over. The liquor flowed over the table and splashed to the floor.

'Like nohkalikai. She became a waterfall.'

When Tei left the table later that evening, Mama Lang lay slumped on his side. Maybe he was asleep. Tei didn't try to find out. He staggered out between the empty chairs and tables as though on a boat at sea. When he reached the counter, he fished into his pocket for money and, with some difficulty, counted out the notes. Bisesh, who was tallying figures on a long sheet of paper, glanced up at him; his eyes were sharp and shrewd like a bird.

'You been sitting with Lang over there?'

Tei nodded. Bisesh crossed his arms and rested them on the counter.

'What's he been telling you? About his girl. What was her name? Mabel. Or Angel.'

'Angela...yes, how did you know...?'

Bisesh laughed. 'He tells that story to any dumb fuck who'll listen.'

'But it's true...' Tei protested.

'Oh, it's true alright. Lang was part of the KSU and all, but there's another version of the story. Where the girl fell in love and ran away with an Akhomia bloke. Hurt Lang's pride, it did. And his...' Bisesh tapped his temple, and laughed again.

When Tei emerged onto the empty street, he realized it had been raining. In Embassy, things like seasons, and Christmas, and changes in weather passed by unnoticed. It was bitterly cold. Tei stamped his feet and blew into his hands, his breath turning white as though he were exhaling ghosts. As he walked, scanning the road for a taxi he was sure wouldn't pass, rainwater gushed around his ankles. It was dark and murky, it could be blood for all he knew. Wounds ran deep in this hill-station town in the middle of nowhere.

# The Discovery of Flight

As always, there was no dearth of premonitions after the incident. Someone had heard the rooster crow five times that morning. The moon on the evening before, conjectured another, was ringed twice. And the symbols in everyone's dreams—from dead cats and dismembered limbs to fallen trees and a flock of birds taking flight—became sure signs that Ezra would walk out of his uncle's house and disappear.

The grandest, most obvious omen of all, however, was the rain. It was raining like the apocalypse had revisited Sohra. The first time was the Great Earthquake of 1897, when entire mountains were whipped and swallowed by faithless tremors and rivers transformed within minutes into magnificent waterfalls. This could easily be the second. The locals were used to rain—every year the monsoon beat relentlessly upon their tin roofs from June to September—but that morning it was the rain of the old days, slap bam briew they called it, rain that wouldn't stop until it had taken lives. It was a living, breathing monster that howled piteously through the hills for blood.

'Why he would go for a walk in such weather, god only knows,' said Kong Syntiew, a housekeeper who'd been in Ezra's uncle's service for over thirty years. She hadn't met him before he left that morning, but she'd been the one to discover the kitchen door unlatched, the kettle that had cooled by the stove, and a teacup washed and placed to dry by the sink. 'He's always been a neat boy,' she added, 'right from when he was a child.'

Janice Pariat

When Ezra didn't return that afternoon, a mild confusion settled into the household. His aunt and uncle were gentle folk, accustomed to a quiet life of careful, impeccable routine. Mama Kes was an averagely important government officer, and Kong Milly ran a small primary school near the Sohra market. When they got back home, at about three o'clock, the maid would serve Mama Kes tea in his study where he'd be reading the newspaper, while Kong Milly drank her cup in the kitchen with Kong Syntiew. That afternoon, Mama Kes appeared at the doorway and stood there awkwardly, unsure whether to come in or stay out.

'Where's that boy Ezra?' he asked.

The women shook their heads. Behind them, rows of streaky smoked meat swayed gently above the large wood fires.

'He may have gone to see Ailad,' said his wife.

Ailad was a car mechanic who ran a workshop nearby, and though he was almost forty, older than Ezra by a decade, he got along well with their nephew. He did most of the talking, while Ezra sat on an upturned pail or a discarded tyre, sipping tea, smiling and nodding.

Mama Kes was reassured by that explanation and trundled back to his study. Later, in between dozing and watching a Doordarshan programme on rural farming, he was shaken awake by his wife who said she wanted him to check Ezra's room.

'What?' He blinked at her, his eyes adjusting to the bright tube light she'd just switched on.

'See if there's anything there that might explain where he's gone.' It was also a man's room and more fitting for her husband to check it, but she didn't need to say that out loud.

'Have you tried his mobile phone?' asked Mama Kes.

'Many times, but no answer.'

They walked to the other end of the sprawling old house, that had grown more vast and echoey after their three children had all grown up and moved away—two daughters in Shillong and a son in Calcutta. They'd given him their son's room, which was farthest from theirs. As Kong Syntiew said, 'Boys like to have their own space.'

Ezra was meant to stay two weeks—that's what Mama Kes's sister had told him when she called to say her son wanted to spend some time in Sohra. 'Before he leaves for Indonesia,' she explained, where he'd been offered a job as a pilot for Garuda Airlines.

Perhaps if someone else had searched Ezra's room in Sohra they might have found a pencil sketch of a bird tucked into a book on the table. But Mama Kes and Kong Milly barely glanced at it, examining his suitcase instead, layered with neatly folded clothes, a pair of fresh socks and underwear placed on top. Everything else was also in place, his shoes under the bed, all in a polished row, the fishing equipment he kept scrupulously clean arranged in a corner. There were no clues to where their nephew had gone—but he definitely hadn't packed up and left for home. According to his aunt Millie he was a quiet boy. 'Polite, well-mannered, though most of the time you hardly knew what he was thinking. He kept to himself, but this is not like him, to just disappear without telling us where he was going or when he'd be back.'

At dinner, a sharp edge of tension knifed the cool August evening. It had stopped raining but the earth was heavily drenched and in the air hung the smell of damp mud, and the sting of a distant winter. The household ate in nervous silence. 'There's still a chance he'll come back now,' said Kong Syntiew, passing around the kwai basket, but everyone knew that could hardly be true. It was difficult enough to travel during the day with all the rain, at night the roads were treacherously unlit, flanked on either side by barren, windswept countryside that suddenly slipped into sheer cliffs and deep valleys. Nobody had said it yet, but it was on their minds—Ezra lying somewhere hurt and helpless.

'It's difficult to decide when something could have gone wrong,' said Mama Kes, puffing at his pipe (it was his only small vice). 'Because you see, you can never truly *know*. It's a question of deciding.'

They decided something was wrong early the next morning, when they discovered Ezra's bed hadn't been slept in and he wasn't in the kitchen, as they were hoping, making a cup of tea. The worse part had been calling his mother.

'What do you mean he's gone?' said Kong Catherine, Mama Kes's sister.

'He left the house yesterday morning, and we don't know where he is.' Her elder brother couldn't have sounded more miserable.

'Have you called the police? Have you arranged for search parties?' She wasn't hysterical, but he could hear fear clutching at her throat.

'We are doing that now.'

'Oh god, Kes...hurry up. Gill and I are coming immediately.'

She hung up. Mama Kes sighed. He hardly got along with Gill, his brother-in-law, and his presence here would only add to Mama Kes's troubles. According to everyone his sister Catherine had done extremely well by marrying into a tremendously wealthy family. Mama Kes had long suspected that this accumulation of riches had something to do with Gill's father being the state home minister for many years in the '80s. Even now, Gill's elder brother was comfortably ensconced as some high-ranking minister or other, and Gill was well on his way to becoming director general of police.

'Oh, why did Ezra come to stay,' he silently lamented. But he had to admit his nephew, who visited as often as he could, was deeply attached to Sohra unlike all the other youngsters in the family who scorned its quietness and old-fashioned ways. He couldn't understand why. Ezra was well travelled, he'd studied in Delhi and then trained at some fancy flying school in Brussels. In fact, at times, he made Mama Kes a little nervous; he was so young and had seen more of the world than his uncle could ever dream of. Why did he keep coming back here? It wasn't something Mama Kes could have asked him; his nephew was a quiet boy, reserved even with his own family. Perhaps, he thought, that's why Ezra liked Sohra's desolation. Mama Kes looked out of the window into a landscape quilted by hills and clouds, the place he'd lived in all his life, and thought about how silence shapes a character. How it forces retreat, and reflection. He wondered what it had done to Ezra.

When news of the disappearance reached Shillong, where Ezra's family lived, it spread through living rooms and tea stalls across town, a place small enough for everyone to be acquainted with almost everybody else.

'Don't know how Ez ended up doing corporate work,' said Chris, who was in school with him at St Edmund's. 'He liked to sketch and paint and all that.' He sniggered. 'I think he even wrote poetry. I sat next to him in class and saw the back of his notebooks...I'm sure he wrote all that stuff.'

He paused. 'Ez was one of those all-rounders, you know, good at everything...football, math, English. He was class prefect and school head boy and won at the science fair and whatnot. We teased him sometimes...harmless kid stuff... 'go put oil in your hair, you Bengali' or we'd throw his gym clothes into the dustbin.' He added, 'I guess we guys always knew Ez would make it big, you know...unlike us.' He laughed. 'He went abroad and all. He got out of this place.' Ezra, Chris said, had few friends, but he'd been close to a boy named Vincent. 'He was from north India somewhere, tall, dark chap.' After they finished school, Ezra left for Delhi and Chris went to Guwahati to attend dentistry school—they ran into each other a few times on the road in Laitumkhrah or Police Bazaar when Ezra was in town. 'I don't know what happened to Vincent—a lot of people thought he was quite sarong, you know, proud.' said Chris. 'I heard he went to Bombay to become an actor or something.' He laughed. 'Never seen him in any movies though.'

After Mama Kes informed the rangbah of the locality, a pyrta shnong was set up, from Nohsithiang to the Sohra market and beyond. Search parties were organized into groups of six to ten but the problem they faced was where to begin looking. Sohra was vast and there were many roads Ezra could have taken. Finally, they each picked a path and walked in hope. One group set off towards Thangkarang, all the way to Khoh Ramhah, the gigantic boulder shaped like a conical basket said to have belonged to an evil giant.

It stood beside a waterfall cascading into the shimmering plains of Bangladesh. Another headed to Daiñ Thlen, and returned with stories of how the place, with a wide expanse of shallow water that curled and dipped into limestone riverbed caves, had seemed even more eerie and surreal than usual. The third search party looked closer, the area around the market, near the cliff from where three boulders stuck out of a sheer rock face, one balanced miraculously on top of the other. It was believed that when these boulders fell, Sohra would cease to exist, struck by an earthquake so mighty that nothing would remain but dust and rubble. The last group made the long trek to Nohkalikai, the waterfall that echoed during the monsoon with the cries of a village woman named Likai who'd jumped to her death off the cliff.

Most of the locals had their own theories—that he'd wandered into Lawkyntang, sacred forest groves untouched for thousands of years, and been whisked away by 'suidtynjang—mischievous spirits that troubled travellers and led them astray. 'Remember last time that dkhar army truck driver went inside the forest? Disappeared for days and then he came out raving mad. Naked as the day he was born.' That story didn't inspire fear so much as hilarity, but the message was clear—you never disturbed the spirits of the forests and if you must pass through their leaf-lined paths, you did so during the day and with the utmost reverence. In the jadoh stalls in Sohra market, where people huddled to take shelter from rain, the story of a certain Bah Bremley was told and retold over cups of sha saw and plates of steaming white putharo cakes. A few years ago, the gentleman had come with his friends, a group of city dwellers from Shillong, to see the root bridges in the valley at Pynursla. The six-hour trail started in Laitkynsiew and wound its way down the mountainside through mildly thick jungle. Much like Ezra, Bah Bremley too vanished without a trace during their walk, lost for almost a week despite frantic sweeping searches by his friends and family. He was found, weak and helpless, on a boulder by a river, and he told a strange story of being in a place he couldn't recognize, guarded on four sides by tigers.

'He wandered into the spirit world,' people conjectured. 'The tigers were his guardians and saved him from death.'

Back in the house Kong Syntiew also remembered that story and hoped that wherever Ezra was he, too, was being protected.

Slowly it was pieced together, Ezra's wandering trail that morning. He'd headed out in the direction of the market, and this was confirmed by Bah Dohling who owned a small roadside kwai kiosk where Ezra stopped to buy cigarettes. It was early and the shopkeeper was surprised to find someone at the counter, especially in that weather. Ezra had asked for a pack of Gold Flake, and they'd made small talk about the weather. 'He said he was thinking of going fishing,' said Bah Dohling. 'But I noticed he didn't have any equipment with him. And who goes fishing during the monsoon anyway?' It was exactly what everyone was hoping he hadn't done. The chances of a body being recovered on its watery descent to Bangladesh were slim.

After that, Ezra joined a group of boys playing football on the road. They'd splashed around in the puddles, fighting for the half-deflated ball, tearing wickedly at each other's shirts. 'He didn't say anything,' reported Thao, a freckle-faced ten-year-old with untidy hair and a snotty nose. 'He kicked the ball back to us and played for a while. He said he was out of practice, but he wasn't bad. He almost scored a goal.' When asked which way Ezra had headed, the boy and his friends pointed down the road that led out of Old Sohra, towards the cliffs.

'We don't know where he went,' Thao added. 'We asked him to keep playing with us but he said he had somewhere to go.'

'The question,' said Mama Kes, 'is where?'

The last person to have seen and spoken to Ezra that day was an elderly Bengali gentleman from the Ramakrishna Mission, who was out taking a morning walk.

'In the rain?' he was asked incredulously.

'Yes,' he said, stiffening up, 'what harm can a little rain do to a man?'

There were stories the locals could have told him that would have turned the remaining hairs on his head white, but this was not the appropriate time.

Through the fog that rolled in dense swathes across the valley, like a giant formless ghost, Mr Dutta had glimpsed a figure walking on the road perilously close to the edge. 'I told him to be careful,' he said. 'That the light could be deceiving and he may lose his footing.' Ezra had stopped for a moment to thank him. 'He was most polite,' the gentleman added. 'A very well-mannered boy.'

Beyond that were a number of paths Ezra could have taken. Down the main road that led to Shillong but that seemed unlikely. To the left up the windswept slopes that dropped to a valley, or to the right where narrow trails wound down to the villages at the foot of the mountains. There was another option that no one wanted to mention—over the sheer cliffs, either by unlucky chance or free will.

Over the next three days, search parties led by nimble-footed men swarmed the mountain trails. 'Nobody just disappears,' Gill was overheard saying, 'not any more. People don't vanish into thin air. My men will find him. And if anyone's hurt him, by God they will pay.'

While most people would have taken this as a sign of a desperately anxious father, Mama Kes knew his brother-in-law had a vicious streak in him regardless of whether it concerned his family or not. He didn't know for sure, but he'd heard rumours that Gill ill-treated truck drivers at toll gates waiting to enter Shillong, had 'illegal outsiders' beaten up periodically, and was generally known to be a man of little patience and small mercy. No wonder then that five days after Ezra's disappearance, people began to mutter about how perhaps the police officer has been visited by retribution—that someone travelling on the road, driver or passenger, had recognized Ezra to be Gill's son and had spared him as little clemency as his father did other people.

Although there were others who disregarded the theory. 'What, you mean someone pushed him off the cliff?' Chris laughed, incredulous. 'In that weather, you probably couldn't make out a man from a dog.'

In the meantime, Ezra's younger sister Liz who lived with her husband and children in Sikkim, informed her parents that she'd received a call from Ezra the morning he'd disappeared, but that the line was disconnected before she could answer it.

'I was busy getting Tanya and Nia ready for school,' she explained. 'I thought I'd call him back later but I forgot.'

It was no secret that the siblings didn't really get along, although nobody knew whether something in particular had happened between them or if, as it so often happens, they were just very different people. Or perhaps, as Chris said, 'She was tired of being overshadowed by her brother. Liz was popular and all, but not what you'd call, you know, outstanding in any way.' Liz and Ezra probably hadn't met or spoken in months. In fact, she was reluctant to make the trip from Gangtok to Shillong—'Knowing Ez he's gone to stay in some godforsaken village somewhere… you remember how he used to keep saying he wanted to renounce the world or something silly like that.' On hearing this, many heads shook sadly in jadoh stalls across Sohra. 'If everyone doesn't truly want him back…especially someone from his own family…he'll never be found.' While a few amid them muttered that perhaps he didn't want to be found in the first place.

After a week, people were beginning to give up hope. 'Even if they find the boy,' whispered Kong Syntiew, 'will he be alive?' The search parties dwindled as people drifted back to the routine of their own lives. 'He's been washed away,' was the most common conjecture, 'a flash flood carried him off.' Yet Gill pushed his men relentlessly while his wife divided her time between pacing her brother's house and sitting in a room clutching at a rosary and praying. 'Until we find his body,' said Kong Catherine, her voice cool and calm as a winter sky, 'there is hope. I'm his mother. I refuse to give up on finding my son. I don't care what people are saying,

229

he didn't harm himself...why, he just got a new job, he was excited about it, h-he...' Her voice trailed off as she tried to stop herself from crying.

All this while Ailad, Ezra's friend at the car workshop, had been away in Jowai on work, and he returned to say he'd last seen Ezra over the weekend, two days before he walked out and never returned.

'We got a bottle of Old Monk...what else to do in this place in the evening...and drank in the workshop. We were pretty drunk by the end of it, or at least I was. From what I remember Ez was quite chatty that night.' He laughed. 'Usually I'm the one doing all the talking. He was telling me about his trip to Bombay recently, where he met up with an old friend...who does theatre or something there. I think he said his friend wasn't well, and he had to go see him... Later,' and here he looked troubled, 'I remember him saying something...maybe I shouldn't tell this to his family...he said that when he died, he wished for it to be in Sohra, and that even though he was Christian, he wanted to be cremated just like the Khasis.'

After this, the ones murmuring words like 'suicide' began to speak louder. And people thought it might have concerned a girl, a tragic affair that came to an end, or unrequited love.

'No!' said Chris. 'Can't imagine Ezra with a girlfriend.' He laughed. 'Of course, I'm sure he had many. After school. It's just difficult to imagine, I guess. He was such a *good* boy, you know? Or wait,' he jabbed a finger in the air, 'I think he used to like this girl, when we were in class ten... Sara, that's it, that was her name. But she drowned at Dwar Ksuid...on a picnic...it was very sad.'

There were people who suggested that Ezra preferred men—'Perhaps,' they muttered, 'he didn't like girls at all.'

Chris's wife, Amy, a pretty, popular girl in school in her time, said she wouldn't be surprised. 'He didn't come after any of us. Or try anything, you know, at parties...' She frowned. 'Although I don't think he ever came to any of our parties. Or maybe he wasn't invited. He hung out with Vincent; very sarong, too proud to have fun with us.'

By now, many people were talking about closure, and how it would be beneficial to the family if they only knew what had happened to him. Even if he was dead. It was important to know, because hope, when it lingers, could be a cruel, dangerous thing.

In the end, one of the search parties found him in a place they were certain they'd checked before. At the bottom of the cliff close to the three precariously balanced rocks. Someone cried out saying they'd seen a white cloth fluttering in the undergrowth. Perhaps, some people conjecture, the wind pushed him over, or maybe, he didn't heed Mr Dutta's warning and had slipped in the rain. 'But why was he off the road and standing so close to the cliff's edge?' asked a few resilient sceptics.

The questions stormed on, and the landscape fell silent under their persistence. On the day of Ezra's funeral, the weather cleared and a mild yet steady sun poured over the gathering at the Khasi cremation ground. As the flames crackled, the heat from the pyre blurred the hilltops and patches of sky; the world was magically hazy, and soon enveloped by heavy, pluming smoke. Later, at the prayer service, the priest's voice echoed through the house—'Dearly beloved, we are gathered here today...'—and gentle hymns filled the rooms. Outside, it started to rain. Over cups of sweet tea and slices of yellow cake, people talked of how the past week had unfolded, and recalled all the other stories they knew of other people who may have also taken their own lives. They huddled together around small coal fires, trying to fathom why. When they returned home, no one fell asleep straight away. They looked at their wife or husband, at their slumbering children, at the patterns on the ceiling, and listened to rain pummel the roof. Finally, they'd doze off and some would dream of birds and other things that could fly.

# Hong Kong

Joshua and I are caught in an early summer storm. Forewarned last night by great slashes of lightning that sliced through a dark, thunderous sky. The kind that, a long time ago, would keep me awake until my grandfather told me stories of a giant named Ramhah who lived on Lum Sohpetbneng, and occasionally liked to rearrange his furniture. I peer up hopefully; as far as I can see there's a dense quilt of grey.

'I told you it would rain,' says Joshua.

I maintain a defeated silence.

No matter the stories about Shillong's prettiness during the monsoon—clusters of dripping pine trees, roadside waterfalls, bright blossoming umbrellas—there is nothing as unappealing as a wet afternoon in Police Bazaar. Endlessly stamping feet turn its roads into a black, squelching mess; there's always the danger of being soaked by rushing taxis and a queer smell hangs in the air, a blend of exhaust fumes and mushroom dampness. This afternoon, out of nowhere, a faint memory stirs of the scent of pine on long walks home from school.

We take shelter under the awnings of Choudhury Pharmacy, which is doing roaring business as usual.

'We should open a medicine shop,' I jest, but Joshua is distracted.

'What?'

I gesture to the pharmacy. 'We'd never be broke.'

It's an old shop, evident from the high ceiling and spacious wooden cupboards that the dkhar attendants stand on stools to reach. Shillong has changed a great deal since I left, now plagued by a host of modern urban atrocities—giant concrete buildings, multi-storeyed shopping malls, rampant traffic— but Choudhury Pharmacy has remained the same, cheerfully doling out medicine and pidgin Khasi to its customers day after day.

'A booze shop,' adds Joshua. 'We'd be millionaires.'

He's right. Even busier, a few stores down, is Economic Wine Shop. Across its grilled counter, a congregation of men, young and old, stand in odd yet amiable silence, as though they're in church and reverently awaiting Holy Communion. They seem unperturbed by the downpour, and I presume they're kept warm by alcohol as much as the anticipation of an impending drink. Joshua offers me a cigarette—he keeps forgetting I quit during the years we weren't together—and I refuse. He drags on it and I watch the smoke curl slowly into the air.

An eclectic group, all sans umbrellas, stands huddled around us. Two young Naga girls in skinny jeans and pointed patent leather shoes text busily on their mobile phones. 'Senti, look what he sent,' says the one wearing a manga T-shirt in heavily accented English, and she holds out her phone to her friend. I strain my neck as much as I casually can, but fail to spy the message. They snicker and continue the conversation in a dialect I cannot understand. I imagine some slick, spiky-haired guy has asked her out for coffee or sent her a declaration of love—'I Luv U 4Eva' or something equally poignant and abbreviated. 'Aru ki koribo pare?' says Senti.

I think she's asking 'what will you do now?' They chatter on in their own dialect. I suppose I'll never know.

At the edge of the party stands a tall man in a bowler hat, with a violin slung over his shoulder. I wonder what kind of music he plays—maybe Indian classical at Aurobindo Hall, down Bivar Road, opposite the stretch of old pine forest—and debate whether he's Assamese or Bengali. He stares out, oblivious, seemingly mesmerized by the rain. He has a peppery stubble and a slim face dominated by a long, hooked nose. He's Bengali, I think, because something about him reminds me of Mr Duttaroy, my history teacher in school. 'History,' he was fond of saying, 'is who we are and...' here he would pause dramatically, 'why we are the way we are.' This to a gaggle of disinterested teenage girls whose minds were mostly occupied by the frustrations of studying in a convent school.

'How's that possible?' my benchmate Damaphi would hiss into my ear. 'I don't see anything similar between Mumtaz Mahal and me.'

'What do you mean?' I'd whisper back.

'She had fourteen kids and I've never even held hands with a boy.'

The musician shifts the weight of the instrument on his back. I notice that Joshua too is looking at him.

'How's the band going?' I ask.

'The usual.'

I can't decipher if that's a good thing or not. I know that he'd had trouble finding a dedicated drummer. 'What do you mean?'

He shrugs. 'That people here have small ambitions.'

I mutter something about starting small, and aiming high. I'm aware that I sound like I'm quoting a self-help book, but sometimes, Joshua makes me nervous. I'm not as comfortable with him as I used to be. It was guilt, perhaps.

'It's not that,' says Joshua. 'I've played with lots of people here. They're not looking to make something of their music… it's a hobby, a fad…a way to make some cash at a wedding reception, playing covers of Michael Learns to Rock.'

'That's a terrible band.'

He concurs.

Next to Joshua is a short-haired, middle-aged lady wearing a rose printed jaiñsem. Its red flowers are impossibly large and elaborate, and stand out against the greyness of the day. She wears her jaiñsem the old-fashioned way—down to her ankles—and is carrying a beige leather bag. A similarly coloured sweater lies draped neatly over her shoulders. For a moment I imagine her life: her name is Mabel, and she's a government employee in faithful service for about twenty-five years, in an innocuous department, like agriculture. She has two children who are now in college at St Anthony's or St Edmund's, studying sturdy subjects like commerce and science. Her doctor husband works in a government hospital and also has his own clinic somewhere in town. Like so many others, he too is judiciously reliant on antibiotics. They live in Malki, in one of those new concrete houses with a cement patch for a lawn, and go for family holidays to Puri and Manali. Their photographs are enlarged and framed at Highland Photo Studio, the largest, most popular one in town, and hang on their living room walls as important testaments to the goodness of God and existence. Suddenly, she looks at me. Perhaps she felt my inspection; I hurriedly look down, feeling guilty for having reduced a life to a string of clichés.

My eyes fall on the mud-splattered boots of the boy next to me. I can tell they'd been carefully polished and have now fallen prey to mud and wet weather. Somehow, that makes me sad. He's in his late teens or early twenties. It's hard to tell. His face is mostly smooth but marked by patches of old pimple scars. Under his fusty black leather jacket, he's wearing an Iron Maiden T-shirt, one of the many sold at the crowded Tibetan Market down the road.

'I'm sure he plays the guitar,' I say nudging Joshua.

'Don't we all.'

I ignore his sarcasm. Perhaps the boy didn't play very well, I thought, but, like so many others, was good enough to keep alive a small, musical dream. He's brushing back his greasy hair and stealing glances at the Naga girls, who pay him no attention. Soon, he gives up, and stares at his boots instead. The usually bustling street in front of us is nearly empty except for a few resilient pedestrians, and an elderly man wrapped in a tapmohkhlieh, holding a black umbrella. I glance at Joshua; he's looking out into the distance; I like the slope of his jawline, the three-day stubble, his tousled hair that curls at the edges. His skin is darker than mine, and he's at least a head taller. I try and imagine how we appear—to someone passing by. Him in his faded jeans and blue sweater, me in my loose cotton trousers and sleeveless pink top. In a moment of affection, I slip my arm through his.

'Do you remember on our way back from Sohra, when we got caught in the rain?' I ask. Three years ago, a dull Sunday afternoon, Joshua's old motorbike, an impulsive plan. We'd made it safely to the Mawkdok bridge, but decided to go no further. Even though I'd visited Sohra many times before, I'd never seen it like this—enveloped in clouds that seemed to begin and end nowhere. We stood at the viewpoint, the only ones there on that mid-monsoon afternoon, and watched the fog glide through the treetops. The world had ceased to exist. Driving back, we were caught in a thunderstorm near Mylliem. I remember the small jadoh stall we stopped at, the coal fire we huddled around. It rained like it would never stop, and we spent the evening dipping butter biscuits into our cups of plain red tea and talking. We did that a lot, those days. Our conversations bound us close because we thought we couldn't speak that way with anyone else. They were, like us, unique. Somehow, it was important to have an opinion on the right books and movies—Camus' devotion to the freedom of the individual and Salinger's pristine, impeccable craft, Truffaut's wonderful, minuscule focus on the everyday and Tarkovsky's sublime, spiritual cinematography.

'I think we finished all the biscuits,' says Joshua.

I agree. I think about how we don't talk like we used to.

We recount all the details of that afternoon, except one—that it was the day he told me he loved me.

I say, 'It was fun.'

'Yes,' he replies. 'And then you decided to leave.'

Raindrops hammer the awning like tiny ammunition.

To study further, to work, I want to say. Things you couldn't easily do in Shillong at the time. Perhaps even now.

'Well... I'm back.'

The rain continues relentlessly, lulling us all into self-absorbed silence. I remember how we'd sat and searched for scholarships. We had a plan, that, given the certainty of youth, couldn't possibly go wrong. We were to study in London, he'd do film and I'd attend classes that would teach me to craft my words. Shillong, even Delhi wasn't good enough for us. It had to be elsewhere, swifter, more exuberant and exciting, one of the great centres of the world, the city around which every other merely circled like satellites. We applied for everything we could find—the Chevening and Charles Wallace, the Jawaharlal Nehru scholarship, Inlaks, and (even though we debated the colonial implications of the title) the Commonwealth.

For months we waited. Then the rejections started trickling in. 'Thank you for your application. We are sorry to inform you...'

'It's fine,' we told each other. We were sure one of them would work out.

They didn't.

I guess the friction started after I told him my parents would pay for my studies in London anyway.

'They said they'd manage it, since I've been accepted by the university,' I added. 'What about you?'

I had no idea it would turn quite so ugly. Something reared in Joshua that I'd never seen before—envy perhaps, or jealousy, a sudden, billowing anger. We argued about it for hours, and days, words flung around like sharp, jagged stones.

'Don't you get it?' he shouted finally.

By this time, I was almost in tears. 'Get what?' I shouted back. 'I won't go if...'

'We're not the same class.'

I remember that word silenced me. Like he'd spat in my face.

Class was something we discussed as a grand theme in films and novels—Austenian characters who struggled to fit in and move up in the world, Renoir's comédie de manières and Buñuel's witty yet ruthless denouncement of the bourgeoisie. I hadn't considered, and didn't imagine it affecting my life in any way. Only after this did I begin to see the differences—between his address and mine, his house and the one I lived in, the jumble of bric-a-brac in their living room and what my mother carefully placed in ours, the way his parents spoke and the way mine articulated their sentences. It disgusted me, the fact that now I noticed.

As soon as it lets up a little, people break away from the group like loosed birds and disappear into the crowd. Joshua has long finished his cigarette. I watch a boy of about eight jump into a puddle. His mother scolds him. 'Ale, Jason... don't be naughty. Ale sha ne.'

'Want some Chinese food?' asks Joshua.

I take it I've been forgiven for dragging him out shopping on an afternoon such as this. About the other things, I could only hope.

'My treat,' I offer, just to be sure.

We walk towards the main road past a row of women selling baskets of soh phi, and stop to cross just before Babla's Clothes Shoppe, where my birthday and school fête dresses were bought. My shiny custom-made patent leather shoes came from Three-In-One in Laitumkhrah, which closed a while ago; the Chinese family who owned it packed up and left when the 'trouble' began and extortion notes were handed out as generously as kwai.

'Come on.' Joshua grabs my elbow and shepherds me across the road. The rain has mellowed to a drizzle and the sky lightened to a pale evening blue. Suddenly, the air is crisp with an after-shower coolness. The streets are damp yet clean.

We descend a narrow flight of stairs lodged awkwardly between two shops, one selling stationery and the other a riot of children's toys. To our left is Kimsang, a dimly lit bar we think is straight out of a gritty noir flick, like something by Melville. Its smoke-filled interiors are dotted with hunched, solitary figures. Faded rock stars, failed businessmen, ex-HNLC and KSU members. Since I've been back in Shillong, almost two months now, Joshua and I have come here a few times for a drink; we proudly place ourselves under those tags of struggling writer and disenchanted youth. Today, however, we turn right into Hong Kong, a lacklustre Chinese joint with thin walls painted a peculiar shade of blue. Unlike other restaurants, Hong Kong has little plywood cubicles to sit in, giving it a private yet slightly dubious air. Joshua heads towards a seat in a cubicle in a corner. I follow. There's barely enough room for me to hang my bag on the chair, yet it's warm, a welcome change from the chill outside.

'What will you have?' asks Joshua.

'Let's see...'

I run my eye down the menu, a laminated sheet of yellow paper framed by twirling red dragons, and choose pork soup chow. He settles for a plate of chicken momos, large.

We place our orders with a shy waiter hovering nearby. His brand new uniform—a silky aubergine-coloured shirt and smart black trousers—seems incongruous in these grubby surroundings.

243

'No, you can't smoke here,' he says in reply to Joshua's question, and points to a poster on a neighbouring cubicle wall which asks, acerbically, 'Tobacco OR Family? Make your choice.'

The rest of the décor consists of faux Chinese fans and tasselled wall hangings, all garish in their cherry red and gold brightness. At the opposite end of the room, a row of plastic ferns hang, suspended from the ceiling. Heavily dusty, they look as though they've been there for years, untrimmed and inorganic. Above the strains of Roxette's 'Spending my Time', I hear distant kitchen sounds: the sizzle of stir-fry, the clatter of cutlery, quickly barked out meal orders—'Segwan chicken' and 'Singapur rice'. The smell of onions hangs in the air like stale, cheap perfume. A cubicle away sit a young couple in awkward silence. She's in a blue salwar kameez and hasn't noticed her chunni sweeping the floor. He picks it up for her and they smile at each other. Dimly, I remember Joshua and I on one of our first few outings together (we never called them 'dates', how uncool and juvenile): he took me to a tea shop in Bara Bazaar, a tiny place in a crowded alleyway I couldn't hope to find on my own. That was what I liked about being with Joshua. He'd take me to joints that I'd never have visited with my other friends and family; it was new, exciting. I realized later that, in my strait-laced bourgeoisie bubble, they were considered unclean and grimy, or just plain dubious. Yet it was in those places—the roadside tea shops and liquor stores, the rumbling market streets and parking lots—where I grew to know my town and pick up its stories. We'd sit for hours and people-watch and he'd tell me, most earnestly, that he wanted to do something for Shillong, but he wasn't quite sure what. On one of those evenings, when he dropped me home, I turned back from the gate, and kissed him, and said whatever he decided to do, I would be there to help him.

I play with the plastic flowers in the vase in front of me. Someone has considerately filled it with water.

In the cubicle behind us two men are discussing Meghalaya politics. I eavesdrop shamelessly.

'You think KSU is against uranium mining? Nonsense. They make a fuss now so the government will pay them off. A few lakhs in their pockets, you see nobody will be protesting.' I can't hear his companion's reply, but the speaker continues emphatically. 'People? What people? Everyone only wants to make more money. Look at that Tasiang woman... made some nine or ten crore.'

I glance at Joshua, who is spinning the salt shaker on the table. The last public protest he'd tried to stage, along with a small group of vaguely interested youngsters, was against the recent Tasiang embezzlement scam: substandard CGI sheets given to the poor for housing that couldn't survive the mad March winds.

'Nothing to be done now,' the voice floats out again, 'this government has gone to the dogs.'

'What did I tell you? This is all people do,' Joshua mutters, as the salt shaker slithers across the table and crashes into the cubicle wall. 'Sit and talk. Nobody gets off their asses to do anything.'

The conversation in the cubicle comes to an end, along with, I presume, their meal. One last apocalyptic proclamation—'What has happened to the world?' followed by a loud burp.

Soon, our food arrives. I'm thankful for the distraction. The chicken momos sit squat and plump on the orange melamine plate like fat, contented priests—while the soup chow is fresh and steaming, topped generously with spring onions. A plate of green chillies and a plastic bottle of virulent hot sauce accompanies the meal. We eat in silence. Joshua's mood improves when I ask him to help me with my rather large helping of soup chow. I fork the vegetables, he picks at the pork. The soup is clear and deliciously wholesome.

'Good, no?' he asks.

I nod as an errant noodle slithers down my chin.

'We can organize another protest,' I offer, 'gather more people. Maybe make a short video…'

'Maybe,' he mutters, non-committal. Yet I know he will. Behind the disenchantment, there was a streak of stubbornness that ran through him like a fault line. He would stick to his job as reporter for the small Khasi daily he worked for, and try and change, not the world, but a small portion of it that meant most to him. I'd help him, perhaps. If he wanted me to.

'How's your article going?' he asks. 'The one on traditional Khasi music.'

'Not bad…but I might need your help with the interviews. My Khasi is a bit thlun…rusty now.'

He nods. 'You should meet this guy who lives in my locality in Rynjah…he works as a banker but he also plays ksing and duitara.'

'Where exactly is Rynjah?' The sprawl of Shillong has blurred my geography of the town.

'I'll take you.'

'Thanks,' I say quietly, trying to catch his eye, but he's intent on swiping the last bit of hot sauce off his plate with half a momo.

Finally, he asks the question I've been hoping he wouldn't.

'How long are you in Shillong?'

I tell him. I have a month left of my sabbatical; I hadn't decided yet whether I wanted to go back to my job in a magazine in Delhi, or stay on. I can hear my parents' voices: *Stay on and do what?*

When we finish, we ask our well-dressed waiter for the bill. It comes on a saucer of stale supari and sugar that looks like miniature cubes of ice. No one collects it for a long while, so we decide to pay at the counter near the entrance instead. There's a middle-aged gentleman in a mustard brown shirt manning the place. His head of thick black hair, done up in a stylish '80s pouf, is oddly mismatched with his tired, wrinkle-lined face. He also has a lazy eye, which adds to his weariness. Behind him, in stark cheerful contrast, are glass shelves lined with pink-rimmed prawn wafers and custard yellow crisps.

'140,' he says, taking the money from me.

I notice he has long, slim fingers. Maybe he, too, is a musician.

'Are you the owner?' asks Joshua.

'Yes,' he replies, counting out the change.

'Do you also own Kimsang?' Joshua points outside.

He shakes his head. 'No, some Marwari man owns it now.'

'And you? Where are you from?'

He seems amused and stops what he's doing. 'China.'

'Which part?'

'Hong Kong.'

'How did you land up all the way here?'

I frown, unsure how Joshua's candidness will be received.

Yet the man laughs as though no one has asked in a long time. 'My family fled during the communist revolution, to Calcutta. My grandparents moved to Shillong in the late '60s.'

'Do you keep in touch with them? Your relatives in China?'

'There's no one left now…everyone's gone. To Singapore, Philippines, Canada.'

There's an awkward pause.

He looks as though he'd like to see us leave.

I pick up my change. 'Thank you… bye.'

Outside, the day has creased into evening, clear but darkened. The sky is a deep, dying blue. A pale sun has set and left behind streaks of silver clouds. We emerge into a busy main road and are jostled by the crowd. Joshua offers me a cigarette. I refuse. He lights one for himself. Puddles of water reflect lights that quiver with every passing step. I feel the weight of everyone's history press down on me like relentless rain.

# The Keeper of Souls

It almost knocks us over. We jump aside just in time and avoid it by a hair's breadth. A battered red Fiat travelling much too fast for these quiet residential roads, and, judging by the cacophonic death-rattle, also for its carburettor. We gaze, speechless, at its retreating tail-lights, speechless, our behinds pressed uncomfortably against a damp, moss-covered wall. We had narrowly missed falling into an uncovered drain swollen with that morning's rain and yesterday's garbage.

'Maniac,' I mutter grimly. I'd never learnt how to drive, but I'm certain somewhere in the handbook is a rule not to kill pedestrians. And their pets.

I must admit I seem more perturbed than Seth, our beagle, who swiftly reconvenes his mission to generously mark the neighbourhood with his scent. Apart from this, Seth has few dogged ambitions—to gnaw on our shoes even though he's long past teething, and to hump my mother-in-law's leg whenever she visits. I have him to thank for seeing her less than five times a month.

'Come on, buddy. That's enough.'

I pull Seth away from Bah Norman's car. He is the colony's rangbah shnong or chief, and it wouldn't do to have our dog spray his tyres. Seth gives me a mournful look, as though to say 'you're ruining my imperialistic plans', and grudgingly follows. Perhaps I can ask Bah Norman who the red Fiat belongs to—my wife and I moved back here from Delhi less than a year ago, and hadn't yet familiarized ourselves with these crucial neighbourly details. The next time I bumped into Bah Norman, which was easy enough in a colony this compact, I'd make enquiries. For now, with the autumn chill sharp and crisp in the air, I decide to head home.

Our house was once a large, dilapidated godown that my wife, Vera, a very able architect, redesigned, renovated and refurbished, all within the space of a few months. Now, it sits squat and cosy at the end of a sloping gravelly drive, with enough open space for a small garden that I'm tending and bringing to life. It's a project that keeps me pleasantly occupied—bougainvillea along the length of the wall, a bamboo thicket in one corner of the square grassy lawn, a stepping stone path flanked by low yellow-flowered purslane and a cluster of large, glossy ferns and wild wood rose by the gate. Perhaps, near the door, I'd place a row of orchids. My wife, who wasn't what you might call horticulturally inclined, said she'd have chosen only cacti, particularly those that needed watering once in a hundred years.

'Gardening is part of architecture, you know, like roofs and walls,' I'd tease her.

'But that would leave gardeners with nothing to do.'

My wife's undisguised lack of interest probably stemmed from having lived most of her life in cities, both in India and abroad. Her father, a reasonably important foreign civil servant, was transferred from one sleek urban centre to another every three or four years—hardly time enough to grow roots of any kind. Even now when he'd retired, he and his wife divided their time between the capital and Shillong—restlessly moving from one to the other. While I, on the other hand, had grown up in a neighbourhood not far from here, in a house that overflowed with people and plants. My fondest childhood memories were of holidays at a tea garden in Assam where my uncle worked—of summers spent close to rich, red earth and sweet-smelling grass. It was one of the main reasons why I agreed to come back, to leave a job and a life I'd spent a decade building elsewhere, cramped in a flat in South Delhi.

'See, I told you it was a good idea,' Vera had declared as I'd nailed the name plaque 'Kynjai' over the letterbox. We'd decided to call our new house after the old Khasi name for the colony we lived in; it was suitable, we thought, for a quiet, peaceful place far enough from the overcrowded centre of town. It was a momentous event marked solely by the two of us with cheap champagne and Chinese takeout.

'Vee, I came up with the name.'

'Yes, you did, but I mean it was a good idea to come back here.'

I'd kissed her forehead and placed my arm around her waist.

Since she'd never really had a place to firmly call home, I knew this was important to her. To have our own house. Where, as we'd been discussing tentatively, we could bring up a child.

This evening, as with almost every other, I pause briefly at the gate. Light spills from the upstairs study—Vera is working—and the path lamps flanking the driveway cast a welcoming glow. Hanging from the rafters, our Indonesian wind chime tinkles softly. The top is in the shape of an intricate dragon, and the striker like a fiery flame; I'd picked it up on our trip to Jakarta after our wedding. People here believe that wind chimes conjure spirits, but we prefer to consider them a frail yet dutiful sentry against the outside world.

'We almost got killed today,' I say, walking into the study.

Vera is sitting at the largest table in the house, blueprints scattered around her like a parchment storm, each page weighed down by whatever happened to be closest at hand—an empty coffee mug, a pair of scissors, a stone I'd once picked up on a riverside picnic.

She doesn't look up.

'By whom? Those catapult boys?'

She's referring to a group of young lads I'd told off about a week ago for hunting blue jays in the forest behind our house.

'Nah, some crazy driver, nearly ran us down at the turning near Bah Norman's house.'

'You get them everywhere.'

I sink into a chaise longue by the window—my favourite seat in the house—and pop open the Diet Coke in my hand.

'Probably a woman driver.'

She puts the pencil down. 'I'd be annoyed if I didn't know you were saying that just to get my attention.'

'Poor Seth forgot to pee...for about ten seconds.'

Hearing his name, Seth gets up from his cushion at the other end of the room and comes snuffling over, his tail thumping against the chair.

'Come here, boy,' calls Vera, and he bounds across, relishing the attention.

'How's it going?' I ask, downing the Coke.

Vera draws her legs up on the swivel chair; she's petite and can do that. 'You know all those horrible stereotypical notions we have about the Jaintias? That they've got more money than taste?'

'Yeah.'

'They're true.'

'And it's not because they're resented by everyone else for accidentally finding coal in their backyards and becoming millionaires overnight?'

Vera holds up a blueprint. 'Why would anyone in their right mind want white marble balusters with gilt-edged floral carvings on their terrace?'

'To make the neighbours jealous?'

'I tried telling them, as politely as I could...you know, beauty in simplicity, zen is so trendy, and all that, but they said they're paying me to do what they want...'

I'd like to say 'Which, to be honest, is true' but decide against it. She looks flustered enough. Instead, I walk up to her and kiss the top of her head.

'Cheer up...that's why you're here. To save Shillong from an onslaught of hideous architectural detail.'

Vera bends over the blueprint and mutters, 'Too late for that.'

'By the way,' I stop at the door, 'do you know anyone in the colony who owns a red Fiat?'

'Nope. Anyway, I thought nowadays everyone only bought tasteless, oversized Safaris.'

'Well, at least we can be sure of one thing.'

'What's that?'

'The crazy driver wasn't Jaintia.'

A few days later, over breakfast, Vera asks if I'd like to meet her cousin Charlie.

'You mean I have a choice?'

She ignores the sarcasm and calmly pours milk over her cereal. 'He called yesterday and said he might have a project for you.'

Charlie works as something or the other in the government. I was never sure what, and didn't particularly care. I find him overbearing in the way government workers assured of fat salaries for the rest of their lives can be.

'What kind of project?' I ask.

'He asked if you were still an animator...'

'He didn't say that.'

'Okay, he asked if you were still making cartoons on the computer.'

It means nothing to mostly everyone here that I am a conceptual 3D artist who worked at a small yet increasingly successful production house in Delhi. I do not make cartoons. I animate fluids and flames—explosions, breaking glass, plumes of smoke, catastrophic waves of water. I am a super-specialist in disasters. A prophet of the apocalypse.

'Better than some useless cog-in-the-wheel civil servant.'

Vera tries to hide a smile. She picks up an apple and slices it into almost identical-sized pieces. 'Be kind, he did help us...'

'...find good workers for the house. Yes, yes, I know.'

It's the standard reason she uses to excuse fat man Charlie for all his crimes against humanity.

After that exchange, a placid silence settles over the dining table. Vera reads *The Shillong Times*, methodically eating fruit, while I listlessly munch on my marmalade toast and watch Seth chase after a bee. He cannot fathom why it keeps flying out of his reach. His jaws click as he snaps after it time and again. Sunlight pours in through the window—the special kind of light I've seen nowhere else, soft and honey gold.

'You've already fixed up a meeting, haven't you?'

Vera folds the newspaper and plants a peck on my cheek. 'Three o'clock. This afternoon.'

Winter days are short in Shillong, and even though I leave an hour before the appointment, the sun has turned weak and mild, tugged gently away to the west, over a line of mist-green mountains. At the bottom of the hill, Bah Norman's car passes by—the flash of a waving hand—and I remember the red Fiat. At some point, I'll drop by to see him, I tell myself. I navigate my way through the town's winding roads, flanked by half-constructed concrete buildings and filled with a steady stream of unwieldy traffic. It is gone now, the old Shillong of Assam-style houses with open verandas and pretty gardens, the quiet, somnolent way of life. My ever-pragmatic wife would say, 'Stop being hopelessly nostalgic. Everywhere, everything changes. What I'm worried about is how they're allowed to build high-rises in an earthquake zone.'

But I can't help thinking of how things used to be when I was growing up in this small town with its little local eateries and family-owned shops. Everywhere else had felt so much further away—while all around me now were hoardings with advertisements for a dizzying array of cellphone connections, direct-to-home television, and super fast broadband Internet. I don't know whether Shillong has caught up with the world or if the world has caught up with Shillong. Everyone seems somehow sassier, comfortable with or oblivious to the eroding power of change. By the time I reach Ward's Lake, I am quite disheartened. I take a moment to peer through the wire fencing and am relieved to find that some things at least have stayed the same—the smooth grassy lawns that slope to lily-strewn water, the courting couples, here and there the bright bursts of red poinsettias.

The Secretariat building opposite the lake stands high and astronomically ugly, painted a curious, undecided pink. It is with no small distaste that I announce myself to Charlie's secretary and take a seat in his office. He's on the phone, one of several placed before him, and holds up a finger to signal that he won't be a moment.

Ten minutes later, after I've been served tea and finished drinking it, he finally concludes his conversation.

'These contractors are such a hassle,' he says. 'Can't live with them, can't live without them. Like women.' He laughs generously at his own joke.

I don't.

'Vera is doing well?'

You spoke to her yesterday, you should know. 'Yes, thank you.'

'Must come and see the house.'

'You must.'

'Heard the workers did a good job.'

'They did.'

'Busy nowadays?'

'There are some assignments coming in from Delhi...'

Not really, which is why I'm here in your office

'Good, good...' One of the phones ring, and he answers, then asks the person to call him back later.

Enough shilly-shallying, I think. 'Vera mentioned something about a project?'

Charlie carefully places the tips of his fingers together. 'Quite so...I don't know whether you'll be interested, of course, but you see, we're revamping the Meghalaya State Tourism website...giving it a new look, more clean and modern...'

I silently object to the use of the word 'clean' in relation to anything concerning the government, but I try to seem keen and interested. For Vera's sake.

'And we're looking for someone to work on it—design and all that. Of course, we'll provide you with the content material. And because this is going to family,' he smiles at me indulgently. 'Our rates will be very generous.'

'How much do you mean?'

When he tells me, I have to check myself from gawking. It's a criminally large amount considering the work itself isn't the most challenging.

'So, think about it, and let me know.'

I say I will, in a few days.

'Tell me, why did you move back here?' He gestures vaguely at the window. 'Shillong is so backward; you can't compare it to Delhi. And Vera has lived all over the world.'

I can tell him that, when it comes to my line of work, he's right. I will have to depend on the kindness of my colleagues in the capital to keep projects coming my way until I can find steady work in town or around the area. But sometimes, I could explain, one makes adjustments and sacrifices, especially for someone they love. That home and ageing parents also matter. That there is such a thing as living a life of grace.

However, I don't need to because the phone rings again. Before he answers, he hastily bids me goodbye. I'm glad the meeting is over. When I step out, the sky is overcast, but it doesn't look like rain. The air is cold yet dry. I take a taxi halfway home to Dhankheti, sharing the back seat with a family from a village near Sohra. I gather from their conversation with the chatty driver that they're in Shillong to have someone seen at the hospital. 'He's meant to visit our village every week,' the man says, referring to a government employed doctor, 'but he hasn't shown up for six months.' They huddle in their places, awkward and uncomfortable, overwhelmed by the sudden, bustling vastness around them. I think of Charlie in his office, his desk, his phones, his short fingers. As darkness rapidly falls outside the car windows, I remember a line in the book on Khasi dreams and mythology I've been reading recently. It explains, most severely, that 'There are nine circles of punishment a sinful soul passes through. The last of which is the worst and called the realm of the dog.' I'm hoping like crazy that this is true.

The next evening, I take Seth for a walk earlier than usual. The house is empty and quiet; Vera has errands to run in town, after she meets, albeit grudgingly, her Jaintia client. Seth is pleased at this unexpected treat. He gallops along and happily greets a group of schoolchildren who fuss over him for a while. As we approach the turning where the Fiat nearly hit us, I see Bah Norman in his garden, giving instructions to a lady watering the flower beds.

'Kumno,' he shouts across the hedge. He's a man with a slight, ageless frame and a booming voice.

'Hello, Bah Norman.'

We make polite conversation, about the weather and how it promises to be another biting winter, the local football clubs, and a little politics in relation to some multi-crore scam in town recently unearthed by an activist. Then I ask him about the red Fiat.

'Why?' he asks, a frown flitting across his face.

'It almost knocked us over,' I reply, gesturing to Seth who is vigorously sniffing at a street lamp.

'I'm sorry to hear that, and in our colony...If I'm not mistaken, the car belongs to Dariti. She lives there,' he says pointing up the hill, 'in the last house near the forest. I can have a word with her, if you like, but...it's strange considering she hardly ever goes out.'

Alarmed that I might have caused more trouble than the incident was worth, I try to tell him not to bother, that I'm sure it won't happen again.

But he won't hear of it. 'She's always been a bit odd...if you know what I mean. Parents died in an accident in Assam... you know how rash truck drivers are on those roads. She lives alone...I don't think that's good for a young girl...'

Vera and I had sworn to keep away from local gossip, but I couldn't see how I'd squirm out of this one.

'Last year, we were having a wall built near the forest, you know to keep all those youngsters out—they come and drink there and create such a nuisance. One day, Dariti came running out of her house, screaming at the workers that they couldn't cut any trees...what could they do? They had to get rid of a few to build the damn wall. Anyway, she stood there and refused to move...for days. Crazy woman.'

'Were the trees saved?'

Bah Norman looks at me as though that wasn't the question he expected.

'Yes, yes, finally the forest department issued an order.'

I want to say I'm glad to hear that, but my rangbah shnong looks slightly peeved, so instead I mutter something about how that must have been terribly inconvenient for the colony. He softens up.

'I'll have a word with Dariti,' he repeats.

'Please don't bother,' I say hastily. 'I'm sorry I brought it up. I'm sure you have other more important things to do.'

I tug Seth away from the lamp post, and politely take my leave. Now, more than before, I am curious about the woman with the red Fiat. We walk past rows of neat houses, until the road curves again and the buildings to our right give way to a deep-green pine forest. The air is cooler, quieter; somewhere far away I can hear the sound of rushing water. I don't know what I will say when I get there, but I decide to pay Dariti a visit. Seth is overjoyed at this sudden expansion of his odorous kingdom.

Where the road ends, a rough dirt track begins, sloping its way up into the trees. In the distance, I can see a tin roof badly in need of a coat of paint. As I climb, an Assam-style house with large windows, lime-washed walls and bare wooden beams looms into view. Parked in the porch is a red Fiat. There are no lights on, even though day has faded into dusk. Seth whines, out of excitement or fear, I cannot tell. I press the doorbell, and wait. It sounds like someone inside is speaking on the telephone. Around me, in the veranda, are stacks of unframed pictures—charcoal portraits and sketches of (what I think are) surreal landscapes. My eye, trained through many classes on drawing and illustration, catches strokes of talented detail—the vividness of the eyes and texture of skin, the tricky play of light. The artist works quickly, I thought. It was the only way the pictures could look this effortless. Above the door, hanging from the ceiling is a small wooden wind chime, with a clapper in the shape of a bird in flight. I reach up and tap it, the sound rings soft and clear as a bell. Suddenly, the door flies open and a woman dashes out. She's barefoot and her hair hangs long and loose. The dress she wears is smeared with charcoal dust.

'It was because I thought I was going to die.'

'W-what?'

She pushes away a strand of hair falling on her face. She's younger than I expected, in her late twenties, with an air of highly strung energy.

'When I nearly ran you over. And your dog.' She points to Seth, who, unusual for him, is sitting quietly.

'But how did you know it was...'

'Bah Norman called.' She sits on a wicker chair, stands up again, and walks out into the garden.

Seth and I follow, hesitantly.

'He told me...and then you show up here.'

'Well, I thought I would—' She starts walking towards me, and I stop.

She wrings her fingers in small nervous gestures. Her eyes are dark and troubled, as though they've been sketched with the same coal dust that's on her dress and hands. Her face is pale and thin, and overcast by shadows.

She speaks again softly. 'You see, the other night, I had a dream...I was sitting there,' she says gesturing to the veranda, 'and sketching, and then at the gate I see my parents, and they're calling me...' "No, it's too soon," I tell them, "I'm too young" but they say, "In your heart you are not." So I follow them, and you know what they say about following the dead?' She looks at me with eyes the colour of burnt coal.

I nod. I'd read it in the book of Khasi dreams and mythology.

'We walk through a forest,' she continues, 'and slowly they start changing...their hair and fingers turn to leaves and their arms and legs grow thick and gnarled...Did you know that people's souls turn into trees?'

She walks away from me to the edge of her garden and stares into leafy darkness.

'I used to hear them at night, you know, whispering in the darkness. And then last year they came to cut them down, all these spirits wandered around me lost and weeping, I had to do something. Now I know what I am...'

She is silent for a long while; I wonder whether she's forgotten we're here.

'That day, after my dream, I drove around for hours, looking for all the places my parents took me to as a child. I thought, maybe, I wouldn't be here long enough to see them again. But even now they're gone...the forest in Motinagar, the stream near Polo Grounds, everything's changed...'

I feel I ought to say something consoling, but my words—'I know what you mean'—drop flat and feeble onto the grass.

She turns around, nervously twisting her dress between her fingers, her eyes wide and distraught.

'But Bah Norman told me I must apologize. I–I'm sorry. He says I must be more careful in the future. I will be more careful...' Her voice trailed off.

'It's alright,' I say. 'Look, we've all driven too fast and reckless at some point of time. There's worse things…I've made too much of this…I'm sorry to have dropped by unannounced.' I hesitate, but thinking perhaps it might make her feel better, I continue, 'Your drawings are very good.' I gesture to the veranda. 'You have an eye for detail.'

She looks down. I cannot tell whether she is upset or pleased.

As we leave, she is still standing outside, framed by a cluster of tall, dark pine.

At home, I find a monstrous black Bolero parked outside. We have a guest. It's our friend Charlie. He is in the living room where Vera is serving him tea.

'Passed her in Laitumkhrah, and offered her a ride back,' he explains, reaching out for a handful of biscuits. 'Couldn't allow my cousin to walk home carrying all that shopping, could I?'

'She usually takes a taxi,' I say.

Vera is trying to catch my eye by way of apology or commiseration, but I stoically avoid her gaze. She throws Seth a cookie, which he snaps up in a second.

'I also get to see your fancy new place. When's the housewarming?'

'Soon, soon,' replies Vera airily. 'Here, have some tea. You look cold.' She pushes a cup into my hand.

'Where have you been?' asks Charlie.

I say I've been out walking Seth.

'Ah, doing your duty, I see. Got him well trained, eh, Vera? I mean your husband, not the dog.'

'So tell us about this new project you're working on,' says Vera hastily. 'The one at Barapani.'

Barapani is a large artificial lake on the outskirts of Shillong. We'd go for family picnics to its once largely untouched shores. Sometimes, if you left town early in the morning, the lake would look magical, overhung with strands of silken mist and framed on all sides by low-lying hills.

Charlie reclines comfortably, his expansive frame taking up most of the sofa.

'We're planning to open an amusement park—multiplex, mall, food court, water sports. You know, draw in the tourists. Multi-crore project. You'll get all the details when you put it up on the website.' He looks at me and winks. The phone rings just then and Vera leaves the room to answer; it's her mother on the line. Seth wanders off after her in the hope of more biscuits. Charlie and I are alone.

'We're hoping to have the website up by March.'

I nod, sipping at my tepid tea.

'That gives us a good three and a half months. You can come into office sometime next week…we'll sort out details.'

I want to point out that I haven't yet accepted his offer, but he begins asking questions on where and how we sourced various raw material for the house. You see, he too wants to build a place, possibly in Lachumiere…with a floor each for all his children. At last count, that was five. I remark that it would be a rather tall house, but he, unruffled by my sarcasm, agrees. Finally, he heaves himself off the sofa and says he must be going. We walk outside, and the roar of his vehicle's engine shatters the still silence of the evening.

Later that night, Vera is working at the table while I sit on the chaise longue with a book on my lap. It's been open on the same page for almost an hour.

'Will you be taking up that website project?' she asks, her pencil busily scratching at a blueprint.

I look outside, at the immense sprawl of Shillong, at the hills lit up by pin-pricks of light. There are barely any left, those dark patches and empty, uninhabited spaces. The town has hardly any room to breathe. I can feel it, its raw, ragged breath. I can hear its vast, gentle heart race like a frightened animal. Suddenly I want to cradle it in my hand.

'I found out who nearly ran us over.'

'What?' There's a flicker of confusion on her face.

'The driver of the red Fiat.'

'Oh, that. Who was it?'

'This woman...who lives near the forest.'

'And why the hell was she driving like a maniac? Where was she rushing to? It wasn't the end of the world, was it?'

Outside, a breeze rushes through the pine trees, and stirs the wind chimes. They keep away the ghosts, they summon the spirits.

'Yes,' I say, 'something like that.'

# An Aerial View

In some places time is fluid. It moves in circles, hoops and swirls, in tiny storms that churn up shipwrecks and lost worlds. At Normandy, they say the sounds of battle can occasionally still be heard, the cry of men and whine of weaponry. In a palace garden in Versailles a doomed queen has frequently been sighted, playing with her children, dressed in summer white.

What about Greenwich, she thought?

Where time ended and began, where it was split and halved and scattered across the earth. Perhaps here it was easier to slip back and forth, slide from one life to the next, clamber into childhood and stay there in a secret place hidden from the withering reach of age and the hours.

The light seemed perpetually frozen as it lay over London, grey yet softly illuminated from within, neither evening nor day but some second before twilight caught and stretched to last for hours on end. In stark sudden contrast, the oak trees in the park stood rich and green, recently drenched in a shower she'd missed as she was travelling on the train.

Where would I go if I could choose a moment, she thought? Which day in my life? In someone else's?

She sat on a bench that looked relatively drier than the others, beside the tarmac path that wound through the park and up a small hill in the distance.

What moment would I choose?

Any time before last night would be alright. She wouldn't be picky. Any time before he told her about Lily.

Lil-lee.

It tripped so prettily off her tongue.

She imagined her pale, white like the flower that heralded death, with leaf-green eyes and a slim, lithe body that had lain under her husband or, as he often preferred, on top.

Can you smell betrayal? she asked herself. Does it linger like the scent of mud and grass after rain? Did it cling to hair and skin? At the airport when her husband had picked her up a week ago, there'd only been a brief, fleeting prickle of awkwardness. She'd put it down to jet lag, and the fact that they'd been apart for three months.

'I love you,' she said, holding his face between her hands.

'I love you too.' He'd pulled her closer. Perhaps he didn't want to meet her eyes.

Then he'd taken her back to a flat in Putney, a one-bedroom place his employers had found for them. They'd made love on the sofa, on the bed. Had they done it there too? Her husband and Lily. She looked up at the sky, framed between the fringes of trees; she felt nauseous.

She'd sensed it a few days after she arrived, after the jet lag had worn off and the hours had settled into place. He hung back in the kitchen not saying a word, she caught him watching her while eating, reading a magazine.

She'd taken his hand. 'What's wrong?'

Was it different, the way they made love? She'd read somewhere that, after months apart, bodies needed time to readjust to each other's rhythms, and contours and needs.

When he was away at work, she spent the day in the flat acquainting herself with the view—on one side a small leafy park, on the other rows of identical terrace houses spread in lines like an orderly army—and the chill in the air even at this time of the year, when back in India they'd be gearing up for relentless summer. She watched strange daytime TV, read *The Guardian* and grappled with the change in the focus of the news. The euro was collapsing. Hapless old men in black suits mourned its demise on screen while printed pages carried lamenting obituaries of Spain, Italy, Ireland, and Greece. When she grew tired of the news, she'd cook the evening meal carefully, worried the splatter of turmeric would never wash off the shiny white kitchen counters. This was alright for a week, she thought, but then what? They hadn't spoken yet of her looking for a job.

Yesterday evening, when she heard the click at the door, she rushed to open it.

'I've been thinking—' she began.

And he interrupted. 'Listen, we need to talk.'

She didn't know how she'd made her way here. To an obscure bench in an empty park in a godforsaken part of the city. She'd left the flat earlier that afternoon and walked aimlessly until she reached an overground station and taken the first train out. Back in the flat—for she couldn't call it 'home'—he was lying on the sofa, asleep, in the clothes he'd worn to work the previous day, the clothes in which he'd told her about his unfaithfulness, in which he'd fought, and cried, and pleaded her forgiveness. Yet forgiveness couldn't be given away like old clothing. It had to be nurtured and coaxed, springing slowly from some sort of understanding.

'Why did you do it?' she'd asked over and over, until the words were ragged and sore, and dripped from her mouth like open wounds.

He couldn't come up with an answer, at first, for why he'd cheated on her less than a year after they were married. Before they'd even celebrated their first wedding anniversary.

Then he tried to patch together an explanation. He'd been newly transferred, she wasn't around, he was lost and alone in a new and strange city, they'd gone out for drinks after work, and had too many tequila shots and danced together, and everything after was a hot, boozy blur.

'Such a blur that you went out with her again and again to clarify how good it was?'

After that, all he did was apologize.

Lily meant nothing. He'd stopped seeing her months ago. He was so glad, he added, to have her back.

She would have liked to believe him. Perhaps she would have if she didn't feel as though she were drowning in a pool of deep, cold water.

A light breeze brushed her face; she was surprised to find her cheeks wet. The cellphone in her pocket beeped, it was a text from a friend in Delhi, asking how she was. 'Fine,' she replied. 'Speak soon.'

She couldn't bring herself to tell anyone. Not yet.

She felt shame stamped all over her body. As though somehow she was the one who'd failed. At her convent school, the nuns punished her once by making her clean the blackboards in all the classrooms—after that, humiliation always smelled of chalk. That dry, dusty, calcium-white odour that clung to her clothes, and hair and fingers. She was glad it had rained most of today in this grey city. The air carried a sharp, uncontaminated freshness.

Last night, after they'd run out of things to say, she stood at the window, watching the lights of an unfamiliar city flicker against an unfamiliar sky. Somewhere far away stood a tall cylindrical tower burning scarlet; otherwise London was low and discreet—waves of roofs and chimneys rising and falling endlessly. He was sitting at a table, laden with two cups of untouched coffee and a vase of flowers, slightly wilting.

'Why didn't you tell me?' she asked. 'Before I made my way here?'

'Because,' he replied simply, 'you wouldn't have come.'

It was a trap, he'd set it up as a careful illusionist sets up his tricks.

*At least he could have given me that choice.*

In the park today, there was hardly anyone around—a couple of children played on the open green and a man in a heavy grey overcoat stood smoking nearby under a tree. It was soothing, she decided, to sit on a bench, in a park and be anonymous to the world. She'd stayed away from the river. It was where he'd taken her first, the day after she'd landed. For her, that was the moment when life had dropped into her hands like a perfectly polished shell. It lay there, bright and shining, this new world that they'd been allowed to enter—the sparkling shops and restaurants, the brisk locals and thronging tourists, the embankment lamp posts, looping around in dark, elegant coils. They had broken away from the crowd back in Delhi with its mess and fury, where they'd met, and their respective hometowns, with their sometimes single-minded regression. Here they were, together, in a city where everything could only be better. Although she'd laughed when she first saw the river.

'All those poems about the mighty Thames seem a bit silly now.'

He'd smiled and said the English poets weren't lucky enough to have lived near a river in Assam. Where they were wide and deep as the ocean.

Perhaps that's where she'd choose to travel back to, the place where she'd grown up. A tea estate in Assam named after an Italian princess—Margherita. Nicer than 'Lily', the word so much more complex and rich on the tongue. The plantation sprawled over low-lying hills that edged the ragged mountains of Arunachal Pradesh. She'd lived there until she was old enough to be sent to convent school in Shillong, after which she returned for long, lazy winter holidays. Lost amid the pink and white bougainvillea that lined one side of the lawn, the colours so bright they hurt her eyes. While they faded, the spring would wake the guayacan into bloom and the entrance to the bungalow would drown in a sea of yellow blossoms, falling like snow that never melted. In the summer, the breeze, delirious with the scent of jasmine and gulmohur, swept into her room through an open window and settled on the sheets. Now, as she exhaled, her breath appeared as a cloud of transparent white. The London air carried no such intoxication.

Across the park, the children squatted on the ground with their father—it looked like he was shooting marbles. They glinted in the light. Marbles! She hadn't played with them in years. How could she have forgotten what it felt like to be a child? Yet slowly it crept back, how they felt against her palm, cool and clear like large frozen raindrops freshly fallen from the sky. And then the smell of dust, of dung and cow feed—a brown husk called bhoosa that she'd help churn in large, black cauldrons in a dark and shadowy shed filled with the gentle lowing of animals. That was where she used to play marbles, behind the cowshed, scuffling around in the dry red mud along with the bungalow servants' children. She'd forgotten their names...Pinky perhaps, a small girl with a coconut tree ponytail on top of her head, Son Son, the eldest boy with a strange white patch on his cheek, and Shambu, the one in the middle, with large black eyes and a gentle smile. They were all better than her; their little hands tough and skilful, and they'd gleefully pocket the marbles she lost. Hers were the prettiest, bought by her father from Dibrugarh, the nearest town, an hour away. They weren't unkind, the rules of the game were fair and simple, but at the end of the day she'd walk back dejected, past the grazing field, behind the garage, humbled by their talent.

One evening she came across a tall man carrying a plank, with a cotton gamucha slung across his shoulder.

'Who are you?' she asked, barely reaching his waist.

'Sharma mistri,' he replied, 'the new carpenter for the bungalow.'

'Oh.' She followed him to the garage where he'd set up a workshop. In the centre of the room was a long wooden table laid out with tools of all shapes and sizes, glinting in shafts of fading sunlight.

'What can you make?' she asked.

'Anything you can imagine.'

She would check on him on her way back from the

cowshed, after she'd helped feed the cattle or lost a game of marbles. It was getting tiring, this habit of losing. After one particularly profitless session, she'd made up her mind, she announced to Sharma mistri, that she'd stick to dolls.

'And why is that?' he'd asked, sawing a plank of wood in half. It came away clean and neat under his hands.

'It's a stupid game.'

'Maybe you don't know how to play it.'

'I do, but...not very well.'

'Wait,' he said. 'I'll show you.'

When he finished, he wiped his face with the gamucha and squatted next to her, digging holes into the mud, drawing lines in the dust. When she had managed to hit a marble squarely on its side, Sharma mistri smiled.

Her husband's smile was startlingly the same. A wide, embracing smile. He was kind. That's what she'd found compelling—his kindness. She remembered an evening when they were taking a walk in their neighbourhood, Shahpurjat—the monsoons had cooled the Delhi summer. The narrow streets were crowded, bustling with shoppers and people returning home from work. A small dog, no more than a puppy, had wandered onto the road.

'Watch out,' she'd shouted, but the scooter ran it over, not bothering to stop. It lay there, twitching, its eyes wide with fear.

'We have to do something,' she'd cried.

He lifted the puppy, cradling it in his shirt and stopped an autorickshaw.

'Friendicoes,' he shouted. 'Jaldi.'

By the time they reached the animal shelter, the dog had died, but he still rushed in to show the veterinarian, to see if, by some miracle, the little creature could be saved. They walked home that evening, not saying much, holding hands, knitted together by the grief of a small tragedy.

*And now, he's been kind enough to tell me.*

She stood up and walked up the path leading to the hillside. There was a damp-dog smell in the air, and a cool freshness stung her face. She'd barely unpacked her things; would she need to put everything away again? Quietly folding up her life into boxes. Would she leave? London? Him?

She thought of him lying asleep on the sofa. The slightly open mouth, the dark circles under his eyes. His ruffled hair and creased, stained clothing. The shawl had slipped off and fallen to the floor, but she hadn't picked it up and placed it over him. She'd stood a moment at the door, looking back, and all time seemed to tunnel towards her like a train racing down the track.

In front of her strolled the man in the grey overcoat. She wondered why he was there, on a Tuesday afternoon. What he'd done, who he'd lost. As they approached the hilltop, he walked straight on while she slipped into a side gate that led to the Greenwich meridian. It was just a line, she thought, an invisible line that divided the world, and gave it time. If there was some way she could take it away, she would, so she'd find herself back at their bungalow lawn that ended where the river began. A gentle slope eroded every July, when the monsoon lashed out like an angry monster. The evenings were her favourite, when she waited for her father to return home from work. The river would change to liquid gold pouring into the sky. Silhouetted fishermen rowed across to the line of huts close by the water's edge, the ones that looked like fallen stars at night. Once her father, a man of not many words, had come up behind her and said, 'It looks like the world has just begun.'

The man and his two children, who were earlier playing marbles, also entered through the gate. A little girl, of about five, stared up, thumb in mouth. She moved out of their way, deciding to walk on.

She eventually did get better at marbles, only with Sharma mistri patiently showing her how to place the glass ball under a crooked finger and take proper, careful aim. To work on lines and angles. Before long, the lessons stopped and instead she'd watch him magically put together shelves, sideboards and peg tables for her mother to place indoors. She'd wait for him to come strolling in through the back gate, running alongside as his long legs took wide, easy strides to the garage. His workplace was filled with sawdust, shavings and odd bits of wood, and it smelled of a forest after rain.

One humid afternoon, too hot even for the hens to come pecking at their feet, Sharma mistri sat on a stool sipping water from a steel tumbler while she drew patterns in the sawdust with a stick.

Suddenly he asked, 'What would you like me to make for you? Tables and chairs for your dolls? Or a little bed? I can make them.'

She looked up, excited. 'Wait,' she said, 'I'll show you.' She ran inside the cool, dark interior of the bungalow, almost bumping into Angad, the old bearer who was on tea duty.

'Help me, Angad bearer,' she cried.

'Ji, baby.'

He followed her to the children's room, the one filled with

toys, a rocking horse, a cot for her dolls, a stack of board games with most of the essential pieces missing and in the corner— what she was looking for. They dragged it across the back garden, the chickens scattering in fright, and into the garage.

'Can you make me this, Sharma mistri?' She pointed to the heap at her feet.

It was an old doll's house, one that had belonged to her mother, made of tough cardboard that had withstood many childhoods but was now on the verge of giving up. Its bright brick-red exterior had faded to a dull pink, the roof which could be lifted off had torn in a corner, and the chimney clung on lopsided. Sharma mistri walked around it in silence, inspected its doors and windows, the little flight of stairs.

'Sometimes I wish I could fit in there,' she said, 'it's no fun moving everything from the top.'

That was the way life felt like at the moment. A puppeteer tugging her into the wrong place at the wrong time. She rounded the corner and the red-brick Royal Observatory building came into view. The entrance was unguarded, and the path took her through a neatly trimmed back garden. On one patch of grass stood a sundial, and further down, an enormous telescope, completed, the information plaque announced, in 1893 and used for research into double star systems thousands of light years away.

*We can look at individual stars, and not into each other's souls.*

Then she chided herself for being melodramatic and ducked into a room lined with shelves filled with old clocks and compasses. The air hummed with the quiet click of pendulums as they swung solemnly from side to side.

*I'm in a room filled with compasses and I'm directionless.*

She looked at the elegant old machinery and smiled. But, at least I know which way is north.

She made her way to the hilltop viewpoint where a small crowd milled around like movie extras. The man and his children were there, as well as the gentleman in the overcoat. The sky had darkened, and London lay in front of her like a fine pencil drawing, smudged into infinite shades of grey. All the walls and buildings and rooftops shivered in the rising mist, twisting and turning like a wretched thing inside her. It rose and howled, and grabbed at smoking chimneys, it tore the hearts of people on the street until it turned and looked her in the face, and left her alone. A cool wind rose up from the river. Where would she go? she asked. And in an instant, she knew.

*Life stands still here.*

She hadn't seen Sharma mistri after that afternoon until her birthday. She'd waited by the gate every day, routinely checked the garage, and even took walks around the chicken coop and cowshed, but for weeks he was nowhere to be found. At her birthday party, though, after she blew out nine candles on a cake shaped like a butterfly, she caught sight of him standing by the lichee tree at the end of the driveway. She cut the cake, handed the knife to her mother, and ran down the veranda steps, ignoring the calls of her parents and guests. Her patent leather shoes crunched on the gravel, the pink satin sash from her dress fluttered behind her. When she reached him, he bent low and smiled, and before she could ask why he'd vanished for so long, why he hadn't told her he'd be away, he asked her to follow him. Down the leaf-littered path that swerved gently to the left, past the heap of sand and abandoned gunnysacks until the garage came into view. He made her wait by the door, peered inside as though looking for a secret and then flung it open. The sawdust had been cleared, the planks and tools out of sight. In the middle of the room stood a doll's house. The wood, still smelling freshly cut, had been varnished to a deep honey-brown, the windows were open; their frames neatly divided like bars of chocolate, a chimney decked one corner of the sloping roof. She walked around it in silence. Peering in she could see a little flight of stairs that led up to four miniature rooms. On the ground inside there was enough space for her to move and stand and sit. The door was tall enough for her to enter. She stepped in and closed it behind her.

# Acknowledgements

Thanks to Meru.

Trisha, my lovely, patient editor, of immense faith and endless patience. Caroline, my inimitable publicist.

Guillermo Martinez and Tom Drury for their *New Yorker* stories that inspired 'Echo Words' and 'The Keeper of Souls'. Jeet, whose *Narcopolis* quietend the tussle between my poetry and prose.

Rohan, for suffering my early stories in silence. Saeed, for bashing my work (and me) into literary shape.

My parents, Danny and Zelma, sister, Deanna, and all my family—words are not enough. My grandparents, who lived the lives I can only write about. I wish you were all here.

Samrat, faithful reader and fellow climber of St Peter's dome. Ranbir, for your unshakeable support of creativity. Deepthi, where do I start? Bah Robin, Bah Ravi—for your tremendous generosity (both with verse and wine). Avtar, who didn't laugh when I said I wanted to be a writer.

My English teachers in school, my professors at St Stephen's—for dotting my i's and crossing my t's. Paul and Jane Carling—you are both irreplaceable. Ghan and 'the others' (David and Ann)—for a room with a view.

All my friends—who've been so uncouraging (on social networking media and otherwise). You know who you are.

Luigi, for bringing poetry to life.

# A Note on the Author

Janice Pariat is a writer from Shillong, India. Her work, including poetry, fiction and articles on art and culture, has featured in a number of national magazines and newspapers. She edits *Pyrta*, an online literary journal, and spends most of her time walking city streets in search of stories. This is her first book.

# A Note on the Type

SABON is the name of an old style serif typeface designed by the German-born typographer and designer Jan Tschichold (1902–74) in the period 1964–7. A distinguishing feature of the typeface was that the roman, italic, and bold weights all occupy the same width when typeset—an unusual feature, but this meant that the typeface then only required one set of copyfitting data (rather than three) when compositors had to estimate the length of a text prior to actual typesetting (a common practice before computer-assisted typesetting).